Cold Country

COLD COUNTRY

Gerri Brightwell

Duckworth

Gerald Duckworth & Co. Ltd.
61 Frith Street, London W1D 3JL
Tel: 020 7434 4242
Fax: 020 7434 4420
inquiries@duckworth-publishers.co.uk
www.ducknet.co.uk

A CIP catalogue record for this book is available
from the British Library

ISBN 0 7156 3207 8

Typeset by Ray Davies
Printed in Great Britain by
Bookcraft (Bath) Ltd, Midsomer Norton, Avon

Acknowledgements

Thank you to Frank Soos for making me the writer I am; to Susan Blalock for her enthusiastic support of my novel-writing; to Rose Tremain for her advice about editing out darlings; to my colleagues in the MFA programme at the University of Alaska, Fairbanks from 1991 to 1994; to Sheryl Clough and Bill McGeary for their friendship, their willingness to read what I write, and their unflagging optimism; to Clarice Dickess and Katherine Bouta for advice on frostbite and freezing temperatures; to Tom and Ray Magliozzi for the perfect truck problem and for making me laugh – a lot; and an especially big thank you to Mike Shaw and Jonathan Pegg for finding a home for this novel.

Finally, thanks to Cameron Esslemont for believing in me, loving me, and giving me the inspiration to write.

I

The Road

the book

One

Vacuums are dangerous: they suck everything towards them. You let the pressure in your life drop and the next thing you know it's filling up with dumb ideas, other people's plans, the sort of debris that comes loose because it's not nailed down.

That was my mistake: not making a plan for myself. I'd grown tired of the freelance work I was doing, churning out pictures of vegetables for menus, pretty feet for footcare products. I'd thought about renting an office just so I wouldn't be living and working in the same small space crowded by our laundry and dirty dishes, but Matt said we should be saving for our future. I wondered what future that was.

One morning over breakfast I'd told him, 'I need a change. I can't live like this.'

He said, 'So let's get married.'

I didn't think he was serious, said, 'Not on your life.'

'Really.' He put down his coffee. 'Where's this going otherwise?'

Which was exactly what I'd been wondering. We'd met a couple of years after Mum moved from England to Seattle so she could marry Ted. Of the three of us girls Claire was twenty-one and was allowed to stay behind and live with her boyfriend but I'd had to come with Mum, and my little sister Laura. Too young to have a life of my own though I was nearly eighteen. Four years with Matt, sharing a flat the last two because it didn't make sense not to. Mum helped us find the place, Ted bought us a second-hand sofa and a bed. That made Matt practically family so even after I told him, 'No, no way, I'm not about to marry anyone,' and moved back in with Mum and Ted he still called around for dinner and no one seemed to mind except me. They encouraged him: Mum asking about his asthma, Ted talking dentistry with him. All I'd done was shift things back to how they'd been before we moved in together.

The summer I moved back home was one of those West Coast summers that never get started, full of overcast days and rain fine as mist. August and I was still in sweaters and jeans. The chill never left my bedroom so I took a flask up there and drank mugs of coffee to keep warm as I sat with paints and inks, pretending this was what I wanted: to be back home, to be churning out corny illustrations while rain slid down the window. I lied to clients that I didn't have enough time for more work, gave them the numbers of friends who'd take it on, spent days on paintings that could have been finished in hours. Mum would call up, 'Everything OK?' or 'Why don't you come down? I'm making sandwiches for lunch,' but I always said I had too much to do and closed the door.

In that big house it was easy enough to keep to myself during the day but for dinner Mum insisted we all eat together in the dining room, and that usually included Matt. Just like before we lived together except now I sat opposite him, not beside him, and I could see even that hurt him.

Mum was big on us all helping out: Laura had to lay the table, I had to clear it and take turns cooking. With Mum there was no point arguing, particularly since she and Ted had this thing going where they never disagreed with each other in front of the rest of us. Our arguments bounced off their joint will, and it made me wonder what was behind it.

One night I'd taken the dinner plates into the kitchen and was going to put the coffee cups on the table when I heard Mum say, 'And I had to pay to have her car repaired last week. She's turning down work – I heard her just the other day. She's running out of money while she tries to decide what to do with her life. It's not like things'll just drop into her lap. She needs to do something.' I stood behind the door, one hand on the handle.

Ted said, 'She's never had to really make a decision, that's the problem.'

'She decided to move back home,' said Matt. 'She –'

Ted broke in. 'That's not a decision, that's a step backwards. The trouble is she just won't commit herself to anything, not even for her career.'

'She's losing all her clients,' threw in Mum. 'I don't understand it.'

'She's not happy,' said Matt.

'She's immature.'

'Yes,' said Mum, 'in spite of everything we've done for her.'

Maybe that was the problem. They'd done too much – they always had. They'd picked out and bought me my first car – on condition I pay them back, which I never did. They'd practically picked out Matt for me – a dentist himself, what could be better? And now that I'd left him they weren't happy. When I'd asked Mum to lend me the money to get my clutch fixed she'd frowned and said, 'This time it really is a loan – right?' But even that had annoyed Ted. He'd come in while she was writing out the cheque and stood right behind her chewing his moustache.

'This is positively the last time,' he told me from over her shoulder.

'Positively,' echoed Mum.

'Because,' and he lifted one finger, 'you've been taking advantage of us. We won't stand for that.'

By the time I brought in the coffee they'd all finished with me. Mum had the application information for yet another university course spread out over her table mat. As though all the different courses she'd taken were going to add up to a career. Ted and Matt were onto their dentist talk. 'I'll bring you a sample of the fluoride gel tomorrow,' Ted was saying. 'It works great.' No one looked at me except Laura.

Matt said, 'I'd appreciate it. I'm not happy with the stuff I'm using now.' He reached for his coffee without looking at me and dumped in two spoonfuls of sugar.

'In fact,' said Ted, 'I'll swing by and pick you up after you finish. How about that? We can go for a beer at O'Connor's – it's on the way here.'

Mum nudged her glasses down and looked over them at Matt. 'Then I'll make pot roast. How's that?' His favourite.

I sat down. 'Hey, Matt can't come for dinner every night. Can you, Matt?'

'Don't worry, Sandra, it's all right,' and Mum gave me one of her flat smiles.

'Maybe I should move back into the flat so he can move in here. That way we won't keep running into each other.'

'Now, Sandra –'

She looked over at Ted who said, 'I've never thought of you as mean-spirited, Sandra. Don't start now.'

Matt shifted in his seat. 'She's right. Maybe it's not such a great idea.'

'We like having you here – *all* of us do. Now, when you come tomorrow bring your laundry. By the time you want to go it'll be done.' Mum picked up her pen and went back to her course catalogue, craning her neck the way she did when she felt uneasy.

Matt made sure not to catch my eye. He said, 'Well, I'd appreciate that.' Sitting there in his creased shirt and hair that needed cutting, every inch of him looking neglected. As though that was my fault. 'There just doesn't seem to be time for that sort of thing right now.'

'Sure,' said Ted. 'They're gonna work you like a dog, you can count on that. This is your chance to prove yourself, and they're not going to make it easy. But you just wait, by the time that contract's up in what – three months? – you'll have a reputation you can use to buy your way into a good practice.'

'I hope so. Oh, by the way,' and he turned to me, 'Mr Russo's made an appointment for this coming week. I'll ask if he has any more work for you.'

'I've got enough for the moment, thanks.'

Ted picked at the end of his moustache. 'Take it, why don't you?'

'I've been thinking about taking some time off.'

'Now? Can you afford to?'

Matt chipped in, 'I'll ask him anyway. Then you have the option of taking it if you want.'

'Really,' I told him, 'don't bother.'

'It isn't any bother.'

Mum and Ted gave each other one of their looks. Mouths pulled down, a slight shrug: I was throwing everything away, I didn't care about Matt when he was so good to me – and so good to them. Helping Mum with the garden, lending Ted his air compressor. Working them onto his side as though they weren't already there.

'Just great,' I said and took my coffee into the living room where I turned on the TV and lay on the sofa. Nothing on but the news. Clinton denying new accusations, an astrophysicist going up in the Shuttle, a dog that could skateboard. A similar look on all their faces: trepidation.

Later Mum and Matt came into the kitchen. I caught their voices over the dishwasher rack rattling in and out. I didn't need to listen to know what they were saying: Matt complaining he didn't understand me, Mum saying he should just look out for himself. She'd be standing with her shoulders back and her head high as though she was peering over the top of something. You can't talk to someone who thinks they can see all the way into your future. She did it to Claire too: she still called her to tell her not to send the twins to the local primary or they'd end up with thick Cornish accents and never get decent jobs, and that she'd regret it if she didn't stay home with the baby while she could. Sometimes she'd beckon Ted over to the phone and he'd stand beside her saying, 'You know, your mother's been through all this herself. You should listen to her.'

Before we moved to Seattle things had been different. We'd sit in the kitchen with a pot of tea while rain pattered against the window and Mum would tell us how she still loved Dad but she wasn't going to wait for him to come back, how she was going to make something of her life even if she had to do it on her own. She told us stories: her first boyfriend who'd taken her out in his dad's car and nearly killed both of them when he went off a bridge; the minister who asked her to marry him the first time he saw her and told her it was God's will. We told her stories back: our plots to get her and Dad to buy us a kitten, the window we broke that she blamed on the boys next door and made their parents pay for; the time Dad bought me and Claire cinema tickets and made us go in by ourselves. From the look on Mum's face as I told her I realised he must have been going to meet one of his girlfriends, and that finding out about his infidelities years after they'd happened still hurt.

Then she'd married Ted. He and Mum were a team. They

13

worked at their relationship. She never talked about him, but if we sat in the kitchen together she'd still want to hear what I was up to, how things were going with Matt, would tell Ted and the two of them would make suggestions, trying to fix my life when nothing had gone wrong. I resented it. She said I'd changed. The truth was both of us had.

The dishwasher had started up. 'Well,' Matt was saying, 'she has to think things out for herself, I guess.' Then he walked into the living room and stopped dead. 'Sorry, I didn't know you were in here.'

'You and Mum seem to be getting on better than ever.'

He stood there in his baggy brown sweater with his mouth turned down and said, 'All she wants is to help.'

'Come on, Matt, she wants us to be a younger version of her and Ted.'

'And what'd be so bad about that?'

I sat up and fiddled with the remote. 'You want to be Ted?'

'I want my own practice, a wife I love and a family I can take good care of.'

'Then marry someone like my mum.'

I'd gone too far. I could see it in the way he blinked slowly, trying not to be angry with me but not quite managing. 'Your trouble,' he said, 'is you're so goddamn resentful. And you don't have any reason to be.'

'You're sounding more and more like Ted. I think it's the way you're getting more patronising.'

He shook his head while he thought of something to say back. But in the end he just picked up one of Ted's dentistry magazines and went back into the kitchen. When I went in there an hour later he was gone.

*

The next Saturday his Honda Civic pulled up in our driveway next to my old rattletrap of a Colt. I was working on an acrylic painting of a hot dog for a new fast food place called Doggity Dog but my heart wasn't in it. The wiener turned out a flashy pink, the mustard a sick yellow. I rinsed my brushes and shoved the painting aside.

14

I only had one other job, a wine bar menu with bunches of grapes dangling over two glasses of rosé and vine tangling up the edges. I was getting good at food. I could paint a provocative watermelon or rambunctious cheeses. That's what clients asked for. I'd note down *rambunctious* and nod seriously. This was my life: rosy ovaries, comforting corn removal pads, enthusiastic garden tools. Sexy hotdogs. It wasn't what I'd hoped for.

When I went downstairs for some coffee the house was quiet. Mum was in the sunroom, Laura in her bedroom, Ted away at some conference in Milwaukee. In the downstairs bathroom Matt was working on the blocked toilet. Instead of calling a plumber Mum had called Matt and he'd come straight round. Of course. I stood in the doorway so he couldn't escape and said, 'Now listen, this can't go on.'

'It isn't going on,' he said. 'You said no, remember?'

I sat on the edge of the bath and rested my mug on my knee. 'So why are you here?'

He flushed the toilet but the water just rose up. 'You don't get it, do you? I haven't come to see you. I like Ted, I like your mom, I even like your brat of a little sister.'

'But here you are,' I said, 'fixing the toilet all on your own. Now why on earth would you be doing that?'

'Because it's broken.'

Always so literal. As though he didn't have the imagination to think any further. I edged away as he worked the plunger up and down. Filthy water slopped out onto the running shoes he always wore when he wasn't working, but he didn't stop. 'Look, you can't keep coming here,' I told him.

Water thrashed in the toilet bowl but none of it went down. 'I love your family, you know that,' he said quietly. 'They're all the family I've got.'

'They're all the family *I've* got.'

He tore a length of toilet paper from the roll. 'When did you get so selfish?'

'It's a family trait. Takes years to come out.'

'You can't even be serious. Not about what concerns other people.' He pulled a sad face – chin loose, eyes big. 'I love you, Sandra, but I'll get over it.'

I knew he was going to come out with something like that. 'Not if you keep coming around here you won't.'

'How can I get through this if I'm suddenly on my own? What do you think I am?'

He filled the small bathroom: wide-shouldered, baggy-looking, with the sort of perfect teeth only Americans have. A terminally nice guy. He'd run into a burning building to rescue a dog but the one thing he'd never do was pull himself together. He blamed it on his mum dying when he was eight and his dad running off with a woman from Dunkin' Donuts ten years later. Since then he'd felt so sorry for himself he'd dedicated his life to rotten molars and overbites. And to saving me from the sort of skin-of-the-teeth life he imagined I'd have had without him.

The bathroom reeked of the cabbagy smell of sewage. I poured my coffee down the basin. 'I didn't do this to hurt you. It just wasn't working out.'

'For you nothing works out. Look at you – you've never had a proper job. You know how much that means to your mom. And just when you were getting to the point of making a decent living, you throw it in.' He was still holding the plunger and it dripped onto the carpet between his feet. 'You need to commit, get a secure job, something to build on.'

'Why?'

'What do you mean?'

'Why do I need a secure job?'

He frowned. 'Come on,' he said, 'everyone has to have one in the end. You can't live without a decent income.' He put down the plunger and picked at the skin around his nails. 'What's got into you lately?'

'Don't you ever get the feeling there might be some other life for you out there? One that's better than drilling teeth in Seattle?'

'You sound like a teenager.'

'I don't want to see the whole of the rest of my life laid out.'

He turned back to the toilet. 'Being married to a dentist would be too dull for you just because it's what your mom did.'

'Right,' I said. 'See, you can be perceptive when you want,' and I closed the door behind me.

Laura was outside in her ballet outfit. With her hair pulled back and some of Mum's lipstick on she looked like a younger and less witchy version of her ballet teacher. She said, 'You guys arguing again? I don't understand why you don't just get back together. He's crazy about you.'

'When you start going out with boys don't pick one who fixes other people's toilets. It's a bad sign.'

'Gross,' she said. 'Are you going to drive me to class? Mum says she's busy.' Except she pronounced it *Maaam*. Something about that accent made her sound so much more grown up than I'd been at that age. She probably hardly remembered England. An American through and through.

'OK,' I said.

'But in Mom's car, right? Yours is a mess,' and she walked off down the corridor swinging her skinny twelve-year-old hips.

The sunroom was brighter than the rest of the house but not by much. Thick clouds hung low in the sky and I wondered if there was a sun up there at all. The summer had been so dreary there'd barely been a chance to open the french windows, and the place still smelled of paint and sawn wood. Mum had taken to sitting out there anyway, in a lounger with her feet up and the telephone wedged between her ear and her shoulder. 'Need the keys to take Laura to class,' I said.

She nodded and pulled out her handbag but she didn't open it until she'd pushed the aerial back into the phone. 'That was Ted. He's met someone in Milwaukee who has contacts with a medical publishing house who might be able to find you a permanent position.'

'Christ, in Milwaukee?'

'Someone he *met* in Milwaukee who knows someone with a company here in town.' She dug through her bag. 'Look at you – you sit up there in your room but you've got hardly any work now. What good were all those years at art school? You need to think about getting a reliable job.'

'That's exactly what Matt just said. You two must have some kind of mind meld going on.'

She slapped the keys into my hand. 'You should start thinking realistically about your life. You can't keep relying on me and Ted to help you out – we just can't keep doing it. You need a house of your own, but you'll never get a mortgage on what you earn.'

'Unless I marry someone reliable. Like a dentist.'

'I doubt you'll ever do anything as logical as that. Tell me, what were you doing with Matt all this time if you didn't intend to marry him?'

Since she'd married Ted you could hear old-fashioned principles clanging away under everything she said. Strange, because it didn't fit the way she looked with her jeans and short hair that made her look so much younger. Except on days when she wasn't feeling so good. The doctor said there was no reason why the cancer should come back, but ever since the operation she'd looked thin rather than slim, and her skin clung to the bones of her face.

She was still beautiful though. Red hair, clear skin, blue eyes. Those genes passed me by, going straight to both my sisters. I ended up looking like Dad: short and olive-skinned with a point of a nose and dark eyes. When we first moved to Seattle and I helped out at Ted's fancy parties I got mistaken for the hired help. Mum laughed about it and said that was because I was doing a fine job but Ted bit his moustache and told me over and over, 'I'm sorry, I feel bad about it.' Now it had been years since he'd had one of those parties. Anyway, at heart he was more of a beer and pretzels man. Maybe he'd just been trying to impress Mum, as though she wasn't already impressed enough to move us to Seattle at three months' notice.

Mum put her handbag back under the table. 'Don't be late. It's your turn to cook dinner.'

'Can you get something out of the freezer? In fact,' and I slid open the door to the living room, 'Matt would probably cook up something if you asked him.'

I stepped through and pulled it closed as she said, 'Just because he's a nice guy, Sandra –' As if that wasn't the problem.

All the way to the dance school I pictured myself waiting for Laura outside Café Marco with a coffee and the paper but by the time we got there rain was rattling against the windscreen. The first heavy fall in days. I pulled up right by the tall windows of the studio so Laura wouldn't get wet. Through the glass I could see

Mrs Tattula staring out at us, scarlet lipstick, dead-white skin, boot-polish black hair scraped back in a bun. She waved and I nodded then turned away. The one time I'd gone in she'd spent a quarter of an hour telling me about her English grandmother in a put-on accent while skinny girls in legwarmers leaned against the walls and made faces.

I put the car into neutral. 'Dracula's waiting.'

'Tattula,' and Laura picked up her bag.

'Right. I'll be back at four to pick you up.'

'Don't be late like last time.'

'Don't vorry,' and I lifted my hands like Dracula before he pounces. 'I vouldn't leave you in ze hands of ze undead.'

She rolled her eyes and slammed the door.

I headed to Marco's anyway. There was no one there except the bloke behind the counter who said, 'You Australian or something?' just as he had a fortnight before.

'Latvian,' I told him then picked up my coffee and moved to the window for some peace.

Before I moved back home I'd come here all the time on Saturdays. Often I'd run into people I'd graduated with or got to know through friends of friends. Sometimes we went for tapas and beer, or to one of the poky cinemas that showed foreign films. That had never been Matt's scene – usually he'd been at work, or off playing badminton with one of his dentist friends. He didn't think my friends were serious, and I got the feeling he thought if I stopped seeing them I'd turn into the sort of live-in girlfriend his friends had: matching skirt and jacket, able to talk retirement plans, and a whizz at making pizza dough from scratch.

That day the rain kept everyone away. I sat at the window sipping my coffee while people hurried past under umbrellas. It wasn't much of a street to look out on. A few furniture shops and a place specialising in maps, a couple of scruffy office blocks full of lawyers and accountants. Seattle was supposed to be more European than most American cities. Though it wasn't as soulless as Austin or Los Angeles, something was missing. But then I was from a town with low sturdy churches, stone houses jammed together against the gales, a cramped harbour full of white and blue fishing boats, pubs with deepset windows and flagstone floors. A real small town full of Mum's relatives and people I'd known all my life. More than anything I'd wanted to leave but the United States was too far. A whole different continent for God's sake, when I'd been thinking of Bristol or London. No wonder that when it came to packing up I was the one yelling at Mum, *How could you? How about us?* Claire had already moved into a flat with Dave, but Laura sat straight-legged on the sofa cuddling her teddy bear and looking ready to cry. Mum filled boxes saying over and over, *Don't worry, it's for the best.* We were all scared – giving up everything for a man Mum had only met twice and got engaged to over the phone. It was the only impulsive thing she'd ever done.

A man wandered in with hair so wet it dripped around his face. The smell of rain drifted out as he shook his coat and hung it up by the door. He took a seat at the counter where he sat tapping one foot to the music, said, 'Turn it up?' and the bloke behind the counter did. Flamenco. It made the street outside look more grey.

When he glanced around I went to the newspaper rack and took the paper before he did. Some man in Wyoming with three wives who all lived in the same street. Al Gore off on some vice-presidential tour of the Far East. The Mariners having a season that was going nowhere. Again.

The rain was coming down hard now with drops splitting against the pavement. I put down the paper and called over for more coffee and an apricot Danish. Across the road a couple ran hunched to a car, coats over their heads. As they drove off the wind caught a plastic dustbin that rolled over and spilled small white bags into the gutter.

There were other places I could go but I just sat and watched it rain. A real wet weekend mood, except I'd been feeling that way for months. The dreary summer, moving back home, Matt's misery, my irritation with him. I should have left him earlier, but there's no such thing as a good moment to leave someone. The least he could have done was to give up on me.

August, but it felt like autumn was coming. Soon I'd have to get a place of my own, though on what I was earning it'd be somewhere cheap and damp, and that meant another winter wrapped in sweaters. I could just picture it: I'd be shivering as I painted scarlet chillies hot as a Mexican noon, or fat tomatoes ripened under a relentless sun. My clients would use words like *sun-kissed* and *flavourful* and *fragrant* because no one wants vegetables that look rained on, especially not when they're being rained on themselves.

That's when I thought, Head south. No danger of painting sodden vegetables in Arizona. Jo had moved down there after we finished art school. She'd come back for Christmas so tanned the rest of us looked like we'd been living underground. I'd give her a call. Ask about work. Be on my way before winter set in if I could find the money – I'd have to get my brakes done, and find some money for rent and a deposit, plus the cost of the drive. I still had a few clients who hadn't paid me yet, but that wasn't going to be nearly enough. I'd have to ask Mum again – how could she say no if it meant me getting work and a place of my own, which is what she and Ted said they wanted?

I could imagine what was going to happen though. Mum and Ted shooting each other looks across the dinner table, Matt sighing as though I was moving so far away just to hurt him, Laura saying, 'What's up? Something's wrong, isn't it?'

Along the pavement hurried a plump old man with the collar of his jacket turned up and a wet terrier racing beside him. The bloke from behind the counter brought my coffee and Danish then stood by the window with his hands behind his back. 'Goddamn bitchin' rain.'

'Global warming,' I said. 'Now we get a monsoon in Seattle.'

'We don't get a monsoon here,' he told me, 'it just rains all the time because of our coastal climate. That's why I'm getting out. Heading for Thailand at the end of the month. Gonna lie in the sun and suck down some fruit shakes.'

'Nice,' I said and picked up the paper again.

'All Thailand's good for these days is some R and R. If you want the real East you have to go someplace else. Go to Thailand, relax, get a visa for Laos. See it before it gets like Thailand.'

'Full of tourists?'

'You've got it,' he said. 'Vietnam's already going that way.'

'I'll cross it off my list then,' and I flicked through the paper to the forecast. Showers, lots of them. Damn. I sipped my coffee and picked pieces off the Danish. Slowly the windows were fogging up. Dampness everywhere like a curse.

It was ironic that if I'd agreed to marry Matt I wouldn't have had to worry about money. Mum and Ted would have paid for the wedding. They'd have helped us get set up in life, as Mum put it. But for me on my own it was a different story. They'd worry I was using their money to be extravagant, living in a fancy flat, buying new clothes, going to cinemas and bars. When I was with Matt they'd never understood why I'd gone out to meet friends. Matt was happy to stay home, other than for his weekend badminton games – why wasn't I the same? I was wasting money. I wasn't thinking about the future. I wasn't responsible.

I could ask Jo to set me up with some work before I left – that way they'd know I was going to be earning money to pay them back. And without this dreary weather and Matt's sad face to weigh me down I'd feel a lot more like working.

It was still pouring when I left. I'd parked the car at the end of the street and had to run through a blinding rain. I turned on the heater and sat there soaked through to my underwear. Shivering, but not for much longer. Soon I was going to be in Arizona.

Two

Ted came back from Milwaukee with the idea that Matt should be the one to buy into his practice when old Mr Feinstein retired. That meant Matt and Ted spent hours in his study with me and Mum waitressing in cups of coffee and neither of them bothering to look up. Ted didn't mention the job at the publishing house – he hardly spoke to me at all. I'd asked Mum for two thousand dollars for the move to Arizona, had told her Jo had promised to find me work and that I'd pay them back in six months, but she'd hesitated. 'I'll have to check with Ted,' she said. And she did. They'd closed themselves away in the dining room. From the kitchen I could hear Mum giving Ted my arguments. I couldn't hear a word of what he said though, so I went back to chopping vegetables and frying them up for sauce. Then I threw in the tomatoes and put on the spaghetti. Fifteen minutes later it was done, and whether or not Mum and Ted had finished Laura had to go in and lay the table.

At dinner that evening Ted looked over at me with his long undertaker's face and said, 'We'll lend you one thousand, though we think even that's too much when you haven't paid us back for the work on your car. This is the last time – do you understand? – whatever happens, whatever mess you get yourself into. We have plans for what to do with our money, and bailing you out every couple of months isn't one of them.' He twisted some spaghetti onto his fork. 'I just hope you know what you're doing.'

'She's *crazy*,' said Laura then turned to Matt to see what he would say. But he just stared down into his plate.

Mum dabbed at her lips with a napkin. 'Honey, I just don't understand it. Why go all that way when you have things set up here?'

'It isn't rational,' said Ted. 'After all the effort you put into establishing yourself here you want to go and do the same thing

23

down in Arizona? And how long are you going to stay there?' He had his hand held up so I'd know not to answer. 'It seems to me you're not moving there because you want to be in Arizona. It's more a matter of not wanting to stay here. Am I right?'

I pushed away my plate. 'If I want to get out of Seattle I have to go somewhere.'

With small, precise movements he cut off a length of spaghetti that was dangling from his fork. 'Don't get smart,' he said. 'I wish I'd had someone sit down and point out my mistakes to me when I was your age. I had to find everything out the hard way.'

He glanced across at Mum for help and she said, 'Honey, we just want you to think seriously about whether this is the mature thing to do.'

'Like rushing off and marrying someone you hardly know after getting engaged over the phone?' I didn't mean it to come out but there it was, hanging in the air between us like a dead thing.

Mum looked down at her spaghetti. 'Sandra,' she said.

We got through to dessert before Ted said in a tight voice, 'Marlene, didn't you say that Fleur called today?'

'Oh yes,' and Mum turned to me, 'that's right. Just before you came home.'

Ted scooped up some ice cream. 'How's she doing?'

'She didn't say. In fact she hardly said anything.'

Ted lifted one eyebrow in a way that he had. 'Huh. Doesn't sound like Fleur. Know what that's about, Sandy?' As though he and Mum hadn't talked this through already. And as though I'd have any idea. I hadn't talked to Fleur in months, and even then we hadn't had much to say to each other. She was his cousin's daughter who'd moved down to Seattle about a year before Mum moved us over here. One day she'd seen his name up on the board outside his practice: Edward B. Satchel – there aren't too many of them around. Apparently she'd come right in, big smile and one hand stretched out, introduced herself as Earl and Hannah's daughter from Alaska going to graduate school and just finding her way around town. Didn't take long for her and Ted to become some sort of family to each other, what with all the rest of their relatives living so far away, hers way up in Fairbanks and his in

Louisiana. They had barbecues, spent weekends putting up a garden shed for Ted or watching baseball on the TV.

When he'd first talked about Fleur Mum had smiled too much and fussed around, said how much she wanted to meet her. Then just before the wedding Fleur rang and said she was going to call round. Mum sat waiting with her hands pressed together in her lap, but when the truck pulled up and Fleur walked up the driveway Mum said, 'So that's Fleur,' and went out to meet her without the held-in look she'd had for days. No wonder. Everything about Fleur was big except her stub of a nose. She was tall and heavy-boned, wore men's jeans and checked shirts, had hair the colour of old paper and a flat line of a mouth. She wore a workman's knife strapped to her belt and drove a three-quarter-ton truck. You'd have thought she worked outdoors but she'd come down from Alaska to study chemistry. I never could imagine her in a laboratory though, not with the slow cowboy way she had with people, nodding hello, talking so politely in that hokey country style of hers.

She'd come over for potluck dinners and Ted would always make sure we sat next to each other. He asked her to take me out and show me Seattle. To her, though, Seattle was Lasso Joe's. What a place. Everyone in clean shirts, ironed jeans and wide hats that hid half their faces, taking their dancing oh-so-seriously, moving together in lines that made it look like practice for the real thing. I'd find a table in the restaurant section and sit with my Coke and burger watching Fleur until she came back and dropped into the chair beside me saying something like, 'Oh boy, that's so good,' or 'I could teach you, if you want.' But I didn't want. I just wanted to be somewhere where a black mini and slingbacks didn't get sideways glances. I think Fleur put it down to being British, and thought that sooner or later my resistance would be worn down and I'd be up twisting and stomping with the rest of them. In the meantime she sat beside me when she was too hot for dancing and told me about Alaska, asked about England, all of it already said on some other evening, and when we ran out of even old things to say she'd start telling me about Clint Black and Randy Travis and whoever the heck else it was she was always listening to. I couldn't tell them apart what with the way they all yodelled their vowels and growled *I* at the start of lines. Songs about *leavin' home* and *long, hard roads* and *home just ain't home without her* in down-home country accents, songs about an America I only recognised from old-fashioned Westerns but that to Fleur was real.

'Integrity,' she said when she drove me home one night, 'that's what they have. Know what I mean? I'm not writing off that other music most folks listen to, but this is music from the heart. It means something.' She really believed in all that stuff: saying please and thank you, treating people the old-fashioned way as though at some time in the past things had been purer than they were now.

'So what does it mean?'

That night she was wearing a black Stetson and she tilted it back. 'That there are values you just can't argue with. Like doing right by the people you're close to.'

I didn't ask what that meant. 'And what if you don't?'

'You end up without a soul who's ever going to help you out. That's the way it goes.'

'So it's some sort of insurance policy? You help others so they help you?'

'No,' she said, 'you've got it all turned around.' And she didn't say any more about it.

Without Ted the whole thing would have petered out and no one would have cared but he had this idea that the two of us should be friends. The truth was that he needed a way out of the routines he and Fleur had fallen into: watching Monday night football on the TV together, spending whole summer evenings at baseball games. Mum couldn't tell one team from another and didn't care, and in the first few months after she married Ted he started following the games less and less. Fleur would still call round but Ted would be off to a restaurant with Mum, or eating popcorn with her in front of one of her favourite films. Fleur would sit on the edge of an armchair and not say much until Ted would look over and say, 'Hey, why don't you and Sandy head out someplace?' And we would because it was too awkward sitting there watching him and Mum hold hands. Soon he had us calling each other so he didn't need to look uneasy if Fleur showed up. She wasn't coming to see him – she was coming to see me. Ted and Mum would look pleased with themselves as they waved us goodbye. Once Laura was in bed they'd have the evening alone and wouldn't need to worry that Fleur or I were lonely.

Even after I moved in with Matt I still called Fleur every few weeks because when I went home Ted would stretch out on the sofa and say, 'Now tell me, how's Fleur getting along these days? Why don't you ask her round next Sunday and we'll have a barbecue?' As though he couldn't call her himself. All those years and he still didn't get it.

Now I shoved my dish away. Maple walnut ice cream. Ted's favourite, the sort of flavour old people like. 'I haven't spoken to her in a while,' I told him.

'Huh, and the two of you used to be so close. You shouldn't let good friends drop. Besides, Fleur's family.'

Next to him Matt nodded like this was something he knew too. I pushed back my chair. 'Well, if it was important she'd have called back.'

Later, though, I rang her. She wasn't there. No one was. A message said the number was no longer in service and I lay in front of the TV working out exactly how long it had been since I'd last called her.

Three

I had to call directory inquiries for her new number, and then it turned out that she didn't have an answering machine hooked up. Several times over the next few days Ted asked, 'Talked to her yet?'

'Nope,' I'd say, and he'd grunt and pick up the paper, or stir milk into his coffee and sip it noisily.

I didn't do any work, sifting instead through my things so that I could fit everything into the back of my car for the drive down to Arizona. When I asked Mum when she could give me the money she looked away, said, 'We want you to promise this will be the last time.'

'What do you want me to do? Write it in blood?'

She glared. 'You have no idea – Ted doesn't have a thousand in loose change he can just hand over every time you need it. He plans everything – what to put into our retirement fund, what to use on maintaining the house, what we need for housekeeping. He doesn't like it when things get messed up. Neither do I.'

Her face had turned pink and her eyes shiny. She'd found some sort of happiness with Ted and his organised life, and I was ruining it for her. 'I'm sorry,' I said. 'I really am.' And I went back upstairs to my room.

It took three attempts to paint a succulent hotdog for Doggity Dog, and though the bunches of grapes I did for Taking the Pip had a cold blue look to them the manager didn't seem to mind. When clients called to ask if I'd take on other jobs I told them I was moving to Arizona and they wished me luck and hung up.

Soon I had nothing to do except hang out in the garage dumping old clothes into rubbish bags for the charity shop, tying up old bundles of paintings that hadn't worked out, putting a badminton racket to one side for Laura if she ever wanted it. It was from the days when Matt had been on the university team and wanted us to have something we could do together. Hopeless. Him whisking the shuttlecock over the net, me batting at thin air. I preferred swimming, the smooth glide-stroke-glide. Once Matt came with me: he got water in his ears and complained he'd get an infection, and never came again. I was relieved. Swimming didn't feel the same with him thrashing up and down beside me like he was in a hurry to get somewhere.

When Laura wasn't at the mall spending her pocket money she spent those last days I was in Seattle in the garage watching me. She brought me Cokes from the fridge and perched on a broken deckchair to see what I was throwing out.

'I don't understand,' she whined one morning, 'why ya going?'

'I'm sick of this place.'

'But it's home. And you only just moved back in.'

'Exactly.'

She scuffed at the floor with the toe of her sneakers. 'Is it because you don't get on with Ted any more?'

'The trouble,' I said, 'is that he's forgotten all about being twenty-five. That's what happens when you hit middle age – you get embarrassed by what you did when you were young, and then you get embarrassed at the mistakes you think other people are going to make just because they're younger than you.'

'So why ya going if it's a mistake?'

I stooped down to a box. 'Maybe it'll be great. For one thing there's no rain – just think of that.'

'You won't come back. It's too far, and you'll say it's too expensive.' She twisted her hair around her fingers and didn't quite look me in the eye.

'That's not true.'

'Claire doesn't ever visit.'

'Yeah well, she's a lot further away, and she's got the twins and the baby now.'

But she swung her foot and picked at her split ends with a frown that only partly hid the way her bottom lip was twitching. 'D'ya think Ted's different now? Is that why you fight?'

'No, he hasn't changed a bit. Nothing's changed except me.'

'You're all so pissed at each other.'

29

'No we're not. At least, Mum and Ted aren't pissed off at each other, and no one's pissed off at Matt except me. In fact, no one's pissed off at anyone but me. Except me. Right?'

'I'm not pissed at you, even if everyone else is.'

'Good. Because if Mum catches you saying *pissed* she is going to be *so* pissed off.'

'Yeah.' And she grinned.

I tugged at a corner of pink material and dragged out a T-shirt I'd forgotten all about. I threw it onto the To Keep pile.

'Hey, I'll have that one,' said Laura.

'It's a keeper.'

'C'mon, you can't take everything with you.'

'Forget it, Doodle.'

She smiled then remembered she was campaigning to have us all forget that nickname. Not dignified enough for a twelve-year-old. 'You said you wouldn't call me that.'

'Oh yeah. But you still can't have it. Sort through the stuff I don't want,' and I pointed at the charity shop pile. She sighed. 'And you can have that badminton racket.'

'Badminton is a dorky game,' she said.

There was no arguing with that.

When Mum came in, an umbrella in one hand and the phone in the other, Laura was pulling one of my old dresses over her head. It was supposed to cling but it hung off her skinny body and came down past her knees. 'Keep it,' I said. 'It'll look good when you have a bust.' She scowled because she liked to think her training bra made a difference, and turned to show off the dress to Mum.

Mum shook her head and held the phone out to me. 'Fleur calling for you.' She stood close by shaking out the umbrella while I said, 'Hello?'

'Sandra? Been trying to get hold of you.'

I leaned against Ted's workbench. 'Yeah, well I've been here. Couldn't get hold of *you* though.'

'Right, my answering machine isn't working.' The phone creaked as she shifted her grip, and in the background I heard a TV. Not like her to have it on in the middle of the day. Not like her to be off work, come to that. 'Anyhow, listen,' she said, 'I've a favour to ask and I'll tell you now, you're my last hope.' Oh shit,

I thought, here we go. 'It's this way – things just haven't gone right this year. And now just to put a cap on it all, I've got my arm in a cast.'

'Oh,' I said. 'Sorry to hear it.' Mum poked through one of the boxes, caught my eye and looked away.

'The thing is, I need a driver. I've got a job lined up back home which starts at the end of the month.' She paused. 'No one else can do it.'

'Alaska? You're moving back? Why don't you just fly up?'

'I've looked at all the angles. No can do. I have to move all my stuff.'

'So ship it.'

'Listen, I can't arrive without a vehicle, and it's a long story but money's kinda tight right now. So as I said, I ain't got no choice but to drive.'

Mum dragged the broken deckchair across the concrete towards me. She sat down at an angle so the rest of the material wouldn't rip and shook her head as Laura held up an old grey sweatshirt of mine. I hoisted myself up onto the workbench and stared through the dirty window into the rain. Fleur was leaving a good job. How could she be broke? I wondered what it was she hadn't told me.

'I'm moving too. In fact, I'm leaving for Arizona any day now.'

Is she OK? mouthed Mum. I shook a hand to tell her to wait but she leaned towards me.

'The drive up doesn't take more than four or five days,' said Fleur, 'and then you could fly back down. It'd be fun. When else are you going to see Alaska?'

'I just don't see how I can fit it in.'

Mum was gesturing for the phone but I turned away.

'You're leaving me stranded,' Fleur was saying. 'I don't have anyone else to ask.'

'Let me talk to her,' hissed Mum.

'I'm sorry. I can't do it, Fleur.'

She said something else, something that sounded thin and lonely in the air as Mum took the phone, but by the time she got it to her ear Fleur had hung up. Mum smacked the antenna back into the phone.

'Couldn't you have told her I wanted another word? What's the big problem here?' The skin around her mouth looked loose, her eyes sunken and tired.

'Sorry,' and I jumped down from the bench.

She followed me across the garage to where Laura was picking through the To Keep pile. I took a suede jacket from her.

'Sorry doesn't cut it,' said Mum. 'What is it with you? Why couldn't you help her out?'

I turned on my heel to face her. 'So you *knew* what she wanted? I bet you already promised her I'd do it too.'

She yanked at the dress as Laura tried to pull it off over her head. 'How could you say no?'

'She said it would take five days – plus I'd have to get back here. I need to leave for Arizona as soon as you can lend me the money.'

Mum pressed the phone against her chest. 'You want something and everyone else has to jump. Once you've made up your mind no one else matters. Isn't that right?'

I dumped the clothes I was going to keep back in a box. 'I'm just too damned selfish, I suppose,' and I pushed past her out into the rain.

Of course Ted got to hear about it. When he got home I had to go over the whole phone call again, explain why I'd said no.

'I don't believe this,' and he leant onto his desk. 'She's family. Why couldn't you help her out?'

I leaned forward too and told him, 'I don't get it. She's so broke she can't fly up and ship her stuff, but she can afford to fly me back home?'

'She has a job lined up, for chrissakes.' He spread one hand over his face, rubbed his brow with his fingers. 'She's had a bad year and this is about the only good thing to happen. She can't lose that job because you won't drive her up there.'

'What kind of a bad year?' I could feel the dampness of my hands on his desk. 'You've already talked to her, haven't you?'

'No I haven't, not yet. But what do you care? You've made it none of your concern. You never call her any more.'

'How come I was always the one who was supposed to stay in

touch with her anyway? We never really got on – did you ever realise that?'

'Now you're being ridiculous,' and he picked up some papers, went out to where Mum was sitting in the sunroom, sat beside her with his knees poking up because his legs were so long, took her hand and didn't look round when she glanced over his shoulder to where I stood watching them.

I called a couple of friends and drove into town. Anything to get out of the house.

*

It was the worst thing I could have done. When I got home just after ten Matt was waiting for me in the hallway. He leant against the doorjamb as I pulled off my shoes and I caught the sweet odour of disinfectant that hung about him when he hadn't showered after work. He'd had his hair cut short and it made his face look naked.

'Where've you been?'

'Out having fun, officer.'

'They've been waiting for you. It's late,' and he led the way into the living room where Ted was peering at some journal and Mum was watching an old Bogart film. I sat on the sofa beside Laura who'd fallen asleep curled around a cushion. Mum turned off the TV. Laura groaned and curled tighter, and I spread myself out so that there was no room for Matt. He went off to the kitchen and I heard the saucepans clattering in the sink. Always making himself useful, as though he owed my family something.

'OK,' I said, 'what's up?'

'We talked to Fleur this evening,' Mum said brightly, then tilted her head to one side and looked at Ted as though not sure who should say what came next.

'Oh no,' I said, 'you didn't –'

'She's desperate, honey. What could we say?' She searched out Ted again, frowned at him. He leaned forward too, bony hands clasped around his knees. It was like a scene out of a made-for-TV film, all those concerned faces and clasped hands, the drama crackling in the air.

'It'll only take a week of your time, Sandy. What else do you

33

have to do before you leave? Surely,' and he held up a hand so I wouldn't interrupt, 'surely you have time to help out an old friend?' He gave a goofy little grin that showed his perfect teeth and waited for me to smile back. I didn't. 'Oooh,' he said then, 'it's not that bad. Come on now, you'll get to see the biggest state in the Union. All those bears and caribou and moose and stuff. A road trip to the last frontier. Most people only dream of doing something like that.'

'Come on,' and I turned to Mum, 'what exactly did you tell her?'

'It's all arranged. We're going to drive you over to her apartment the day after tomorrow. She says it'll take about five days to get to Fairbanks, and then she'll buy you a ticket home.'

'And how about me already telling her no? Did you just forget about that?'

Mum pressed her hands between her knees. 'Honey, I said you'd changed your mind. I know you didn't mean to let her down. Besides, the money's in a high interest savings account – if we don't wait until the end of the month we'll have to pay a penalty.' She smiled but it made her look more guilty. 'So when you get back, we can get the money out and you can head off to Arizona.'

I wanted to say, *How could you?* but there was no point. They'd tied the whole thing up tight. If I wanted the money I had to drive Fleur home.

'Just great,' I said. 'Don Corleone would be proud.'

Four

When I came down for breakfast I found Mum and Ted fussing around the car. I grabbed some coffee then put my bag in the back. There on the seat I found a small rucksack. 'What's this?' I said.

Ted looked over. 'A few things you might need – maps, sleeping bag, matches. Your camera.'

'I've already packed,' I said. 'I won't need much besides a couple of changes of clothes. Besides, Fleur'll have all that stuff.'

'You can never be too prepared.'

It's a Boy Scout mentality, thinking you need to know how to build a fire from a few damp twigs or skin a rabbit and eat it in case, by chance, you find yourself having to survive utterly alone in the wilderness. It's manly, needing to always be prepared – not for the day-to-day cleaning and eating and shopping but for larger, catastrophic events. Fleur was the same, but then a great deal about Fleur struck me as manly, from the way she walked to how she kept her nails clipped short so oil wouldn't get stuck under them when she worked on her truck. It wasn't a matter of independence, at least that wasn't how it seemed to me: more like she had something to prove about how tough she was, how she could survive if she had to, without help from anyone.

I headed back towards the house to say goodbye to Laura, and Ted called, 'We're already behind schedule. Let's get going.'

Laura was at the door in her slippers. 'Don't go getting eaten by the bears,' she said, and she hung her arms around my neck.

'I'll be back in a few days.'

'Not for long,' she said. 'Then you'll be off to Arizona. It's not fair – everyone gets to live where they want except me.'

'And where do you want to live?'

'With you guys,' and she laughed at herself.

Ted started the engine and beckoned to me. Mum was already

beside him with the city map spread out over her knees. I waved to Laura and got in the back with the two bags leaning against each other like a couple of drunks.

'I put those maps of western Canada in the backpack for you,' said Ted over his shoulder. 'You can never have too many maps, especially where you're headed. In places there won't be a gas station for a hundred miles at a time. You're gonna have to really think ahead.'

'I have been,' I told him, 'and it isn't a pleasant prospect. Five days on the road.'

'It'll be an adventure – all those places you'll see. How many people d'you think get to go on a trip like this? Huh?'

I didn't say anything, just watched out the window as he took the slip road down onto the highway.

'Aren't you even going to look in the bag I packed for you?' he said at last.

'I'm sure you thought of everything – waterproof matches, survival kit, flares for if we get lost.'

He glanced at me in the mirror. 'This isn't some kind of day trip.' As though we hadn't spent an hour looking at maps the night before. He'd been disappointed I hadn't got them out myself, had told me I wasn't prepared. But then, as I reminded him, Fleur had done this trip God knows how many times. To Ted that was missing the point. Why go unless you've spent hours bent over maps tracking your route beforehand, arguing about which road to take and which places to stop at? That was half the fun. Except to me this trip wasn't any fun at all. I'd watched him run a finger up the Alaska-Canada Highway – the Alcan, he'd called it, as though he'd driven it himself – through British Columbia and the Yukon into Alaska. With most of the BC towns gathered along the border the rest of the province was vast and empty, and that brought home to me how dangerous this trip might be: breaking down with no town to walk to, no phone box to call a tow truck from. We could be stranded. We'd be in danger. I think that was the point. Those nights in Lasso Joe's Fleur had told me about the long drive home, the bears she'd heard snuffling around her tent, the puncture she'd had in the middle of nowhere in the middle of a storm that she'd had to fix herself, and I'd realised that the trip wouldn't have meant a thing to her if she'd just driven it rather than surviving it. Me, though, I just wanted to get it over with. I didn't have the sort of survival skills I could show off out there in all that wilderness.

I didn't recognise the road Ted took to get us to Fleur's. When he pulled up I asked, 'This it?'

'Yup, sure is.' As though he hadn't noticed the sad buildings, the broken paving stones, the cars propped up on bricks.

'Venice Mansions, one hundred and thirty-three Statton Road,' read Mum. The three of us looked up at the sign covered with swirls of spray paint. That's what it said all right.

The building had rust stains running down from window frames and rubbish spilt over the pavement. Grass grew in the cracks at the edge of the main steps as though no one lived there. But they did – Metallica boomed from an open window a couple of floors up and from further away a baby's scream echoed out.

'Christ almighty,' I said because one of us had to say something. Ted tucked his expensive sunglasses into the glove compartment while Mum buttoned up her coat and pushed her hand through the handle of her bag. The way she was dressed up in a coat, skirt and heels she must have been expecting something different.

The front door of the building had been propped open and we trooped in and up the stairs as the lift had a sign saying *Out of Fucking Order AGAIN*. The stairs smelt of old plaster and stale cooking. On the landing a square-built man in sweatpants and a stained T-shirt squeezed past us carrying a box. His nose had been knocked flat against his face and he had a tooth missing right in the front.

'Hi,' he said, 'she's in 3C. This is about the last of it.'

'Thanks,' said Ted. He laid a hand on Mum's shoulder and held onto her until the bloke had gone down the stairs.

On the third floor one door was held open with a dumb-bell. In the doorway a woman with a parrot tattooed on her arm was taping a plastic bag around a box. When she looked up and brushed back her bleached hair a whole curtain-rodful of rings shone along her ear. She looked tired, as though she wasn't usually up at this time of day. She pointed into the flat. 'Fleur's inside.'

We stood in the living room between a low scarred table and a lumpy sofa. Its nylon covers were torn and the original red cushions showed through like wounds. From somewhere close by came the smell of hot fat.

'Fleur? Where you hiding?' called Ted.

A door opened. Fleur, in jeans and a man's checked shirt, her left arm at an odd angle in its cast. Her stub of a nose, her small mouth, her grey eyes, all looked lost in her wide face. Her hair had grown and she'd combed it back, away from her brow.

She smiled, said, 'Hey there,' and stepped into Ted's hug. She hugged Mum too, then me, squeezing me tight as though to make up for bringing me into this. 'Good to see you,' she told me, and I just nodded. 'Good to see you all – it's been a while.'

It was the way she said it: she was different. More hesitant. She sat on the edge of the sofa and jumped when Ted put his hand on her shoulder.

'So what's the story with your arm?' I asked.

'Oh,' and she looked down at the cast. 'Had an accident the other week. Got a bad wrist fracture and they slapped a cast on it. Real pain in the butt,' and she grimaced. 'Anyway, Mandy and her boyfriend from next door have been great helping me get packed up. Not much more to do now except carry these down and tie the tarp on.' She nodded at a couple of boxes against the wall just as Mandy's boyfriend came in. He piled one box on the other and lifted them both, veins mapping his thick arms.

'Well now,' said Ted, 'what can we do?'

Usually she'd have said something like, 'Got it all under control already, Ted. Been up since six getting the last few things boxed up and loaded,' but instead she just muttered, 'Nothing much.'

Ted sat back with his arm along the top of the sofa behind her. 'You're gonna enjoy this trip. Wish I could come along but Sandy here beat me to it,' and he winked at me. 'Next time you'll have to ask me. I always wanted to see Alaska.'

'Yeah,' she said, 'next time I will.'

He sat there smiling at us and tapping one foot on the worn carpet. When he turned his smile on me I looked away. 'You're lucky, Sandy. This is a once-in-a-lifetime opportunity.'

'I hope you're right about that.' My voice came out strangely high and I coughed to loosen my throat. It got to me – the way he was sitting there looking so pleased with himself when that night he'd be eating dinner at home and sleeping in his comfortable bed, his life running on its usual tracks while mine was shunted off onto a siding. Mine didn't matter – after all, it wasn't really going anywhere, was it?

Mum sat in one of the armchairs by the window with her hands around her knee and her handbag in her lap. 'It'll be nice for you to be home.'

Fleur fiddled with the fraying end of her cast. 'Yeah, it sure will. It's been too long,' and we all nodded and smiled though I for one had no idea what she was going back to. She'd talked about Fairbanks and Denali National Park and cold winters but she'd hardly mentioned her family. I wasn't even sure what family she had up there apart from her parents and a brother she doted on who had a band. Country, naturally. Did she have another brother too, or was it a sister? I couldn't remember.

Fleur fidgeted, crossing and uncrossing her legs before she said, 'Well, I'd better just check everything's packed.'

She disappeared into a room with a beaten-up door and I caught a glimpse of ceiling tiles stained and drooping, and a carpet peppered with cigarette burns.

The counter between the living room and the kitchen was stacked high with old newspapers, half hiding a coffee machine that looked new and expensive. 'How about the coffee maker?' I called. 'Isn't that coming?'

Fleur came out of the bedroom with a towel in one hand and a hairdryer in the other. Strange, I'd never imagined her needing a hairdryer. 'Oh yeah,' and she forced a smile. 'Looks like I forgot a few things.' A joke that she of all people had done a bad job of packing. I went over and cleaned the machine while she hunted for its box in the cupboard, found her vacuum cleaner and had to pack that too.

This was not the Fleur I remembered. That Fleur would have had everything packed and labelled, would have had coffee made for us and the coffee maker in its box still warm from being used. But then the Fleur I remembered didn't live in a place like this.

She'd had a good job with a big pharmaceutical company, a bland flat with pine furniture, and had given up driving her old rattletrap of a truck for a brand new red Chevy pick-up that she loved more than anything else in the world. Except maybe country music.

It took nearly an hour to get the rest of her things together. Mandy and her boyfriend carried stray bags and boxes downstairs with cigarettes poking from the corners of their mouths while the rest of us looked around the flat for anything else that might be Fleur's.

In a car park full of dented cars young boys were hurtling around on bikes, making them rear up like horses and whooping as they came past. Fleur's truck fitted right in: paint flaking off the sides, a bumper hanging at an angle. Above us dirty curtains licked out of windows.

'Must be pretty reliable,' said Ted. 'You've had this old thing for years.'

'Hope so,' said Fleur. 'We have one heck of a long way to go.'

Mandy's boyfriend was grinning. 'Had hardly been driven in months. Just needed a jump start then she was roaring like a big cat. Man, that thing's got an engine.'

Despite the sun Mum kept her coat buttoned up. She stood on the broken concrete with her feet together, her arms folded at her waist, every part of her tucked in. When the kids came back past on their bikes she flinched but didn't move out of their way, just held the collar of her coat with one hand.

Mandy lit a fresh cigarette while her boyfriend showed Ted the truck's engine. Ted was nodding and saying, 'Right, yup,' though he hardly knew a carburettor from a distributor cap. He paid a man to fix his car so that he didn't get his hands dirty. No one wants a dentist with oil under his nails.

The breeze blew Mum's hair across her face as she unhooked the bag from her arm and pulled out a small package. She said, 'This is for you, honey.'

I pulled off the gold tissue paper. Inside was a guidebook to Alaska. 'Thanks,' I told her though I doubted I'd have time to use it. A guide to Arizona would have been more useful, but she hadn't thought of that. She'd never been much good with presents.

She took hold of my wrist, said, 'You be careful. It's a long way and the roads aren't good. Make sure you stay in decent motels and don't overtire yourself or you'll end up having an accident. And for God's sake don't do anything silly like picking up hitch-hikers.'

'I never have.'

'You can be so soft-hearted, Sandra. You have to take care of yourself, and Fleur. We're all counting on you.'

'Yeah,' I said, 'I'll keep the doors locked the whole way and drive like the clappers.'

She took a deep breath but didn't let go of my wrist. 'Sandra, I just want you to arrive safely, and have a nice time.'

'There won't be time for a nice time. Fleur wants to be there by Sunday. All we're going to do is drive and sleep – you should know, you helped set all of this up.'

'Don't be so mean-spirited,' she said. 'It isn't like you.'

'Yes it is.'

No one had mentioned Fleur's new truck. When I put the guidebook on the driver's seat I asked her, 'So what happened to that red Chevy you used to drive? Did you sell it?'

'Had an accident a while back. The truck was a write-off.'

Ted said, 'Anyway, this one's just fine, isn't it, Fleur?'

'I hope so,' and she went back to watching Mandy's boyfriend fiddle with the engine.

Ted beckoned me away. 'Fleur's had a rough time. Go easy on her, OK?'

'You still haven't told me what sort of a rough time.'

He put his arm around me. 'I know she really appreciates you doing this. You're a good friend to her, and that means a lot to me.'

'You're doing it again,' I said.

'What?' and he looked genuinely surprised.

'Not telling me what's going on.'

'Is that the price for helping her out? The right to invade her privacy?'

'No, but if that's the way you see it why don't you just go ahead and tell me?'

He stood there with his jacket flapping in the wind. 'You're nervous, I understand that. I would be too with that long drive ahead of me, but don't you worry about a thing.' He gave me a small smile. 'It'll be fun. In fact, I really do wish it could be me going.'

'It could have been.'

He laughed, said 'I guess that's right.'

I didn't laugh back.

He was right about one thing: I was nervous about that long drive. So much could go wrong, especially with Fleur's old wreck of a truck.

Ted's hair looked thin on top where the wind had blown it to one side. In the pale light he looked older, his skin like a crumpled paper bag. 'I'm sorry about how this has worked out, Sandy, I truly am. I know you hate being pushed into things, but you don't understand – there's a lot at stake here.'

'And just think,' I told him, 'all you had to do was tell me all about it. You still could.'

I waited but all he said was, 'We just went over this.'

I pushed my hands into my pockets and walked back across the tarmac to give Mandy and her boyfriend a hand with the tarp. Ted lodged the bag he'd packed for me in the bed of the truck along with a couple of jerrycans. Between us we got the tarp tied over everything while Fleur watched. When she tested our knots with her good hand she tugged them hard, no-nonsense, one of the men. This was the real Fleur. Competent. Never worried.

Nearly half past nine and we were ready. Mum hugged me. 'Take care,' she said. 'And don't forget to call when you get there.'

'I'll be calling before that if anything goes wrong.'

'You do that.'

When I hugged Ted I got a face full of jacket and a strong smell of deodorant. 'Bye Sandy,' he said. 'Be good. We love you.'

I didn't say anything back, just climbed into the cab and started the engine. It roared as we crawled through the car park, coming dangerously close to Ted's silver Infiniti on a tight bend. Only then did Fleur tell me to use second gear because you don't start trucks in first, and that the release for the emergency brake was the knob under the dash. Once I had that sorted out we rushed past Mum and Ted's worried faces and took off up the road trailing a dramatic cloud of dark smoke. But we only got as far as the petrol station a couple of blocks away. We needed oil because the truck had a leak, and the cooler between us, the water container, and the jerrycans Ted had just put in the back were all empty. He must have noticed when he lifted them in. He didn't say a thing, though.

It was well past ten before we got going. On my own I hadn't been able to pull the tarp tight again and as we sped along the highway one corner flapped like a sail. Three times it came loose and I had to swerve to the side of the road to tie it back on. All we had in the cooler was white bread, processed cheese, chocolate, six cans of Coke, and a bag of ice to keep it all cool – the petrol station didn't have much else. Fairbanks was an impossible distance away, and it felt ridiculous to be taking the road north in that clapped-out truck, so badly prepared we probably wouldn't even get to British Columbia.

I wanted to ask Fleur, *So do you really think we can make it?* just to hear her tell me this truck was in far better shape than it looked. But I didn't because I saw her hand tight on the edge of the seat.

Five

There was a queue to get into Canada. With the sun glaring down it was too hot to sit in the truck so I turned off the engine, grabbed a Coke from the cooler and got out. Two lanes of cars and trucks leading up to the *Welcome to Canada/Bienvenue au Canada* sign, licence plates with *Washington* against a background of blue mountains, or boasting *Beautiful British Columbia.* One cramped brown car's licence plate said *Friendly Manitoba*: what else was there to say about hundreds of miles of dead-flat prairie? I walked up towards the front of the queue and passed a high-riding truck. An Alaskan licence plate in yellow and blue: *The Last Frontier.* A wolf-dog peered out the window of the extended cab, eyes the colour of old jeans. From under the bill of his cap its owner watched me, smoke snaking from his cigarette, until I moved away.

Only a couple of hours to get to the border but already I felt stiff. The seat had rusted fast and I had to strain to reach the pedals. That together with the way I held onto the wheel so hard had cramped my muscles from my shoulders down to my thighs. I walked to stretch my legs, sipping my Coke and looking at the cars, my head buzzing from concentrating on keeping the truck between the lane markers.

No one else got out of their cars. I got within a car's length of Canada then turned back to find suspicious faces staring at me through windscreens. You'd have thought I was trying to sneak in ahead of them.

The other vehicles varied between sleek and wretched but only Fleur's truck was so loaded with boxes that it looked like it was squatting on its heels. I walked back and leant in the window. Fleur had put on her hat, the old Stetson I'd only seen her wear in

Lasso Joe's or driving around town in her truck, and had it tilted so it covered half her face.

'What's the hat for?' I asked. 'Stopping me from seeing in, or you from looking out?'

'Keeps the sun off.'

'So it's not just a fashion accessory then.'

She stared at me from under the brim with one of those slit-eyed cowboy looks. 'No,' she said, 'it's not,' and tugged it further forward.

'Don't fall asleep – we might have to circle the wagons at any moment.' Of course she didn't laugh, didn't look up again, so I said, 'Pass me some chocolate, would you?'

With a sigh she rummaged in the cooler. 'We'll soon have nothing left at this rate.'

'We didn't have much to start with. A loaf of Wonder bread and a pack of cheese slices isn't enough to get us to Alaska.'

'This isn't some kinda holiday. We can't stop every ten miles for you to use the washroom or buy more candy. You don't get it – we've got two thousand miles ahead of us.'

'Oh, I get it,' I said. 'I looked at the map. The whole of Canada's empty apart from where all the towns huddle up against the border. There's nothing between here and Whitehorse except a couple of petrol stations.'

'Gas stations,' she said.

'What?'

'You've been here long enough – it's gas stations.' Getting back at me for what I'd said about her hat.

'Right,' I said. 'You gas up in gas stations, and wash up in washrooms. I'm sure I'll get the hang of it one day.'

We spent the rest of the hour it took us to get to customs and immigration with the radio on. Country music. I said, 'Can't we have something we both like?'

'But this is great,' and she turned it up.

Songs about *walkin' away* and *not runnin'* and *runnin' out of time* that she hummed along to. Desperate love and desperate lives in corny rhymes while sweat crept down my neck and I moved the truck forward. When I leaned over to get out my passport my

T-shirt stuck to my back. 'We're driving to Alaska,' I told the officer.

'Any guns?' she asked.

I opened my mouth to say no but Fleur called across, 'A handgun. Got a licence for it.'

'OK,' said the officer. She made a note of that then looked at me. 'How much money do you have?'

'Fifty in Canadian, plus my credit card.'

I passed them over and she looked at them, stamped my passport and handed everything back with, 'OK, then. Have a safe trip.' Her vowels were too short to be American. Right at the border already the accent was different.

The road ran along a flat valley bottom full of pastures and barns and horses nodding over fences. At last this was summer: the smell of warm grass, sunshine pouring down. I couldn't relax though. The truck was bigger than anything I'd ever driven, so wide that if I didn't hold it straight the wheels strayed into the dirt at the side of the road or across the centre line. On top of that the gun nagged at me.

'So you've got a gun?' I said.

'That's what you heard me say.'

'Oh yeah, I heard. But that was a conversation opener.'

'If you want to know anything, you can ask me straight. I don't hold with this roundabout way of getting to things.'

Good ol' Fleur, straight as an arrow, shooting from the hip, corny as those songs she was always listening to. 'Right,' I said. 'So tell me, why do you have a gun?'

'None of your goddamn business,' she said. She smiled just in time but I knew not to ask again.

With a warm breeze rushing through the windows we passed shiny red tractors, a donkey in a shabby horse-box, got caught behind massive supermarket lorries heading north. Soon the valley narrowed to squeeze between the hills and there was no more room for fields, just a wall of rock on one side of us and the river gorge on the other. We stopped for coffee in a town called Hope. Trees all around, motels called The Alpine Lodge and The Swiss Chalet with steep roofs and window boxes full of bright flowers. Maybe they looked less out of place when there was snow.

It was easy to believe Hope was days from the nearest city, not just a couple of hours outside Vancouver. It was cooler up here and the streets were lined with pick-ups and people who looked tough in a way city people never could. The only clothes shop we passed had a window display of down vests and woollen hats. *Winterize yourself* said a yellow banner, and Fleur stopped and peered in. 'What's hot this winter?' I asked.

'They've got a good deal on Carhartt's.' She pointed at padded overalls the colour of mud.

'Earth tones,' I said. 'Nice.'

'They'll keep you warm at forty below.'

Functional. Like everything people walking past us were wearing: thick shirts, jeans, work boots. Already Fleur fitted in and I didn't.

The restaurant, though, was something else entirely: a waitress in a white apron and lace cap, a menu with scones and sponge cakes. England fifty years ago alive and kicking out here in British Columbia.

Beyond Hope the road narrowed. Lorries and those houses-on-wheels they call recreational vehicles thundered down at us, swinging out across the centre line as they took the curves wide and missed us by inches. Nothing felt right: my feet were sweaty in my leather boots, the slick soles were slipping on the worn pedals, my tight jeans were damp and clung to my legs. My head pounded from too much coffee and the effort of watching all that road coming at me but there was nowhere to stop with the road slicing between the rockface and the low wall bordering the gorge. From out of tunnels dark as boreholes cars rushed at us with their lights ablaze. Darkness swamped us, then bright sunlight, while down below the Fraser River frothed and tumbled with a summer's worth of rain.

Fleur fiddled with the radio, found a station, lost it, caught it again. Country, of course. 'Travis Tritt,' she told me.

A song about paying taxes and Uncle Sam stealing what you earn. A song from the heart. 'Yeah,' I said, 'I've heard of him. Isn't he the one that wears a black hat?' It was a good guess. Most of them did.

'No hat. He has a beard, and brown hair down to here.' She held a hand to her shoulder.

'That really narrows it down.'

Coming around the curve up ahead an RV swung into our lane, coming right at us, filling the road. Impossible to avoid it. No room between us and the wall but I wrenched the truck over anyway and kept my foot hard on the accelerator to pull us past. No impact, just an ugly tearing from the passenger side, and the pale length of the RV flashing past with its doors and windows and curtains. Then it was gone.

I kept going. Didn't even slow down because we had a sports car right on our bumper sliding out every few seconds to scout the road ahead. When I tried to change gear my leg jerked so stiffly I changed my mind and kept us in fourth. It was a while before I could look away from the road long enough to glance over at Fleur, and when I did my neck hurt from the tendons pulled tight by what had happened, and by what could have happened. Her face was flushed and she had a foot braced against the dashboard. 'I hope the damage isn't too bad,' I called out over the noise of the engine. 'He was coming right at us. He didn't even try to keep out of our lane.' My voice sounded thin.

'Yeah,' she said but she kept her eyes on the road as though if she let her attention slip again something worse would happen.

I oversteered around curves as though I expected the RV to come at us again, but more than anything it was the way Fleur didn't say anything that got to me. I wanted her to tell me it wasn't my fault. Instead she just sat there and watched the road.

*

The first petrol station I saw I turned into. When I switched off the engine the truck coughed, kicked forward dangerously close to a wall then stopped like something shot dead. Neither of us spoke. Then I reached for the doorhandle and jumped out.

Fleur was faster. Before I could get around the truck she was out of the cab and crouched down to get a good look at the damage. She kept her broken arm against her chest and peered at the long graze running through the dull yellow paint. Beneath gleamed raw metal. Still, given a couple of months it would rust over like all the other dents and scratches.

'Doesn't look so bad,' I said. 'It's mainly just the paintwork, and it's not as though that was in such good shape to start with.'

She pointed to the three ragged holes by the passenger door. 'Lost the mirror.'

'I can manage without that. Didn't even notice it was gone.' With the sun glaring down the tarmac had turned into a hotplate. I'd knotted my hair into a plait. Now I lifted it to let the breeze touch the back of my neck, and wondered where I'd put my sunglasses.

'Fairbanks is a long way from here. Another four days if we don't mess around. There are hazards like you wouldn't believe – bears and gravel, and long drops off the road. I need to know – do you really think you can handle it?'

'Great time to ask.' I pulled my bag out of the cab and looked through it.

'There's no point you doing this unless we get to Fairbanks in decent time. And in one piece. So if you can't do it, you just tell me now.'

Brave Fleur who'd go on alone if I backed out. 'What, and we'd turn around? Or would you somehow manage to drive yourself?'

She stood and wiped her hand on her jeans. 'I wouldn't have asked you if I didn't think you could do it, Sandra. Don't let me down.'

'You asked me because no one else would do it.' My sunglasses were at the bottom of my bag. I wiped them on my T-shirt and slipped them on. The world turned a shade darker.

'And you,' she said, 'didn't have to say yes just to please Ted and your mom. Your mom's worried, you know.'

'So she should be. I don't feel great about this trip myself.'

Her eyes pinched closed against the sun. 'No, about you leaving Matt.'

'That's just because she had her heart set on him as a son-in-law.'

'I wasn't surprised you changed your mind about coming,' she told me, 'not when your mom said you'd moved back home. You and Ted never did see eye to eye.'

I came closer. 'Let's not start this trip without getting some-thing clear. It wasn't my choice to drive you home. They forced me into it to help you out.'

She pushed back her hat. 'That's ridiculous, Sandra. No one can *force* you into something like this.'

'It was the only way they'd lend me the money to move down to Arizona.'

Her lips pulled in and she blinked at me. 'That's just not true,' she said softly.

'Oh yes it is,' and I got back in the truck

Six

Canada always made me think of forested mountains, or vast prairies where only silos and telegraph poles broke the horizon. Here there was nothing but mile upon mile of hilly scrubland. All along the road, though, we passed stalls selling cherries and peaches and apricots. I couldn't work it out.

Just beyond a bend I pulled up at a stall and got out, more from curiosity than hunger. I didn't see the river until I got close, nor the rows of trees beside it. I didn't see the woman either because she came out of the shadows so silently. She looked East European: narrow eyes, thick waist, scarf tied over her hair. Stranded out here in this desolate country.

She weighed the cherries – half a kilo – took my money without a word, thrust some change into my hand. A blue five-dollar note, a red two-dollar note, a golden one-dollar coin with a bird on one side and some small change. Then she settled back into her deckchair in the one part of the stall still in shade. I had no idea if I'd got a bargain.

When I glanced back she smiled so I waved. 'You take care now,' she called. No accent at all.

I put the cherries on top of the cooler. A peace offering. Fleur ignored them but I lifted them out by their stalks and dropped them into my mouth, bit off the flesh, spat the stones out the window as I drove. They were still warm from the sun, with sharp-tasting skin, a sweet burst of juice then the smooth stone inside.

For the first time all day I let my hands settle at the bottom of the wheel. This trip wasn't so bad. The heartening smell of earth, the road unpeeling in one long strip under a sun turning the bare hills gold. We passed small towns along the river, their fenced cemeteries and football fields, their farm equipment yards, their churches, everything so warm and clear I could have driven for ever even in that old wreck of a truck. My bladder put an end to that, though. The coffee in Hope, the Cokes I'd taken from the cooler since. There was nowhere to stop so I stepped harder on the accelerator and ignored Fleur's glances.

The next petrol station was half an hour up the road. I swung in and Fleur said, 'Out of gas already?'

'No, I need a toilet.' I left the truck at an angle and raced across the forecourt. The toilets stank. That seemed wrong in a country where waitresses still wore pinafore aprons and lacy hats. Only one of the toilets had been flushed, and as I crouched over the seat I read *Sue's A Cunt, Karen 4 Ray, Go Canucks.* Nothing original except they supported hockey up here not baseball, and that wasn't much of an improvement.

One winter Matt had got hooked on the National Hockey League. For months we had whole evenings with the TV buzzing under our conversations, and Matt looking past me at the screen while we ate dinner. He'd leave me the washing up and settle into an armchair for a better view, his feet on the table, a bowl of popcorn in his lap. When I glanced over his head would be outlined against a screen full of bundled-up players chasing something I couldn't even see. I called friends and arranged for us to go out but Matt wouldn't video the games – he said it wasn't the same. No matter what time I came home he'd be there, one hand on the remote, the other fumbling in his bowl of popcorn, like a middle-aged man with nothing else in his life.

The next season he didn't watch a single game.

Over the cracked basin hung a small mirror. I peered at myself, saw eyeliner smudged beneath both eyes. Must have been that way for hours. Fleur hadn't told me, but then she wasn't the sort of woman who would. My hair was a mess too so I undid my fancy plait and tried to retie it. My fingers were stiff from driving and my hands sweaty. In the end I gave up and put my hair in a pony tail.

Outside the sun was scorching the hills. This could have been southern Italy, a place where old women dressed in black and donkeys sulked along dusty paths, except for the huge petrol station sign and, behind it, a patch of green so bright it didn't look real in all that dried-up earth. A well-watered, perfectly clipped lawn tucked around a house – out here where even the people pulling up at the diner looked withered, like the woman who came past with two young kids: tight, bleached curls, tight, bleached jeans, trying to light a cigarette despite the breeze, her bone-thin husband close behind wearing a cap advertising a septic tank service. Old faces on young bodies, cheap denim even on their little boys trailing behind them.

This town was nothing more than a few petrol stations and a handful of convenience stores but the people could have been straight out of Venice Mansions: thin as sticks, discount shop clothes, skin rough from too many cigarettes and too much drink. It made me wonder what had happened for Fleur to end up there when she'd had such a good job. The other places she'd lived in had been so clean they were stark. Not as good as she could have afforded on her salary, but then it wasn't like her to spend her money on anything except her red Chevy pick-up or CDs of Clint Black and Dwight Yoakham and God knows who else. And now she was on her way back to Fairbanks when no job up there could match the one she'd had.

When I climbed back in and started the engine she was picking at her cast. I checked the map, decided to get petrol, and pulled up at a pump. 'We can't keep stopping like this,' she told me. 'You drank too much coffee. Could have seen that one coming.'

'Yeah,' and I looked away. A man in a green cap was slouching towards us so I wound down the window. 'Fill it up, would you?'

I leant back with my eyes closed and rested my arm on the cooler. The sun blasting through the windshield burned my face, turned the colour behind my eyelids red. After a summer of rain and cloud it felt good.

'We have to get to Prince George by tonight,' Fleur said.

'Or what?'

'Or I won't get to Fairbanks on Sunday. They're expecting me at work on Monday, and I have to find a place to live and all.'

'Fleur, you're cutting it fine, aren't you?' I sighed. 'Plus we left Seattle late, you know that.'

She shielded her eyes against the sun. 'Whenever I've driven home I've always got to Prince George the first night. I know a good campground there.'

'All we need is a place with a patch of ground and a shower. We've passed dozens of them.'

'Everything I own is in this truck. I can't afford to lose it by camping just anywhere.'

The man was at the window and Fleur was fumbling in her wallet for her credit card. I passed it to him. 'Is that why you've got the gun?' I said. 'To shoot anyone who tries to steal your stuff?'

'Out there,' and she pointed up the road, 'no one's going to come to our rescue. There aren't any phones to call for help if someone tries to rob us, or rape us. Out there you're on your own.'

A man trying to rape Fleur: it had never occurred to me. She was one of the boys. Jeans, checked shirt, never wore a skirt or make-up, never had a boyfriend as far as I knew. A tomboy grown into a plain woman, always cheerful as though it didn't bother her that men didn't ask her out. She treated them like brothers and now I wondered – did she feel she had to? Was she happy being no-nonsense Fleur who watched football and could change a tyre on her own? Had she ever been in love? Had anyone fallen in love with her?

'Besides,' she was saying, 'guns are perfectly safe.'

'Except for whoever you shoot.'

The attendant was back. He handed me the card. 'Can't use this,' he said. 'It's been cancelled.'

'What?' Fleur leaned over and looked at it, turned it over and looked at it again. She said, 'What d'ya mean?'

'Been cancelled. Sorry. Do you have another card you can use?'

'No,' she said, 'no, I don't. This one's fine. I used it a couple of days back.'

He gripped the top edge of the window. 'Then you have cash, right? Forty-four dollars sixty.'

She blinked. 'Give us a minute, would you?'

'Sure,' and, just in case, he walked away towards the exit, casually kicking at the dirt.

'Give him cash,' I said. 'What does it matter?'

She had her wallet out and her money spread over her knees. 'Can't,' she said. 'If I do that we won't have anything to pay for campgrounds and food.'

'Then give him American.'

'That'd pretty much wipe me out.'

'So how exactly were you thinking of paying?'

'By credit card.' She looked up. 'I used it on Friday and there wasn't any problem. He must have made a mistake.'

'Go on, tell him.' But she just sat there picking at the end of her cast. 'Fleur, how much cash do you have on you?'

'About forty dollars Canadian, and the same in American.' She leant forward with her elbows on her knees and her fingers at her mouth.

The attendant was watching us from under the bill of his cap. I looked away. 'You couldn't have been planning to drive all that way with only one credit card and so little in cash.'

'Things have been tight.' Her face was flushed, and when she pushed her hair back some strands stuck to her forehead. 'You must have brought your cards, right?'

'Of course I did. Well, my one remaining card.' I rested my hands on the top of the wheel. An RV pulled up at the next pump. A man got out, shorts, short legs, a cap tipped back. His belly hung in front of him like a balloon full of water.

'I'll pay you back,' said Fleur.

'Come on, I'm moving to Arizona next week. I can't pay for petrol all the way to Fairbanks.'

'Then you think of a way of getting us out of here.'

She was waiting for me to say that we should turn back, willing me to come out with it, but I didn't. I didn't want to be to blame when we arrived back in Seattle – I knew what that would mean to Mum and Ted, and I wouldn't get the money I needed to move to Arizona. I opened my bag, searched through it saying, 'Shit, how could you not know it was cancelled? What the hell did you buy the last time you used it?'

'I'm sorry,' she snapped. 'I didn't mean for this to happen.'

'This isn't like you. You've hardly prepared for this trip at all.' I waved the attendant over then handed him my card. 'This one's OK.' Self-righteous, but it didn't make me feel any better.

'I'll pay you back,' she said. 'You know that.'

'Yeah, right after you pay for my ticket home. Or is that going to come off my card too?'

She propped one foot on her knee. It tapped tapped tapped. 'Haven't you ever helped anyone out before? I mean, *really* helped them out?'

'It's supposed to be something you do out of the goodness of your heart, not because someone forces you into it.'

'You don't get to choose when you help people depending on whether it's convenient. You've no idea, have you? You've always had it so easy, never had to really make it on your own, never had people rely on you.'

'If you're trying to make me see how unpleasant life can be you're doing a great job.'

The attendant passed the slip through the window and I signed it, handed it back, took my copy from him. 'Have a nice day,' he said, not all in one rush the way you hear it at the 7-Eleven or McDonald's, but as though he'd just thought of it.

'It's too late for that,' I told him, and I started the truck.

Seven

Fleur wasn't kidding when she said she wanted to make it to Prince George. Night came down but we kept going. Tiredness made me see things: shapes stepping into the road that turned out to be tree shadows, lights coming at me that shrunk to moonlight on water. For dinner Fleur had passed me a sandwich of white bread, stale mayonnaise and limp cheese slices. Lots of calories and not a single vitamin. Afterwards we had Coke and a Hershey bar, just to make sure we'd eaten a well-balanced meal.

'This isn't so bad,' she said.

'Compared to what?'

But she couldn't tell me.

The whole time I was thinking: at least thirty US dollars each time we stopped for petrol, four stops made well over a hundred dollars a day plus twenty for food, ten for a campsite or maybe forty for a motel. Four more days at least to get us to Alaska. This trip was going make a big hole in my card – an even bigger one than I'd already made from a whole summer of charging my petrol, paints, paper and postage and only paying off the minimum every month – and who knew when Fleur was going to pay me back. I thought, I should leave her now before I dig myself in too deep, and imagined her standing by her truck as I walked away, her hands jammed into her pockets, her elbows sticking out. Maybe she'd shout something: *I should have known I couldn't trust you.* I'd have to yell something back, but all I could think of was the same: *I should have known I couldn't trust you.* And it was true: she'd always been too good to be true.

When we came to a place called Shirley's Gas & Diner I pulled in. 'I need some coffee or I'm going to fall asleep.'

She sighed, didn't object though I knew she wanted to keep moving as though this was some kind of race.

I pulled up close to the long window running down one side of the diner. Over platefuls of steaming food faces peered out at us, pale in the fluorescent light. It looked like everyone was wearing hats or caps, even the women.

'I'll get take-out,' she said, 'it'll be quicker,' and as if she didn't trust me she got out before I'd even turned off the engine. In the dark I watched her walk over, push open the door, lean on the counter and talk to one of the waitresses. There'd be a smell of frying burgers, the murmur of conversations, the gleam of light off the tabletops. That's what I'd wanted, not just the coffee: time off from staring through the dark at the road. She glanced at the clock, tapped her fingers against the countertop. Five hours without a real break but she still didn't want to stop. When she turned towards the truck the electric light made her face looked flat and stupid.

In a couple of minutes she was back. One cup of coffee, no doughnut to go with it. She passed it to me then slammed the door.

I popped open the lid but the coffee was scalding. 'Listen,' I said, 'we should stop at the next campground. I'm getting really tired.'

'You're doing just fine,' she said.

'You won't be saying that when we're wrapped around a tree.'

'Don't kid about things like that,' she told me, but I wasn't kidding. I was dog tired and was sure she knew it, but she found both ends of her seatbelt and clipped them together. 'We could be in Prince George in another hour.'

But we didn't get there until after eleven – everything shut for the night, including the campground. Fleur got out of the truck anyway and stood at the padlocked barrier. I leant my head against the wheel. It was cool where I hadn't touched it in a while. When she tapped on my door I couldn't be bothered to reach for the handle and instead let her pull it open. 'I can't understand it, I've always stayed here,' she said. 'They don't lock up til midnight.'

'It's late.'

'Goddammit, it's not that late.'

'Get in. We'll have to find somewhere else.'

'There isn't anywhere else. Not around here.' She rattled the barrier then waited with her fingers looped over the top bar. No one came.

We drove up empty streets, back past a huge rough-cut statue of a logger with an axe over his shoulder and a stare fixed on the far distance, found ourselves heading out of town the wrong way and had to turn around. On the way back in I spotted a motel and slowed. Marcie's Motor Lodge. A prim place with blue window frames and tubs of flowers by the office door. 'Here, this'll do.'

'We can't afford a motel.'

'You're not paying, remember?'

'But I aim to pay you back. It'll be at least fifty bucks. Anyhow, we could camp outside town someplace for free.'

I felt itchy from sweating in my clothes most of the day, wanted to at least change and have a shower. 'Camp in the middle of nowhere? You're joking.'

'We can drive around town looking for another campground but I'm telling you, there's nowhere else.'

'It's worth a try,' and I pulled away from Marcie's Motor Lodge, saw its lights disappear in the rearview mirror before I realised – even a campground with showers wasn't much good this late at night. We'd have to put up the tent in the dark, root through the bed of the truck for the bedrolls and sleeping bags, lay them out. Or at least I would. Fleur wouldn't be able to do much with her arm in the cast. No wonder she didn't mind camping.

We drove up and down dead streets with lit-up signs for pizza, oil changes and pet grooming but she was right, there weren't any other campsites. No other motels either, just a few hotels we couldn't afford. 'Take a right here,' she said. As though she knew where she was going. Instead I took a left because I thought the motel was back that way. More dark buildings, then a flash of red and white neon advertising Molson. 'This isn't the right way,' she told me.

When I went through a red light and just missed a car that blared its horn I wasn't scared. Was hardly there at all, to tell the truth, more asleep than awake, dulled by all the road coming at me. Fleur hissed, 'Goddamn, be careful,' and I slowed right down. Ghostly lit supermarkets, a boutique, a convenience store window bright as a TV screen.

We crawled along, me looking for a motel and Fleur watching for God knows what. She had her feet against the dashboard. 'Driving around town's a waste of time. This is the road north. We might as well keep going.'

It was nearly midnight and Marcie's Motor Lodge had vanished. Maybe I'd missed it – I was losing snatches of time as waves of tiredness swamped me.

This was the biggest town since we'd left Seattle: banks, supermarkets, hairdressers, restaurants. As though no one had noticed that all around was nothing but hundreds of miles of forest. I didn't want to leave and head back into the dark. Already the town was thinning out with smaller buildings and bigger gaps between them. When I saw a side road I swung into it and there, right in front of us, stood a gaudy, yellow-painted motel with a lit-up vacancies sign. Primrose Court. More decrepit than Marcie's Motor Lodge but only fifty dollars for a room, hot water, cable TV and free ice.

'We can't afford this,' Fleur said.

'Free ice,' I said, 'we'll fill the cooler and get our money's worth.'

'Fifty bucks. It's ridiculous.'

'It's open and it has vacancies – what more could we want?'

She scowled, looked away.

I unbuckled my seatbelt. 'Christ – my treat, all right?'

Of course it didn't work out that way. Right there in front of the clerk she insisted on adding the fifty Canadian dollars to the list she'd started, then she stood on the concrete outside our room looking grim as I drove the truck over. In the headlights she looked old and washed out.

Inside the air was stale, the beds covered with shabby nylon sheets, and the TV picture had a strange green tinge. 'Fifty bucks for this,' she said.

'It's a bargain compared to being comatose in a ditch.'

She unzipped her bag. 'You should have said if you were that tired.'

Instead of answering I shut myself in the bathroom and rested my aching head on my knees. I didn't bother with a shower. Instead I brushed my teeth and changed my underwear, then sunk into bed with the covers pulled up around my neck. It took Fleur quite a while to get out of her clothes and maybe I should have helped her, but I kept my eyes closed against the light and tried to sleep. No matter which way I lay I couldn't get comfortable because the road kept rushing towards me, and when in the end I did fall asleep I dreamt I was still driving.

Eight

I wasn't used to driving long distances. I'd only been on a couple of road trips – a journey down to Texas with Jo one summer after her good-for-nothing boyfriend moved there, and the time I drove to New Mexico with Matt to meet some long-lost uncle who was his only relative who hadn't died or disappeared. We'd planned to spend a week but after two days we made some excuse and left. All those polished antiques we had to keep our feet off, the expensive rugs that couldn't be stepped on, the ashtrays that turned out not to be ashtrays but ancient Chinese ceramics. As I drove out the gates Matt whooped and put his feet up on the dashboard. We threw rubbish on the floor and smoked until our throats were sore. We stopped as often as we wanted, saw the landscape rather than just speeding through it. Small desert towns of flat-roofed buildings and wide pavements, roads ruled straight across deserts spiked with agave. The biggest surprise was the colour, all the reds and yellows and greens that ripened in the shade: on flowers and T-shirts, in murals and salads and mouth-scorching sauces. We stopped for cold beers and tortilla chips in dark bars and for the first time Matt told me stories about his grandmother who'd come down from Nova Scotia, his grand-father who'd fought in the Spanish Civil War whose wife thought he was dead and married another man, his brother who died when he was one and Matt was four and just old enough to remember. He told me how he'd tried to track down his runaway father and had found a woman who'd rented a room to him a few months before in Oklahoma. That was as close as he'd got.

For those few days on the road Matt reached down inside himself: setting a neighbour's shed on fire when he was twelve, running away to San Francisco and living with the Hare Krishnas until the police found him, going to a brothel with one of his friends. He told me these stories when I was driving and couldn't look him in the face, and I got the feeling he told them to watch me, to work out what I really thought of him. He must have known it wasn't enough to build a life on. Maybe that's why he didn't want to hear my stories, and why afterwards he never talked about his past again. His secrets were still there though, and we couldn't talk without bumping into them, soft but resistant, unmentionable but there, his sad past that I should pity him for, love him for, at least stay with him for.

Fleur told me stories too but they weren't about her. When I came out of the bathroom towelling my hair dry she was perched on the edge of her bed pulling on her jeans one-handed. She said, 'Just another four days and we'll be there. I can't wait.'

'Right.' I dug through my bag for fresh clothes, pulled on a clean pair of jeans and a sweater.

She gave me a smile. 'Fall will just be starting. Maybe getting a frost at night, though the real cold won't come for another couple of months. But then in Alaska you never can tell. Winter can catch you out.' She watched me brush my hair and plait it, then run a little liner around my eyes. 'I don't know why you're bothering when we're just gonna be in the truck all day. No one in Fairbanks uses stuff like that. Besides, when it's real cold your eyes run and your make-up would end up all over your face.'

'I won't be there when it gets cold.'

'It's something to experience,' she said, 'there's nothing like it.'

While I pushed my dirty clothes into my bag and hunted around the room for anything I might have left behind she told me that Fairbanks has a dry cold from being in the heartland, that it can get so cold trees explode, that at fifty below boiling water thrown into the air vanishes into vapour with a whistle. By the time I was tying the tarp over our bags she was telling me some story about two people getting caught on the mudflats outside Anchorage, the woman sinking into the mud, getting stuck, how the fire service could do nothing to save her except lay on pipes of air as the tide came in but in the end it was hopeless and she drowned with all the emergency crews and her husband looking on. Fleur was full of stories about strange accidents – a woman in high heels losing her toes to frostbite, a bull moose that trampled a snowmobiler who wouldn't get out of his way, a shooting in a small town near the Arctic Circle that left five people dead. Stories about other people's mistakes.

Despite the sun the air was cold. I pulled on my suede jacket and climbed into the cab. Felt like winter already, and Fairbanks would be colder. Snow maybe, despite what Fleur said. As she walked back from the motel office the thick shirt she'd put on over her T-shirt flapped because she hadn't done up the buttons. She got into the truck and fiddled with them as I pulled out onto the main road, trying to do them up one-handed. She didn't ask me to help so I didn't offer.

I drove up the road to a diner in the heart of town and she kept right on with her stories: about her dad going hunting and being sneaked up on by a moose; how her brother Ryan had gone out snowmobiling on a lake one spring with a bunch of friends and one of them had gone off the trail onto thin ice and was never found. Stories about how dangerous Alaska was, how mistakes were deadly. After the mistakes she'd made I wondered if it had struck her that she'd changed, that maybe she'd be the one who went off the trail and was never found.

The diner smelled of fresh coffee and stale grease. I chose a table by the window and a skinny waitress with a mournful face had our cups filled before we'd even opened the menus. I ordered bacon, eggs and toast but Fleur said she wasn't hungry, she'd stick to coffee, then carried right on about Alaska being the biggest state, Alaska having the highest mountain on the continent, Alaska having the lowest temperatures, the biggest coal reserves, the most oil, the greatest ranges of temperature. The most super- latives. She was proud of them, as though they proved something about her.

It was nearly nine o'clock and most of Prince George had already eaten breakfast. Only a few tables still had customers, mostly men in worn work jackets with caps pulled down over their faces. Caps that said things like *Deschamps Lumber Yard* and *Deloitt Fertiliser*. Over in the corner three waitresses were drink- ing coffee and smoking. From speakers at the end of the room country music sighed out so softly all I could hear was a moaning slide guitar and snatches of a man's slow voice.

Just about everyone who came past the window was in boots and jeans. I only saw one woman in lipstick and heels, nothing fancy, but enough to stand out as she picked her way across the pavement towards an office door. She wouldn't make it in Fleur's Alaska. She'd be one of the women who walked through the snow in thin shoes and lost their toes to frostbite.

I'd brought the guidebook along and looked through it as Fleur talked but soon she took it from me. 'There,' she said and pressed open the pages, 'that's Fairbanks.' A double-page spread, headlights looming out of thick fog, snow violet in the twilight, a couple of neon signs that made everything else look lost. *Fairbanks at midday, 1st January* said the caption. 'That's right downtown. The ice fog can get real bad. Anyway, in January there's not much daylight to speak of.'

'Lovely,' I said, 'this will do a lot for tourism.'

She smiled to herself as she took back the guidebook. 'All that darkness and cold can get to you. People end up drinking too much or doing drugs, anything to get through the winter.'

'What did you do?'

'Me? Winter didn't bother me too much. In fact, I kinda liked it. Used to go mushing with my friends who kept dog teams, or skiing sometimes. Weekends I'd go dancing somewhere like The Wild Dog Saloon.'

Of course she would. And of course it would have a name like The Wild Dog Saloon.

The waitress brought over my breakfast and the coffee pot. She slid my plate in front of me and bent close to refill our cups. Rose soap. Hint of cigarette smoke. Her skin thin and wrinkled like used wrapping paper, though she couldn't have been more than forty. 'Eggs over easy, bacon, wholewheat toast, blueberry jam.'

'Thanks,' I said.

She looked across at Fleur. 'You going to change your mind about breakfast, sweetie?'

'No, thank you.'

She nodded and walked over to the next table, her loose shoes slapping her soles. The man pushed his cup towards her but didn't look up from his paper until she said, 'Aren't they missing you at work by now, Ron?'

He tilted back his cap. 'Doubt it. Besides, I'd rather sit here and spend the morning watching you. You're looking better every day, Marie.'

'Well, you're not,' she said. 'You'll turn to fat if you spend half the day sitting around eating,' and she walked back with more of a swing in her hips, picked up her cigarette and leant against the counter. Through her own smoke she stared out into the street where cars and trucks slid past, some with dogs in the back, others with wood piled high. Getting ready for winter though it was only August.

While I ate Fleur read out parts of the guidebook, telling me what she thought they'd got wrong, how some of the motels they mentioned had closed down or should be closed down, how the ferry service from Seattle to Haines had changed. The sun came out and made everything look fresh. Soon the diner had emptied except for us. Though it was barely half past nine the board outside the kitchen had been turned over to show the lunch specials. Fleur bent forward over the guidebook as she read. In the sunlight her hair looked dull and unwashed.

'Must be difficult showering with that cast on your arm,' I said.

She looked up, let the book close. 'Sure is. Can't get it wet.'

'So how do you manage?'

'I have sponge baths.'

I speared a piece of bacon. 'How long have you been doing that now?'

'Oh.' She looked straight at me. 'About three weeks.'

'Is it fractured?'

'What?'

'Your arm – is it fractured?'

She shifted forward and picked up her coffee. 'Yeah,' she said. 'Broke the ulna pretty bad. Have to keep the cast on another month at least.'

'Bad luck breaking it just before you wanted to move. Wrecking your truck too.'

She just nodded. Picked up the book. Opened it and frowned down at the first page she came to. End of conversation, just like the day before in Seattle when Ted had told me not to pry. But then Ted was too careful. He never chewed ice in case he cracked the

66

enamel on his teeth; he unplugged the TV before he went to bed; he filed away the guarantee of every electric appliance he bought.

'Did you break it in the accident?' I said.

She turned the page. 'No. That was a while back.'

'How long back?' but she didn't say anything. I spread butter and jam on my toast, and the waitress came by to refill our cups. Someone turned the music up in time for the end of a song telling us *If love's a fool's game, I'm a fool*. 'Shame we didn't think of taking the ferry as far as Haines,' I said. 'It would have cut down on the driving.'

'We'd have had to book at this time of year, and I didn't have time for those kinds of arrangements. This was all decided at the last minute.'

'Even the job?'

'Yeah.' She glanced at her watch. 'We're running way behind this morning. Ryan can do this trip in four days. I usually take five, and it shouldn't take any longer than that.'

Usually. As though she did this trip once a month. 'Right, but I bet your brother doesn't do the trip in an overloaded old three-quarter-ton truck.'

She pushed the guidebook back towards me. 'This isn't a vacation, Sandra. I've got to get home, find a place to live and get ready for work, and I haven't much time for any of that.'

Almost no time, in fact, but I didn't say so. Instead I said, 'You know, you still haven't told me what this job is.'

For a moment I thought she was going to ignore me again, but she said, 'Working as a lab tech in a high school. The pay's not bad, and it's something different.'

Different from earning good money as a chemical engineer in Seattle, that was true, but then there probably wasn't much else she could do in a place like Fairbanks. And I wondered – why did she want to move back so badly? What had happened to her?

Fleur was saying, 'I have to be back as soon as I can – they're expecting me to call in on Monday morning if I can.' She glanced at my breakfast. 'We can't waste time like this.'

'So maybe you should have flown Ryan down to Seattle. He'd have driven you home in four days.'

'He's got a job,' she said. 'It wouldn't have been fair to ask him.'

I finished my coffee. 'Did your whole family have better things to do?'

'This is only going to take a week of your time, Sandra.' She watched a truck pull past, not looking at me though I could see her face reflected in the window. Round and bright as a coin. Hard. 'You always think of yourself, you know that?'

'And who do you always think of?'

'This isn't some kinda joke. This is people's lives.' She shifted in her seat, settling in to tell me all about Life. 'Don't you care at all? I mean, we're talking about people's feelings here and you just run all over them. Matt loved you and you kept him hanging around just as long as it suited you, then you dumped him. You can't treat people like that.'

I leant onto my elbows. 'And what makes you an expert? When have you ever had anyone to dump?'

She sucked in her bottom lip and blinked. I shouldn't have said it but I was provoked and I don't take well to that. So we sat there staring past each other while plates rattled as tables were cleared and someone shouted from the kitchen. Didn't say a word because there was nothing else to say.

*

It was lunchtime when the signs started: Northern Lights Motel, Mac's Deli, Frozen Delights Ice Cream, Northern Towing Service. That last one made me wonder: what if we broke down? The engine could seize up, a tyre blow out, and we'd be stuck out here. Forest all around. Nothing but this road and a sign announcing twenty-five kilometres to Fort St John.

The air was so clear the trees bristled with sharp lines of sun and shadow. In their shade I caught flashes of sunlight on fur. Animals looking out at us. Deer maybe, though they looked too big. I'd have asked Fleur but she'd curled up and hadn't opened her eyes for over an hour. She looked smaller, as though I'd knocked the breath out of her with what I'd said in the diner.

When we'd gone out to Lasso Joe's she'd always had plenty of men nodding hello. Though they made room for her at the bar and bought her beers they didn't change the way they stood when she came up, not like when a woman in tight jeans passed and they all shifted slightly to watch. I'd always thought she preferred being one of the boys in her jeans and plain face, fitting in without changing a thing. Now I wondered: did she see the man she wanted turn to watch other women cross the room? She'd never let on, as though she didn't need anyone or anything. Unlike the rest of us.

More signs but still no town, not even a thinning of the trees. Nothing but hills, straight stretches of road, and in places ghostly curves of the old highway snaking past, silted up now with weeds. The guidebook said this road had been built in just a few months back in 1939. Preparation for the war, in case the United States was invaded from the Pacific, which of course it was. Japanese troops in the Aleutians, out on that tail of islands stretching so far into the west they don't even make it onto maps of Alaska without being stashed in an empty corner. Come to that, Alaska doesn't make it onto most maps of the US unless it's lowered into a box somewhere just off the coast of California. A giant icy island just out of sight of the beaches.

Fleur slept with her broken arm in her lap and her hair straggling across her face. When we'd left Prince George I'd waited for her to say, *You shouldn't have said that – who the heck do you think you are?* And I'd have said, *I didn't mean it – it just came out,* though that wasn't true. I'd been longing to say it for years, just to get back at her for all her remarks about my short skirts and tight jeans. Instead we both stared through the windscreen and when eventually I looked across she'd curled up with a pillow, leaving me to drive with nothing for company except the radio. A couple of times I'd said, 'You still asleep, Fleur?' She didn't move, even when I found a country station and turned up some number about how *a big-hearted woman needs a big-hearted man.*

When the road turned from tarmac to rough dirt her head slid to one side and bounced against the window. With the sun hitting her full in the face she looked soft and vulnerable. As gently as I could I pushed her head back towards the pillow. She sniffed and turned away.

All those stories she'd told, and not one of them had said anything new about her. I'd been listening for some hint to explain how she'd ended up without a job and living in a place like Venice Mansions. There'd been a crash that had written off her Chevy, and some other kind of accident three weeks ago that left her with a broken arm. How could anyone be that unlucky? But then maybe it wasn't luck. Maybe the two were connected. Ted knew what had happened, and probably Mum did too, but they hadn't told me. Hadn't trusted me to keep it to myself.

Construction up ahead. A woman in a bright orange vest got up from a deckchair and held out a stop sign. Beyond her roared earthmovers, some of them so big they belonged to a different scale of things. Their wheels were taller than the truck, the earth they carried enough to bury us so you wouldn't even have known we were there. The air was fogged red with dust and the woman had to raise her voice. 'Be another few minutes,' she told me. 'Then you'll have to drive through real careful. Construction goes on for about five clicks here, but the road's up for another ten so you'll have to go slow right the way into town. Construction vehicles get the right of way, so make sure you keep an eye on them. The way some of these guys drive, chances are they won't even see you.'

'Thanks,' I said. I wanted to wind up the window to keep out the dust and noise but she rested her arm on the edge.

'Where're you two headed?'

'Fairbanks.'

'That's a long drive,' she said. 'What's up there?'

'My friend's family. And she's got herself a job there.' The seat creaked as Fleur shifted, woke. 'She's broken her arm and can't drive.'

As she looked past me to Fleur she lifted off her hard hat and pushed her fingers through her hair. Her forehead was white where the dust hadn't got to it. 'How did you do that?'

Fleur rubbed her face and yawned. 'Had an accident.'

'Car accident?'

'Nope, it wasn't no car accident.'

'So how did you do it?'

'I fell – the whole thing was dumb.'

70

'At home? You know, that's where most accidents happen.' The woman wiped her face with one hand. The sweat she missed was brown. 'Well then, you're lucky you have someone to drive you.'

'I guess,' said Fleur.

'You bet you are.' Up ahead an RV came lumbering out of the dust, tiny beside the construction vehicles. The woman looked at her watch then went back to her deckchair. She spoke into a walkie-talkie, plugging her left ear with a finger and raising her voice. Then she waved us on, shouted, 'Good luck, girls.'

'So you fell?' I said as I rolled up the window. 'How did that happen?'

'I passed out.'

A giant dumper truck came roaring down an earth slope and into the road right in front of us. I braked to let it past. Up in the glass eye of the truck the driver looked tiny and remote. 'Were you ill?'

'Yeah, I was ill.' The pillow had slipped down and she tugged it back behind her head then closed her eyes.

'Fleur?'

'Yeah?'

I was going to ask her again, *What happened?* Instead I told her, 'I'm sorry about what I said earlier. I shouldn't have said it.'

'But you did,' and she turned away to the window.

'What – didn't I apologise the right way?'

'You meant what you said, so how can an apology put that right?'

She was right, but that wasn't the point. I wanted to patch things up so we could get through another three days together, but to her it didn't seem to matter: we were stuck in this cab and if we hardly talked it wasn't of any concern. Maybe it was punishment for my saying what I shouldn't have, and for letting her know that if it wasn't for Mum and Ted I wouldn't be driving her home.

*

There wasn't much to Fort St John. Not that I'd expected any different. At the end of the first block we found a restaurant with nylon lace curtains and walls hung with paintings that had orange price tags on the frames. A stiff moose in a glade. A bear drinking from a blue smudge of a waterfall. Winter scenes of snowy hills that looked as flat as chalk. The bigger the painting the higher the price. Paintings priced by the square foot, like back in the Renaissance. It wasn't such a bad idea.

A sweet-faced girl with a middle-aged body laid a menu on our table. While we looked at it she folded her arms under her breasts and stared out the window. Behind me two women were talking. 'Doesn't have arms, the poor little thing,' said one of them.

'It's not as if they can't do something for them nowadays.'

'But what sort of a life will it have? If you ask me, they should have decided not to have it.' There was the chink of metal on crockery, then she added, 'They were going to name it Alice after her mother. They've decided against that now.'

I looked over my shoulder. Both women were spreading butter on sliced fruitcake, their faces pulled tight around pursed lips.

Fleur didn't even open her menu. 'Coffee for me,' she told the waitress.

I handed back the menu. 'Yeah, me too, and I'd like a ham salad sandwich on wholewheat.'

We'd barely started this trip and already we were in a rut: she'd get coffee while I ordered breakfast or a sandwich. She'd look sour because, as she'd told me when we left Prince George that morning, we had bread, cheese slices and chocolate in the cooler for when we got hungry. Afterwards she'd get out the receipt and her list of Money Owed To Sandra, and add it on with a sigh.

I opened the guidebook. Inside the front cover Mum had written, *Have a wonderful trip – and see as much as you can while you're there!* above a black and white map of Alaska. It only showed a couple of roads because that's pretty much all there was. I flicked through to the section *Around Fairbanks*. Denali National Park, Chena Hot Springs, Circle Hot Springs, a town called Circle, another called North Pole – one of the many places Santa was supposed to come from – Fox with its great bar, Tok shortened from Tokyo that was set up for Alcan construction workers and that had nothing much of anything nowadays. Little else besides a disused gold-dredging operation that did the best breakfasts anywhere in the state. Fairbanks itself had a few fast food franchises, something called Alaskaland, a university and its museum, an airport, a few main roads with arrows pointing out of town, though unless you went east or south there was nowhere much to go.

A Musak version of 'Cracklin' Rosie' filtered down at us. It matched the cheap wallpaper, the lacy curtains, the fake flowers in their Woolworth vases. No surprise then that the coffee was instant and the cream was creamer. But the sandwich was a surprise – two thick slices of fresh bread stuffed full with ham, lettuce and tomato, and just enough mustard to give it a kick. It was inspiring – it would have been a sandwich to paint. I took a couple of bites then slid half across to Fleur. Trying to prove her wrong. She slid it back, said, 'I'll make myself a sandwich back in the truck. We have –'

'Bread and cheese slices. I know.' As though a few dollars was going to make a difference when we were putting over a hundred dollars of petrol in the truck every day. Or at least, I was.

I spread one of Ted's maps on the table and took another bite of the sandwich. It wasn't like her to be mean like this. She'd taken me to Lasso Joe's and insisted on buying me drinks and bowls of chilli, had taken me to see the Mariners though I hadn't a clue about baseball, had always come over to the house with pizza or ice cream. But now I wondered: had all that been an act? Had she just been generous when she could afford to be, or when she thought she ought to be? Besides, she must have been earning good wages in that pharmaceutical plant on the edge of town, full benefits and no one but herself to look after. Now, out here in the middle of nowhere, she didn't care any more. I was supposed to live on Wonder bread and cheese slices and drive hard all day to get her home.

I found Fort St John in a crease of the map, said, 'Where're we aiming for tonight?'

Fleur was dipping her head to a violin version of 'Stand By Your Man'. 'Somewhere around Pink Mountain. At least we will if we keep moving,' and she glanced at my sandwich.

As though we were taking our time. Day Two and we were two thirds of the way through the vastness of British Columbia. The rest of the province stretched above us into a few small settlements, a couple of roads and not much more. Then there was part of the Yukon to get through before we even reached Alaska. It was hard to find anything to the north of us that looked like a decent-sized town. Canada was massive – and most of it was empty.

It took me some time to find Pink Mountain. It was way to the north, a tiny circle with the name printed in letters it strained my eyes to read. Most likely it wasn't more than a few shops and a motel or two along the highway. I said, 'I don't see how your brother can do this trip in four days unless he drives eighteen hours a day.'

'That's about it. He doesn't hang around, not for anyone or anything. Plus he used to be a truck driver.' She gave me a small smile then made a face at the coffee. 'Recently he's been doing this trip a couple of times a year. His ex-wife Cassie moved back down to Bellingham and took little Mike with her so if he wants to see him he has to come all this way. Usually he brings the band and they play a couple of gigs.'

I nodded and looked away but she kept on talking as though she'd forgotten we were irritated with each other.

'The band's had more luck over in Idaho and Montana. He's got friends that fix him up with gigs. Ends up playing places out in the sticks, but one of these days he's gonna really make it. His songs are just as good as anything Clint Black ever wrote, and that's the truth, but he has to take on carpentry work and stuff to get by. He cut a record a couple of years back but he couldn't get the air time. He'll try again soon, that's the plan.'

She smiled, not for me but because she adored him. I got the feeling she expected me to as well though he sounded like an arrogant son-of-a-bitch, walking out on jobs when he felt like it, taking off for weeks at a time without telling anyone where he was going, thinking he was some hotshot singer when all he got were small-time gigs. I'd have bet anything he had the same *Howdy pardner* way of talking as Fleur. Another fake cowboy.

'We can't get all the way to Pink Mountain today,' I said. 'Not unless we drive until eleven tonight, and I'm not doing that again.'

'Sure we can, I know it.' Back to cornball Fleur, all goodwill and optimism. She even smiled at me. 'You have to put a lot in to get a lot outta life. You just don't have enough confidence in yourself, Sandra, that's why you're dragging your feet.'

'I'm digging in my heels,' I said. 'There's a difference.'

She waved to the waitress for the bill, pulled out her wallet and slapped down a ten-dollar bill before I could get out my credit card.

'Keep it,' I said and pushed it back towards her, 'we might need the cash later.'

'I can cover it.' She was on her feet before the waitress came over, out the door before I had picked up the map and the guide-book. I handed my card to the waitress and put the ten dollars in my pocket. Stupid of her to insist on paying cash when we didn't have much to get us through the rest of Canada.

Fleur didn't wait for me. When I came out she was walking back to the truck and I followed, noticing how she walked with a roll, how she leaned slightly to one side to make up for not being able to swing her broken arm. A cowboy walk, and it annoyed me. Fleur pretending to be something she was not, listening to that music, talking about Life as though she had some special insight.

As I climbed into the cab she stood on the pavement and pushed back her hair. She called over, 'If you want to eat in restaurants you'll have to pay your own way.'

'I'm paying both our ways, Fleur.'

'I said I'd pay you back. But I can't afford for you to eat out the whole time.'

'I could stop eating,' I said. 'That would cut down on expenses.'

Getting into the cab she said something. Sounded like *Screw you* though the first word could have been anything she said it so quietly. I pulled out behind an old red pick-up with that *Screw you* keeping me quiet as we headed out of town and back onto the thin strip of road.

Nine

The mechanic was so wild and grizzled he should have been out trapping beaver, not poking around in the guts of the truck. He had a grey beard down to his chest and a nose pocked with blackheads. Still, he strutted across the yard with his arms swinging, his oily handkerchief dangling jauntily from his back pocket as he headed towards the pumps and the car that had just pulled in – an MG that looked small and fragile out here. It was the only vehicle that had stopped since we'd lurched off the road and onto the forecourt, and that had been a good two hours ago now.

From a low wall by the roadside I watched the driver get out and stretch with hands pressed into the small of his back. He looked around, looked at his watch, folded his arms. Impatient to be off in less than a minute.

It was already well past lunchtime and I was starving. Day Three of the trip and what I'd feared had happened way past the town of Fort Nelson, past the single motel and petrol station of Pink Mountain, out in an area that was pure wilderness except for the road. Now we were stranded here while the Mountain Man fiddled around inside the truck. It felt like we could be stuck here for ever. And just to add to the misery I'd caught a cold thanks to Fleur insisting we camp out the night before.

I'd hardly slept. The smell of Ted's sweat on the sleeping bag. Cold creeping up from the ground through all the clothes I'd pulled on, Fleur murmuring in her dreams while my breath froze on the sleeping bag. Right then I hated her. She'd refused to stop in Wonowon – never mind that the sun was going down – so on we'd gone, out to where there were no towns, no motels except one with rooms for more than even I was prepared to pay. I'd suggested we turn back to Wonowon and she'd laughed, said, 'Wo*no*won? It's not Indian, it's One-Oh-One. You know, mile one-oh-one of the highway.' The first time she'd laughed all day, and it irritated me.

I didn't know if this place where we'd broken down even had a name. It was just a garage-cum-petrol station. How could anyone settle here? And why would they want to? The further north we'd come the more the towns had shrunk and the less solid the buildings looked. This garage was just a patch of cracked tarmac with weeds pushing through and a couple of buildings listing to one side, losing their balance out here in all this emptiness. Places like this ended up scattered along the road where people had broken down or given up, putting up a house then finding a name for the place. They stayed because they couldn't go on and had no way to get home; they watched other people with better places to go drive past, and surely that would make them bitter enough to screw whoever broke down for all the money they could. People like us.

A couple of RVs passed in a rush of air and dust. When I turned back the mechanic wasn't at the truck, only Fleur who was leaning against it, yawning with one hand up to her mouth. Everything so still, the RVs heading down the hill like houses broken off the edge of a city and washed away by a flooded river.

By the time we'd driven up this hill the temperature gauge had tipped over as far as it could go. I knew we shouldn't go on, had been holding my breath for miles as I looked out for a garage – for something – out here in the middle of nowhere. Just when I was giving up hope the garage had appeared beyond the brow of the hill – a miracle – and I'd laughed as I'd pulled up on the forecourt. 'What,' I'd shouted to Fleur, 'are the chances of that?'

All morning the temperature gauge had been creeping over until it finally dipped into the red, and I'd pointed it out to Fleur. Naturally she leant close to spot what I was doing wrong. That made me tense up just when I needed to be gentle with the truck. I'd said over and over as we passed garages, 'How about here?' or 'This place looks like it's got a mechanic,' but she'd snapped back, 'Just don't push it so hard up the hills.' As though something I was doing was making it overheat.

Careless, and that wasn't like her. She'd always been a stickler for oil changes and tune-ups. But then that was for her Chevy, not this old bone-shaker. I was the one who ignored strange rattles and whines until it was too late because I never had the money to fix them, and had Matt and Ted tut-tutting at me as they leant under the bonnet of my Colt with the mechanic. As though they had any idea what he was doing.

At first I'd stood around with Fleur and watched the mechanic lean into the engine, come back up and wipe his face, pause to light a cigarette, knock the ash of it, relight it when it went out. Every now and then he wandered away then came back grimacing. He spread his rough hands along the edge of the truck and stared at the engine. 'Goddamn,' he'd say. Then, when smoke from his stub of a cigarette stung his eyes, he'd spit it out and grind it flat under his boot.

I'd waited until he'd disappeared into the workshop before whispering to Fleur, 'Do you think he has any idea what he's doing?'

Fleur pushed back her hair. 'He's a mechanic, isn't he?'

'I don't know,' I said, 'is he?'

Eventually he came back with a wrench and used it to knock some part loose, fiddled deep in the engine and came back up with a blackened part dangling pipes. He held it up for us to see. 'Water pump's leaking coolant. That's your problem. Gonna need a new one.'

Fleur nodded. 'Do you have one?'

'Nope, not for this truck. But maybe I could fix this one up. Might get you where you're going.'

I didn't want something fixed up. I wanted a new water pump that wasn't going to give out on us somewhere even more remote.

Fleur watched him. 'We'd sure appreciate it.'

'Gonna have to charge you extra if you want it done now,' he said. 'Got other jobs lined up.'

'No problem,' said Fleur.

But I said, 'How much more?'

'Double. That's the standard for emergency work.'

There were two other cars on the forecourt. One of them was up on bricks, the other had sunk down on flat tyres. Both looked like they had rusted solid. 'Where are those other jobs?'

Fleur smiled across at me. 'It's fine. We just need to be out of here as soon as we can.'

'Oh, that's right,' I said, 'money's no object.'

'We're in a hurry,' Fleur told the mechanic.

He gave us a slow smile I couldn't bear. I wrenched open the driver's door then rooted in the cooler until I found the last bar of chocolate. I slipped it into my pocket then strode away to the road. As though I was leaving, when there was nowhere to go.

Since then I'd been sitting on the wall. I'd eaten half the chocolate but it had just made me long for real food. A burger. Even a Wonder bread sandwich with pre-sliced cheese. But we'd eaten the rest of that for dinner the night before. The sun had grown harsher and now I shielded my eyes to watch the MG pull out onto the road. Gravel hissed under its tyres as it accelerated up the hill and out of sight. Ten minutes later it reappeared, a bright spot of reflected light sliding through the green, blinking then gone. When I looked again I couldn't even find the road.

Hills covered with grass and scrub, trees tucked into their folds, the world ending twenty miles away where earth dissolved hazily into sky: we'd been shipwrecked here. Behind me on the oily forecourt the truck sat low on its wheels with its bonnet open and its engine exposed while an MG – of all things – had left us behind.

Still, we'd been lucky and we didn't deserve to be after setting out in that old rusting hulk of a truck. What had Fleur been thinking? Or Mum and Ted, come to that? They'd let me drive away though they must have seen how ridiculous it was to think that truck could go two thousand miles without breaking down. They'd forced me into this when I'd known better. And I hadn't protested. How could I when I wanted to get to Arizona? A thousand dollars – surely I could have saved up that much myself if I'd tried.

A bird floated down, hooked head and wide wings. It hovered, then slipped off the current to sink along the slope of the hill. Effortless. I kicked at the dirt and managed to loosen a stone that I booted away. It tumbled a few feet then stopped. I unwrapped the rest of the chocolate and threw the paper at it.

Sitting in the sun the chocolate melted quickly, so I stuffed it into my mouth. Couldn't taste anything though, just a thick sweetness because the inside of my head was tight from the cold: my nose, my throat, my head, everything sore and swollen. I should have saved half of the chocolate for Fleur but I felt mean: it was her fault we hadn't stopped somewhere with real food, aspirin and a motel. I licked melted chocolate off my fingers and stared out into the distance.

Slowly the sunlight turned from white to yellow and the breeze swirled dust along the roadside. A couple of times the mechanic got behind the wheel and started the truck. It moaned sadly but started. The last time he got out he shoved his hands into his pockets as he talked to Fleur. As I watched I blew my nose on what was left of my tissue. I was full of hope: the mechanic's cap shaded half his face, Fleur had her back to me, her hands on her hips, her head nodding. I thought it had been settled, that the truck was fixed and we'd be going any minute. But when Fleur looked across at me and her head bobbed at what he said I knew it was bad news.

She came over with her rolling cowboy walk and sat beside me with her broken arm on her knees. 'He's tried putting some sealant into the water pump but it's still leaking.'

'So we have to wait?'

'Delivery truck should be here in a day or two.'

'We can't stay in this godforsaken place. There's nothing here.'

'No choice, is there?' Sensible Fleur, reasonable and calm. Her hand, though, was pulled into a fist and wedged between her knees. 'Maybe we can make up some time if we don't stay the night in Delta Junction. It's so close to Fairbanks we could probably push on and get into town late.'

'Christ,' and I folded the tissue over to find a drier patch. There wasn't one and the wet paper was cold against my nose. 'You aren't still hoping to make it by Sunday?'

'The school's expecting me to show up on Monday, remember.' The chocolate wrapper blew up against her foot. She kicked it away and watched it roll along the grass by the road. 'Besides, the longer we're out here, the more likely it is something'll go wrong.'

'It already has,' I said. 'We've broken down.'

'That's not what I meant.'

'Then what did you mean?' Silence. I kicked at the gravel.

'Great trip. Drive Fleur all the way to Alaska, don't ask why, and oh – pay for everything along the way. You should go into the holiday business. All the masochists in the country would sign up.'

'One mistake and you won't let me forget it. I said I'd pay you back – why do I have to keep telling you?'

'Because you're so broke.' Yet another comment that I should have kept to myself, but out it came. Not surprising because it had been nagging at me: if she was so broke just how was she going to buy me a ticket out of Alaska? She gouged at her cast with her thumbnail. 'I don't doubt you'll pay me back,' I said, 'but just when is that going to be? I'm supposed to be moving down to Arizona next week. Jo's got work lined up for me.'

'I know it.'

'Have you got some money at home in Fairbanks? Is that it?'

She said, 'Trust me.'

*

The mosquitoes were whining just beyond the netting. I'd already been bitten despite jeans and repellent so I sat in the tent with a tissue held to my nose and my throat burning, watching the sun go down and the green of the hills being swamped by shadows. Darkness flooded up from the valley and soon it was too dark to read. That left nothing at all to do. Misery.

At least Fleur had gone back outside. The mosquitoes, she said, didn't bother her, and she'd managed to make it sound as though if only I knew how I wouldn't get bitten either. So she sat out on the grass and I was glad she wasn't beside me shifting this way and that on the sleeping bags, propping herself up on one elbow to pick at her cast. I kept thinking: none of this would have happened if Mum and Ted hadn't forced me into it. Or if Fleur hadn't messed up her life because, surely, that's what had happened. Now here I was, caught up in her screwed-up life just when I was about to do something with my own.

A light came on in the mechanic's office and lit up everything like a TV screen: the untidy piles of paper on the desk, the corkboard, the three plastic chairs, the small rack of chocolate bars, the drinks machine by the far wall. I couldn't go without her. 'Fleur?' I called. 'You still out there?'

'Yeah.'

'Want to get dinner?'

'What? The chocolate in the cooler?'

'No, that's all gone. We could get something from the office.'

In the breeze leaves hissed on the trees behind us. 'You ate it all?' she said. As though she hadn't noticed the wrapper blowing against her foot on the roadside.

'We can get more.'

Her face appeared at the screen. 'You just took it?'

'Yeah, I just took it.'

'You can't only think of yourself. We're in this together. We have to share, right down the line.'

I wondered what she thought she had that she could share, but for once I didn't say a thing, just unzipped the flap and fumbled my feet into my boots, then zipped the tent back up to keep out the mosquitoes. There were too many of them to waste time doing up my laces but as we walked to the office I realised how I must look: bootlaces flapping loosely, crumpled clothes, my eyes watery and my nose sore.

The radio was on loud. Some country station. 'Evening,' said Fleur. The mechanic nodded. 'Any word on that delivery? Are you sure they can get us a new water pump in the next day or two?'

He looked up from a catalogue. 'If they can't you're going to have a long wait, aren't you?' He gave us a grin of grey teeth.

'I guess,' said Fleur.

'Got any change?' I nodded towards the machine and held out Fleur's ten-dollar note.

'This ain't a bank,' he said, but he dumped a handful of change onto the counter.

I fed two of the dollar coins into the drinks machine. I liked them: the weight of them, the elegant loon on one side. They felt like real money. Two cans of Coke rumbled down a chute while from somewhere close by came the smell of frying onions and roast beef. My stomach twinged: real food.

There wasn't much to buy except a packet of tortilla chips and some more chocolate. 'You two are going to get bad skin eating that shit,' the mechanic said.

'Have you got anything else?'

'Nope,' and he leant on the counter to watch us leave.

Outside the air smelled of damp earth. After the electric light the night was darker and we had to walk carefully over the rough ground. Some stars were out, pricks of light sharpened by the cold. 'You took my ten dollar bill in the restaurant yesterday, didn't you?' Fleur said.

'Yeah, because I used my card. We should save the cash for when we need it. Like now.'

'And you didn't say a thing – it's like you always have to be sneaky.'

'What does it matter? It works out the same.'

'And how much of a tip did you leave?'

'You think I stole the tip? Christ,' and I pulled out the wad of toilet paper I had in my pocket, tore off a few squares and wiped my nose. 'OK, I give up. I made ninety cents on the deal. Here,' and I held out a dollar coin, 'with interest.'

She slapped it away. 'You're always too busy trying to be clever to understand,' and she walked on ahead.

The tent's blue nylon was just a dark smudge on the dark of the night. I heard her unzip the flap but of course she didn't zip it back up behind her so when I got in and closed it mosquitoes buzzed around my head. I got bitten on my neck, my cheek, my knee where my jeans were pulled tight against my leg. Painful bites that hurt like bruises.

Fleur hadn't given up. Now she said, 'You hate to be obliged to do anything, even when it's done to please you. The way you used to sit there and look so bored when I took you places.'

'That's not true.'

'You bet it is. One hundred per cent true. How do you think I felt taking you out? I didn't mind doing it for Ted, but you couldn't even try to have a good time.'

'The only places you ever took me were country bars.'

In the light of Ted's small torch she tore open the bag of tortilla chips and dumped them between us. 'You think I'm some kinda hick because I dress differently from you and like different music.

You just can't see any further than that, can you?' She took a handful of chips. 'Even Ted – you wouldn't make an effort to get on with him. Always disagreeing with him as though it'd kill you to see he talks sense.'

'He doesn't always talk sense,' I said. 'Spending all day fixing rotten teeth doesn't mean he's right about everything.'

'The only thing he was ever wrong about was you, believing we could get along for his sake when you didn't care at all.'

'That must be why he made me come on this trip – so you could tell me all the things I've done wrong. God, I must have done some awful things to deserve this.'

She sat there eating the chips, rummaging in the bag for more. 'Someone had to tell you,' she said.

I slapped the air as a mosquito whined by my ear. 'Well, just so long as you're doing this for my own good and aren't getting any satisfaction out of it.'

'You can't let things be. Where I'm from people aren't like that. They don't count everything they do to help you as something you have to pay back. And they don't think it's better to have a sharp tongue than a good heart.'

'Is that a line from a song?' I said. I shouldn't have. I couldn't see her face but I knew she'd turned away. 'Sorry. Sometimes things like that just come out. I can't help it.' As though I should be the one to apologise for all that had happened.

She got into her sleeping bag and pushed the chips away. Then she switched off the torch and the night closed in around us.

*

There's something unsafe about sleeping in the open with only a thin sheet of nylon between you and what's outside. That night I lay curled inside Ted's sleeping bag with a tissue pressed against my nose, breathing through my mouth though the chilly air made my teeth ache and grazed my sore throat. It wasn't a freezing cold like the night before but a damp cold that worked its way into me without much effort. Coke, tortilla chips and chocolate for dinner weren't much of a defence.

Somehow Fleur could sleep on that hard ground, in that cold, with mosquitoes buzzing around us. I pulled the sleeping bag over my head but soon the stale air got to me. I must have fallen asleep for a while though because I woke up with my nose running and had to blow it on what little toilet paper I could find.

The second time I woke up it was much darker and my heart was beating fast. I listened. Nothing except wind in the leaves. Then I caught it: a whisper close by, the sound of breathing so faint I had to hold my own breath to hear it. A snuffling, closer now, and I lay still and waited for something to come crashing through the thin wall of the tent. Bears were attracted by food. And raccoons. And God knows what else. And right beside me lay the open bag of chips.

I turned over and felt for the torch. Whatever it was heard me and stood still. Then it gently moaned, an unearthly sound from deep in its throat that made me afraid even to feel for the button on the torch. Just above my head a nose pressed against the thin fabric and sniffed. Then claws rasped against the tent wall. I hurled the torch, yelled, 'Go away.' Whatever it was ran off and I sat there shaking.

Fleur shifted, murmured sleepily, 'What's that?' In a few moments her breathing had slowed and she was asleep again.

I waited for it to come back with the torch in my hand, as though that would do any good if it attacked. I didn't fall back to sleep until it started getting light.

Ten

A delivery truck was parked by the office and the mechanic was leaning against it talking to the driver. I wanted to ask him about the water pump but he didn't look my way so I kept walking, right past him into the office where country music chirped out of the radio, fresh coffee gurgled through a stained machine, and a plastic dome covered fresh doughnuts. I put some money on the counter then piled two onto a paper plate and pulled out the jug to slop coffee into a polystyrene cup. No milk, just packets of creamer and plastic sticks to stir it in but that didn't matter, especially as I'd spotted a *Time* magazine on a chair by the drinks machine.

If the mechanic got the pump in straight away we could leave before most of the morning was gone. Maybe our luck had changed. I spread the magazine on my knees and dunked a doughnut. The Middle East. Another threat of war. With my head aching from my cold the story didn't make much sense but that was all right: I had hot coffee and food, and within a couple of hours we'd be heading north again.

I even got up and poured Fleur a coffee when she came in. 'Look,' I said, 'and there are doughnuts too.' As though I'd forgotten what we'd said to each other the night before.

She sat in my chair and picked up the magazine. 'Why're you reading this?'

'The whole of the rest of the world could have been blown up and out here we'd never know.'

She dropped it back on the table. 'It's a year out of date.'

I didn't bother to stir in her milk and sugar, just handed her the sachets and a plastic stick along with the cup. She peered into it, didn't say thank you. A DJ came on the radio, then a slow song that rhymed *Texas* with *fetch us* and *worry* with *story*. She hadn't

86

reached for the second doughnut so I took it. 'Well,' I said, 'looks like we'll get away this morning after all.'

She raised her eyebrows. 'How's that?'

'Delivery came,' and I held up the doughnut as proof.

'Yeah,' she said, 'we've got doughnuts. Just ain't got a water pump yet. Last time I checked grocery companies just delivered groceries.' She proved it by saying to the mechanic when he came in, 'No water pump, huh? My friend here thought maybe it'd been delivered along with the doughnuts.'

He tucked a stained hand into the waist of his jeans and laughed. 'Nah,' he said. 'Truck won't come until at least tomorrow. Won't have left Prince George until yesterday.'

She gave me a sour what-did-I-tell-you look. 'I'll be outside,' she said, and let the screen door slap closed behind her.

I finished my coffee slowly so I wouldn't have to go outside where she was sitting on an old oil drum. But that meant I had to put up with the mechanic. When I looked his way he gave me a grin and said, 'Yup, them bakeries is just turning out engine parts these days. You can get 'em to bake you up just about anything.' I slipped the old *Time* onto my lap and concentrated on that instead.

From the way I was sweating I knew I had a fever. Already my T-shirt was damp and my hair lank. With a hot shower I'd have felt so much better. Here, though, the only place to wash was the toilets just beyond the garage. Broken window, old cracked mirror, a floor engrained with dirt, and a basin with only cold water. When I'd flicked through the magazine without finding much to read I chucked my cup in the bin, grabbed my day bag and headed up the path to wash. In the mirror I looked pale except for the pink around my nose and eyes. My face was still creased on one side from the pillow, and was shiny with sweat.

I couldn't be bothered with liner. My eyes looked smaller without it, as though part of me had retreated inside. This place was like something out of the past: bad food, bad company, and nothing to do except pass the time waiting. I imagined arriving here in a cart and having no way out. Every day the same stale food, the same people to talk to, no news from outside for weeks at a time. Further north, in Alaska and the Yukon, it would have been worse. The long hard winter, the few months each summer to search for gold or trap for furs. Everyone hoping their lives would change for the better so they could leave for a place where their money would buy them the comforts they'd been doing without.

I packed my brush and make-up back into my bag and pulled open the door. Outside sat a Rottweiler, head tilted for a better look at me. It sniffed then made a noise deep in its throat. This was the first time I'd seen one up close and unleashed, and I found myself gingerly closing the door – as though the dog hadn't notice me. It jumped and I shoved the door closed against its weight, then held it shut as it threw itself against the glass, barking angrily. The door shook. The shape of its paws showed through the frosted glass, then its nose. It barked again. I leant back against the door, heard its claws scratch the glass then snuffling as it sniffed at the gap at the bottom.

Then all was quiet. The tap dripping. The breeze in the trees outside. I looked over my shoulder at the shapes beyond the glass and waited for them to change. They didn't. I imagined the dog crouched back on its haunches, ready to leap, and shifted my weight against the door. My nose started running again and I had to feel in my pockets for some toilet paper.

Ten minutes must have passed. I doubted a dog could sit still for that long so eventually I opened the door a crack. No dog. I crept along the wall of the building peering around me but it was gone, and I felt a fool.

Eleven

You wouldn't think you could get claustrophobia in a place where you can see for miles, but I managed it. By the third day of waiting I'd discovered every place to sit: our small blister of a tent, the low wall, the plastic chairs in the office. The office didn't have much to buy, and had even less after we'd been there three days. I bought cans of Coke, Babe Ruths, Hershey bars, M&Ms until the mechanic held up his hands and said, 'Whoah now, no more candy until the next delivery.' We were running out of Canadian dollars anyway.

In the daytime I wandered around the place but there was nothing much to see: the view over the valley, the road leading off in both directions. Most of the traffic came from the north, RVs rushing down towards warmer, more populated destinations, the occasional truck, once a motorbike that sounded like an angry fly. The mechanic's house was attached to the garage and after I'd explored the rusting wrecks and locked sheds I ended up around there, more out of boredom than curiosity. When I came around the corner the Rottweiler jumped to its feet and strained against its chain, barking frantically. But as I came closer it stopped and licked its chops, glancing around, unsure. It still had a puppy's feet big as lily pads and a head too big for its stocky body. I held out my hand but it growled until I backed away.

'She'll take your hand off.' Through the screen door I glimpsed a girl standing back in the shadows of the house. She couldn't have been more than twelve or thirteen, and was in the sort of housedress old women wear: flowered cotton, loose, shapeless.

'What?' I said.

'That's a Rottweiler. They're bred to be killers.'

'But this one doesn't look too dangerous.' The dog's face wrinkled into a frown as it looked between me and the door.

'She's a bitch, and they're twice as vicious as the males. If I let her loose she'll have you.'

'Why would you do that?'

She touched the screen with her fingers. The tips showed pale against the mesh. 'Her name's Attila.'

Through the netting she was little more than a ghost. I thought there was something strange about her face, something not quite right. I stepped closer. 'And what's your name?'

'Who's asking?'

'I'm Sandra.'

'None of your goddamn business, Sandra.'

'Why's that?'

'You look like a *witch*.' Then she was gone. A moment later a door slammed somewhere deep in the house. The dog snuffled as it stared back to where she'd stood. Then it leapt to the end of the chain with a sudden bark. I jumped and hurried back down the path to the forecourt.

The girl's presence haunted the place. I felt her staring from the windows as I came up the path to the toilets, or as I sat on the low wall looking over the valley with a pad of paper on my knees. I rarely drew just for the hell of it. Drawing's work, work that I love but not something I do to pass the time. Still, with nothing else to keep me busy I'd rooted through my things for some paper, found a pencil in the glove compartment and made a few sketches.

Later when I looked at those drawings I noticed I'd made the valley wider than it really was, the pencil so light across the paper it left only suggestions of lead in the grain. I'd done cobwebby drawings of the garage and the house behind it that left the page mostly blank space, and from that blankness something crept, a watchfulness, an illwill. I drew in a shape at the window, turned it into a ghost draped with a sheet before it became something else.

That's what happens when you have too much time and nothing to fill it. Your mind turns up all kinds of odd fears the same way it does when you sleep. I'd let that girl get to me. Too many films about isolated places where a car breaks down, the people can't get away, strange things start to happen, horrific things, and before they know it they're living a nightmare with some maniac who won't let them go. We, though, were still in the first few scenes when the characters aren't sure if they're in danger – the audience knows it and wills them to leave while they still can. Of course they never do.

On the Sunday we should have arrived in Fairbanks Fleur persuaded the mechanic to let her use his office phone to call her parents. The next day she rang the school to tell them she wouldn't be in until the end of the week at the soonest because she was stranded in northern British Columbia. Afterwards she sat on the grass and chewed at her thumb. She looked worried, as though she'd ruined things already.

I watched the road for delivery trucks. I tried sleeping, in the tent, out on the grass, but I was too uneasy, as though I'd be stalked lying there defenceless. Sometimes Fleur came and sat with me and even if we didn't talk it felt better than being on my own. She spent a lot of time with the old guy, watching him work or trying to find a decent station on his crackling radio. I didn't like the dirt or the stink of oil so I waited for her to find me to ask, 'Any news?' She'd sit down and lay the guidebook on her knees. 'No,' she'd say and turn the pages, her pencil ready. She was finding mistakes and had begun a list. I had no idea what she planned to do with it.

In the evenings we lit a fire with the few old branches we found lying around. The smoke blew over us and made our clothes reek, and the warmth on our faces made the coldness at our backs sharper. It didn't matter. We sat there in its swimming light drinking Coke and trying to think up things to say to each other. The fire spat sparks at my suede jacket and that more than the cold, and the way our conversations were all first lines, made me curl up early in Ted's sleeping bag.

On the morning of the fourth day I sat by the road looking south for the delivery truck. My cold had left me with a headache and a cough, but at least my nose wasn't running. I'd got out the hat Ted had packed for me, more to cover my hair than to keep warm. A red skier's hat shaped like a pocket, as though wearing a ridiculous hat doesn't matter when you're skiing. It made me look stupid, but that hardly mattered when my clothes smelled of smoke and sweat and I hadn't showered in days.

There'd been nothing to eat for breakfast – no delivery so no doughnuts, just the mechanic's wretched coffee. I'd carried my cup outside, away from the hot smell of frying food coming through from his kitchen. I hadn't seen the girl again. Maybe she was the one cooking. Maybe it was someone else, someone I hadn't seen. I didn't care any more. I wasn't even thinking about the water pump – all I wanted was an omelette, or potatoes soaked in butter, or a sandwich filled with sliced turkey and salad. The mechanic must have realised we'd eaten nothing but snacks for days. He didn't mention it; neither did we. Maybe he hadn't ordered the pump but was waiting, weakening us until we reached the point of despair. And we were going along with it, sealing our fate because we weren't quick enough to understand what was really happening.

I sat on the wall and watched the breeze comb through the grass in the valley below. In the distance a white dot slid along the road, blinked out then came back into view bigger than before. Another RV fleeing south. Five minutes later it rolled up at the pumps and the mechanic ambled over. The driver climbed out and walked the length of the RV, hands in the pockets of his white shorts, a peaked cap pulled low, a captain inspecting his ship, at least until the door halfway along its side opened. A woman stood there with a curtain held to one side saying something. Then she passed him a lead and the small dog attached to the end of it. The dog skipped at his feet and he grimaced. It had a red ribbon in its long hair and when he didn't crouch down to stroke it it yapped. He looked away when it squatted next to the wheel of the RV and wasn't prepared when it finished and trotted away. The lead slid out of his hands and he strolled after it as the dog dropped its nose to the ground and traced a scent across the forecourt with the lead slithering behind.

From around the corner came the girl, the Rottweiler loping beside her. She was in loose jeans and a sweatshirt that came down nearly to her knees. Even from where I sat her hair looked badly cut, her face pale and lopsided. She went up to the mechanic while he pumped petrol into the RV and folded her arms to say whatever it was she had to say to him. Mouth working, hair blowing, not watching Attila who spotted the small dog, stiffened, and in the same motion of turning her head took off in a long-legged bound. The mechanic caught the movement, shouted to the girl, 'Get hold of her, quick.' Attila dipped her head to the small dog's neck just as the owner yelled, 'Hey,' so loudly that Attila hesitated. The small dog darted away barking shrilly with its owner chasing behind, his sandals slapping the concrete and Attila ducking out from under the girl's hand. Of course Attila was faster than any of them. She caught up to the small dog a few yards away from me, plucked it from the ground by its neck and gave it a couple of shakes. When the girl caught up she hit Attila hard with the flat of her hand and yelled, 'Drop, drop goddamn it.'

Attila let go. She looked at the small dog twisting on the ground, then slunk away to the mechanic who hooked his hand through her collar and held tight, though it was too late for that. By the side of the road the owner crouched over his dog. He scooped it up and held it to his chest. The legs kicked but when he stood I saw blood on his shirt.

The mechanic beckoned the girl closer. 'Get Floss out of here,' he hissed, 'right now. Tie her up.'

Floss. Not Attila after all. I watched the girl drag her away, her legs stiff until she gave up and trotted beside her around the corner towards the house.

The mechanic disappeared inside the RV, and it stayed on the forecourt for half an hour. When eventually he came back out he swaggered over to the office and let the door slam behind him. Then the RV started up, lumbering over the forecourt back to the southbound lane. The woman glanced out at me. It looked like she'd been crying.

*

Fleur missed the whole thing. After the RV had gone she came stumbling out of the tent with her hair sticking up on one side. 'What was all the shouting a while back?'

'Dog fight,' I told her. 'The Rottweiler got hold of a small dog from an RV.'

'Was it hurt?'

'Yeah. The owner had to carry it back inside. It was bleeding.'

'Oh.' She looked out over the valley. 'That's too bad.'

'The Rottweiler followed the girl out. It wasn't on a lead.'

'You can't have dogs like that running loose.'

'Yeah.' With the sun climbing it was getting warm. I pulled off my hat and ran a hand through my hair but it stayed flat. 'Who's that girl anyway? The mechanic's daughter?'

'He never said.'

'You didn't ask? What on earth do the two of you talk about?'

'Stuff.'

'What stuff?'

'You know – cars, hunting. Music.' She shrugged.

Strange – her being able to talk to that old guy half the day but when the two of us sat down we hardly had a thing to say to each other. When she got up and headed to the office I followed her. 'Do you like him?' I asked.

She shrugged again.

'I know there's not much choice here but he's – well –'

'You won't give people a chance, will you? He's a hard man all right, but how else can anyone survive out here? You gotta respect that.'

Being able to survive. That's all that counted for Fleur. 'Where's he from?'

'Spent time away out east but he's from up the road in White-horse.'

'Time away doing what?'

'In prison,' she said.

'Let me guess – for robbery? Or did he attack some customers who got stranded here?'

'He killed someone.'

We were almost at the door. Through the window I could see the mechanic sitting with his boots up on the desk and his news-paper curtaining off the rest of him. 'Christ, Fleur. And you sit around half the day talking to this bloke?'

'What difference does it make? It's not like he's about to kill *us*,' and she stomped up the steps.

*

Sometime around midday a truck pulled up. Later, when the stock had been unloaded, the mechanic manoeuvred Fleur's truck back into the middle of the forecourt and propped open the bonnet.

94

Fleur perched on an old box, swinging her heels to some country song as she watched him work. I went over and stood beside her.

'Did that dog die?' I asked.

The mechanic straightened up. 'It didn't look too good last time I saw it.'

'No, I suppose not.' He looked at me and I fidgeted. 'Is she your daughter? That girl?'

'Nope.' He stood there with a spanner in his hand. Didn't move. 'Anything else you want to know? Or should I get on and fix this truck?'

'Is it going to be ready this afternoon?'

'That depends on how long I have to stand here answering dumb questions.'

Tough guy. Adapted to survival in the middle of nowhere by becoming sarcastic and self-righteous. 'Well,' I said, 'I'll leave the two of you to talk about more important things while I take down the tent.' I tried to look relaxed as I walked away but my legs felt clumsy.

Fleur should have backed me up, that's what I thought as I rolled up the bedding. Instead she'd sat there without saying a thing. I unhooked the top cover of the tent, pulled out the rods and telescoped them down to short sticks, then crammed the tent into its bag. The whole time Fleur sat watching the mechanic drop his rag, search his pocket for it before he realised it was gone, whack at something in the engine with a spanner, stand back every couple of minutes to look at the truck. He was here because he wouldn't survive anywhere else, but that was something she couldn't see.

*

The heat of the day had faded by the time he'd finished. I packed our things into the truck and turned it around to head north. Then I waited. He came out with a charge slip and handed it to Fleur. She looked it over and didn't say anything as she passed it to me. Six hundred and twenty-six dollars. 'This can't be right,' I said.

'I didn't try and fix up that old water pump of yours for nothing. And you wanted it all done quick, remember?' He smiled. 'And,' he added, 'there were two international calls, plus the camping fee. Thirty bucks a night.'

'Thirty dollars for a patch of ground?'

'And the use of the facilities.'

'I didn't notice any facilities. Only the toilets, and they're filthy.'

A flush had crept up Fleur's neck. 'Pay it,' she told me.

'No way. This'll take my card close to its limit.'

He leant back against a crippled car. 'Then I guess I'll just have to take that part out again.'

'Pay it,' said Fleur quietly. So I did.

'Thank you, ladies,' he said, and as we climbed into the truck he stepped back and bowed. 'Come again.'

I pressed hard on the accelerator and we lurched out onto the road. All the way up the hill and over the brow I kept glancing in the mirror.

'Expecting someone?' said Fleur.

'That place gave me the creeps.'

'Me too.'

'And it looked like the two of you were getting on so well.'

She brushed some dust off her jeans. 'Someone had to keep an eye on him.'

'Yeah,' I said, though I knew it had been more than that. 'So what was all that stuff about having respect for him?'

'Well, you gotta, right? For living way out here.'

'Even if you don't trust him?'

'I guess,' she said, 'even if he gave me the creeps.'

'You have the weirdest taste in men,' I told her, and she laughed like it was the funniest thing she'd heard in weeks.

Twelve

By the second day back on the road we'd fallen into a routine again – getting up at seven, taking down the tent, stopping to buy take-away coffee, eating sandwiches for breakfast as we passed mountains as grey and wrinkled as elephant hide, or mountain goats, or long tracts of marshy land flat as maps. Evenings we'd find a campsite and I'd put up the tent, unroll the sleeping bags, leave Fleur to find the office and pay. Sometimes we drove out to get something to eat. We'd compromised at hot food from petrol station microwaves if we could find it – better than sandwiches though none of it tasted real, too salty, too cheesy, with a taste that'd still be in our mouths the next morning.

After those four days waiting for the truck to be fixed, whatever had been strung across our silences had gone and we could talk or not talk and it didn't matter. I didn't bitch about all the money piling up on my credit card; she didn't complain when I pulled in for coffee and toast at a café with caps nailed up all over the ceiling that made it look like the lining of a stomach, or when I stopped for lunch by a lake so flat and blue it looked too like a backdrop to be real. It was as though we'd come through something and were grateful.

As I drove she'd stare out the window. I'd ask, 'All right?' and she'd say, 'Sure.' I didn't believe her. She must have been expecting things to turn out differently. From the way her face had gone stiff when she saw the charge slip I knew she hadn't expected the mechanic to rip us off. No matter what she said she had trusted him because she respected the place he lived, and the music he listened to, and more than anything because she'd thought she could make things come out right.

We didn't talk about it again.

*

Our last stop in Canada was Haines Junction, up in the Yukon. The next day we'd reach Alaska and from the border it was a short hop to Fairbanks – at least, compared to the distance we'd already driven. That was something I hadn't expected – that the biggest state in the Union wasn't anything like as big as British Columbia. I pointed this out to Fleur and she just nodded, said, 'I guess that's right.'

We got to Haines Junction as the sun was going down. That far north it sank at a slant so night didn't fall so much as seep in. From one side of the town loomed a broken wall of mountains with patches of snow like peeling paint. We stopped in a campsite where those mountains blocked out one third of the sky. At last I thought I understood why Fleur was going back to Alaska. Against that sort of scenery, what else could matter?

Fleur came back from the office, said there were hot showers. Turned out there were washing machines too, though she wanted to wait until Fairbanks to do laundry. I didn't. I threw in all my sweaty, smoky, creased clothes then locked myself in the shower. The water came out hot and strong and I let it rush against my face. Eight days on the road. I hadn't felt clean since we left, and had resorted to wearing anything that came to hand just to stay warm. That wasn't me: hair dirty and flat, face bland without make-up, clothes crumpled and stained – that was who I would have been if I'd been brought up in the wilds of Alaska, a plainer version of myself that I didn't like at all.

I stayed under the water for as long as my three Canadian quarters lasted. I brushed my hair and plaited it into a damp, cool strand that lay heavily against my neck, then drew liner around my eyes and combed mascara onto the lashes. I came out wrapped in my towel. A T-shirt and my black mini were dry enough to wear. Fleur had a magazine in her lap. She looked up, said, 'Make-up?'

'Yeah, why not? I look pale without the dirt.'

She looked about to say something else but I was glad she didn't. I closed the door again and looked at myself in the mirror: clean clothes, clean hair, clean skin – I looked good. Part of me hadn't expected this, as though the way I'd looked for the last week would show through.

I gathered up my things. The trip hadn't been so bad. It would be something daring to look back on though really, apart from that first day's drive, the worst of it had been the four days waiting for the truck to be repaired.

Our luck had changed after that. We'd seen an eagle, a beaver, a bob cat trotting beside the road. We'd spotted elk and, crossing the road, bears. Three of them. A mother and cubs. I'd braked though we were a way off, watched the mother walking so heavy-footed across the tarmac I expected the ground to shake. She swayed and checked her cubs were following, then led them off the road. I drove past peering into the undergrowth but they'd gone. Only a few thin trees, some tall grass, but there was no sign of them. That amazed me more than seeing the bears themselves.

I'd started believing I'd get to Arizona soon after all. Fleur had said to trust her so I did. Mostly. It was hard, though, not to ask her how she planned to pay me back. And all the time more money was piling up on my credit card from petrol, and food, and that new water pump. Close to a thousand US dollars so far, according to her list. Nothing else I could do but keep paying if we were going to get to Fairbanks. I had to believe that Fleur would pay me back, that she was honest and trustworthy because treating people properly meant a lot to her.

Fleur was still sitting there when I came back out. 'Guess I should wash,' she said. 'Difficult with this though,' and she held up her cast.

I perched on the seat beside her. 'You don't want to arrive home like that, do you? You haven't washed your hair since we left, and –'

'I know it. I'm beginning to smell.'

'We could tie a bag over your arm.'

So we did. I took her things as she undressed: the man's shirt, the T-shirt, the jeans that had turned brown along the thighs, the pale blue underpants. She wasn't wearing a bra. 'Can't manage the clasp with one hand,' she said.

'Yeah.' I looked away and piled her clothes on the chair.

Dressed she looked blocky – square-shouldered, wide-hipped, not much waist to speak of – but without her clothes she had unexpected curves. 'You look better without your clothes on,' I said.

She looked up. 'How come?'

'Well,' and I taped the bag around her arm, 'you know, you wear jeans and men's shirts all the time.'

'They're comfortable,' she said.

'Not flattering though, are they?'

'They're not supposed to be for show.'

'Yeah, I know.'

'You wear jeans,' she said, 'but they're so tight they're uncomfortable for driving. So why wear them? D'ya think people won't like you if you don't look your best all the time?'

'No, but they'd treat me differently.'

'You're talking about men, Sandra.' She unfolded her towel. The middle had turned grey.

'I like to feel good about myself. Everyone does.'

'Is that all it takes? Looking good? And if you don't look good then you can't feel good?'

'No,' I told her. 'That's not what I said.'

'You can't be fashionable out here,' and she stepped into the shower. 'It's who you are that matters, and how you treat people.'

I closed the door and sat outside. She was manly in how she behaved, and whether that was because of the way she wanted to be or because of her plain face, it meant she never was going to care much about how she dressed. I wondered, then, what made her feel good about herself. Her Chevy that had got smashed up? The music she couldn't live without? Being able to survive somewhere as harsh as Fairbanks? Or was it people liking her for being kind, cornball Fleur?

But kind, cornball Fleur didn't really exist, not any more. Fleur had turned into someone who could be mean and small-minded. Had she noticed that? Or the way that she used people, like she was using me to get home?

The miniskirt was a bad idea. I sprayed on repellent but even that didn't keep the mosquitoes away, and in the end I ran for the tent. The mosquitoes whined on the other side of the netting, motes against a sky turned all the colours of a ripe peach.

Thirteen

Mosquitoes got into the cab the next morning and bugged us all the way along the cold blue of Kluane Lake, past Destruction Bay's *WELCOME!* sign and big bulldozer with its blade raised in a salute to visitors, right up close to the Alaskan border at lunchtime. The bites on my arms and thighs throbbed. In the mirror I saw that the one on my neck had turned purple.

Here in the Yukon the road twisted like a length of old rope dropped across the wilderness. The edges had frayed so badly I had to steer the truck over the fading white centre line to keep it on the tarmac. Every now and again the road suddenly smoothed to new, straight blacktop that sliced through old curves clogged with grass. We came across people peering through theodolites, all dressed up in fluorescent vests and hard hats – as though anything was going to fall on their heads out here. In places construction crews were laying new tarmac. Soon, though, the cold and the wilderness would eat away at it, trying to turn it back into wilderness.

There was nowhere to stop and buy food, nothing at all for tens of miles except for the occasional construction truck and the huge lone whales of RVs migrating south. Somewhere along the way Fleur had bought a packet of jerky. All those complaints about buying sandwiches then she spent ten dollars on dried beef. Now she tugged a strip from the bag and held it out to me.

'Isn't there anything else?' I said.

'Nope. Not unless you want a slice of dry bread.'

I took it. 'This stuff's reminds me of that Charlie Chaplin film where he's starving and eats his shoes.'

'*Gold Rush*. Then he chases the other guy around the cabin with a knife because he thinks he's a turkey. Cabin fever. People can go nuts during an Alaskan winter, cooped up all that time.' She took

101

a piece of jerky for herself. 'It's the lack of sunlight that does it. Means your brain doesn't make enough serotonin, and that causes depression.'

She went on but I wasn't listening. Alaska this, Alaska that, as though it was all she could talk about. Up ahead something small and white was running along the roadside. 'Look,' I said.

'A dog – that's a dog.'

It was a terrier of some kind, short-legged but determined as it jogged along with its stump of a tail twitching from side to side. It didn't even glance round as we drew up close.

'Probably some old folks with an RV brought him north,' Fleur said. 'They let him out and he took off to chase a squirrel or something, and they lost him.' Already we were past him so I pulled over. 'What are you doing?' she said.

'Waiting.' And sure enough, a minute later the dog came trotting up the road, legs working fast, head up to gauge how far it had to go. I undid my seatbelt.

'There's no point,' said Fleur. 'What can we do to help it?'

'We can't leave it here.'

'Can't take it with us either.'

It was still going. Typical terrier, the sort of determined dog that'll yap at the wind all night, or take on a pack of bigger dogs for the hell of it. 'It won't survive out here.'

'Leave it be. It's got this far, Sandra.'

'Only because nothing bigger and faster has caught up with it yet. There has to be a town somewhere around here. We can drop it off.' I jumped out and whistled but the dog didn't stop, so I jogged along behind it with the jerky in my hand. 'Dog,' I called, and it turned to stare. 'Wait, you can't run around out here on your own.' I held out the jerky. It came close and sat a couple of feet away, staring at the meat. I said, 'Come on, I know you're hungry,' but it didn't move.

It had eyes as big as a starving child's, both of them ringed with patches of brown that added to its sorrowfulness. A Jack Russell, thin, white fur turned grey, its nose dusty, its ribs showing through. As I crouched I caught a whiff of dirty fur. Maybe Fleur was right. It wasn't a great idea to take him with us.

He kept his eyes on the jerky as I waved it close to his face, but he wouldn't take it. 'Stupid dog,' I told him and turned back to the truck, but he followed, staring at the jerky in my hand.

'He's well trained at least,' Fleur said. She was leaning against the door. She'd put on her Stetson and had it pulled low over her eyes.

I crouched and held out the jerky again but the dog just shifted his feet. 'Yeah, I know it looks like leather, but Fleur eats it so it can't be that bad.' He didn't move. 'Great,' and I stood, 'a picky dog. It's gone native and probably won't eat anything but road-kill.'

Fleur sighed. 'You haven't got a clue, have you?' She took the jerky and said, 'OK. Now. Eat.' He fixed his eyes on the jerky and trembled. 'Go,' and he pounced forward, snapping it up, chewing and swallowing in a couple of seconds then standing poised for more. 'Someone's put a lot of time into training him. Shame he's in such a bad way. I'll bet he's full of ticks and fleas.'

'Yeah. And he's filthy.'

In the end we didn't get to decide his fate. He squirted a neat jet of piss onto a clump of grass and without being invited jumped into the truck. Perched on top of the cooler he waited for us.

'Only as far as the next town,' said Fleur. 'There's no way we're taking him home with us.'

'Right. And if he barks or farts he's going back out to fend for himself.'

'We have to be realistic, Sandra – he belongs to someone. Besides, small dogs don't do well in Alaska, it's just too cold for them.'

Alaska. Survival. From what Fleur said you'd think that anyone who couldn't make their own clothes out of caribou hide or build a cabin single-handed would freeze to death in the winter. But according to the guidebook Fairbanks had McDonald's and Pizza Hut. Not civilisation, granted, but if you could get fast food there had to be supermarkets and central heating. Fleur hadn't mentioned them.

I drove on with the dog panting beside me. That whole morning the landscape didn't change: muskeg, stunted spruce trees, willow, grasses turning yellow in the late summer. It rolled past like a short loop of film, making nonsense of all my driving – the same bent tree again, the same broken section of road I recognised from a few miles back.

Fleur fiddled with the radio but it squealed and shrieked so she turned it off and settled back with her hat over her face. Beside her on the cooler the dog crouched down, head on his paws, eyes straight ahead. Watching.

'Did you have a look his tag?' I asked.

She sat up with a sigh and pushed back her hat. Strands of hair clung to her forehead. 'Harlequin Bob,' she read. 'Telephone 488-8990.'

'Your owners didn't have any taste,' I told Bob, 'but we're sending you back to them anyway.'

'There's no area code.'

'Oh great.' I shifted down as we came to a sharp curve. 'They're probably back in Florida at a fancy RV site by the beach, drinking martinis and playing bridge. I bet they've forgotten all about him.'

'We'll have to get rid of him.'

'You're out on your ear before we get to Alaska, Bob.' He looked at me, ears pricked at the sound of his name, and I felt bad for getting his hopes up. 'No boy, got nothing for you,' and I patted his head. His fur was sticky with dirt, and I rubbed my hand hard on my jeans to get rid of the feel of it.

The map put the Alaskan border at Beaver Creek. Just after lunchtime we drove into town, past the Northern Skies Hotel, the High Country Lodge, the Moosehead Lodge, TJ Tours & Accommodation, Leclerc's Hunting Supplies.

All the businesses had a monied look about them, and even the motels weren't the usual dilapidated places sinking into the ground but a proud line of neat white buildings, way out here in the middle of nowhere. There had to be a lot of money in shooting wild animals.

We stopped at a petrol station on the far side of town that the hunting boom hadn't reached. The pumps were painted red where the rust hadn't got to them, and the dials were the type that spin around. The building sagged as though it had been sat on and its windows were so powdered with dust I wondered if the place was deserted until a man in overalls came out. He glanced at our number plate as he wiped oil from his hands, and I wound down the window to say, 'Fill her up, would you?'

Some places cleaned the windscreen while you waited but most didn't. I'd got into the habit of jumping out and doing it myself, washing away the dust and smashed bodies of insects with a long-handled squeegee. Here I'd hardly taken the sponge from its bucket when a cloud of biting, whining insects whirled around me, flew into my face, made me drop the sponge and run for the office slapping and shaking my head. Bob chased after me barking happily and together we stood panting on the other side of the screen door looking back out. At the pump the attendant slowly waved a hand through his grey halo of insects.

'Christ,' I said to Bob. 'And people pay to spend time here?' He sat to listen. 'And you need to stop looking so bloody clever. You're a small-brained dog. You were bred to go down holes after rats. You don't fool me.' I chose a couple of chocolate bars, one with peanuts, one with nougat, counted out the money plus some for tax and left it on the counter.

Fleur had decided to brave the swarm and was trying to clean the windscreen one-handed while the attendant talked to her. 'No,' I could hear him saying, 'not 'round here. Reckon you'd be best off taking him with you when you head back down to Washington.'

She lifted the wipers and rubbed beneath them. 'Home's Fairbanks.'

He considered this, one stained hand rubbing his chin. 'Don't want a dog like that in Fairbanks,' he said. 'Don't want a dog like that 'round here neither. Cold gets 'em.'

'I know it,' said Fleur. 'That's what I've been telling my friend.'

It sounded like a threat. I peeled the wrapper off one of the chocolate bars and took a bite as I watched her struggle one-handed with the squeegee. Her mouth cramped into a straight line. Unforgiving.

There was nothing else for it but to take Bob north with us, past the sign saying, *You're leaving Canada. Thank you for your visit / Vous quittez le Canada. Merci pour votre visite,* then the twenty miles of land where there weren't any signs let alone any houses or petrol stations before we reached the US Beaver Creek customs and immigration office. Bob stayed out of sight at Fleur's feet and we didn't ask about dogs, just drove through when they waved us on. 'Who knows what you're getting us into,' she said to me. 'We've no idea what the regulations are.'

'Dog smuggling's probably a federal offence,' and I shifted up a gear. 'If there's a lack of small dogs in Alaska then maybe he's worth something.'

'Yeah, right,' but at least she smiled, just for a moment. Humouring me before she put her hat back on and the top half of her face disappeared.

This side of the border the road was sleek with crisp white lines. The signs, though, were pocked with bullet holes. Distances in miles, garages with cheap petrol, woodframe churches, shoddy houses with decomposing cars in their yards, and shops advertising cut-price beer. Alaska. The landscape stayed the same all the way to the scattered buildings that were Tok and on to the end of the Alcan highway at Delta Junction. For a while the mountains of the Alaska Range heaped up on our left before disappearing into the evening and leaving us with a landscape of low hills around a floodplain. The sky ripened from turquoise to orange to deep blue so gradually that time must have slowed down.

I hadn't mentioned it to Fleur but I was starting to itch. Fleas I was sure, plus I'd spotted something small and pea-like stuck to Bob's ear. I'd never seen a tick, but what else could it be? I pressed my hands against my itches rather than scratch them, tried to shift a little further from Bob who eventually yawned loudly and jumped across to curl up at Fleur's feet. She didn't say anything, didn't scratch either. Maybe she knew how to deal with fleas too.

From some bleak petrol station that a winter wind whistled through Fleur phoned her parents again to let them know we'd soon be there. No one answered. I imagined us showing up to find a dark house and having to drive around town searching out campgrounds and dingy motels. 'Probably gone to bed already,' said Fleur.

'They know we're arriving today, don't they?'

'Yup, and they don't wait up for nobody. We'll just wake them when we get in.'

I couldn't imagine it – their daughter moving back after so long and they went to bed. What sort of people were they? 'Isn't there anyone else we can stay with?'

'Why?' she said. 'They'll be there.'

Maybe it was just as well they didn't answer. It took twice as long as we thought to make it to Fairbanks. We got caught in a jam, grinding slowly forward for half an hour until we were close enough to see red flashing lights. Lots of them. Must have been bad. All three cars had been hoisted onto trucks to be driven away. So badly smashed up they couldn't be towed. 'Sweet Jesus,' muttered Fleur and kept looking back even when the wreckage had disappeared into the darkness.

'Didn't look like anyone could have made it through that.'

'No,' and she sat with her broken arm against her chest, staring at the road ahead.

Sometime around eleven we went through the biggest town we'd seen all day, and I caught a glimpse of a huge lit-up Father Christmas. 'Look,' I said, 'what on earth is this place?'

'North Pole,' and Fleur yawned. 'Nearest town to Fairbanks.'

Across the night neon spelled out *Santa's Wash 'N' Dry, Santa's Mechanic, Santa's Plumbing Supplies*. Another sign said, *Christmas 24 Hour Sale. Beat Santa to the Rush!*

The air had a chill to it. I tried closing the window but the smell from Bob was overpowering. He'd jumped back on top of the cooler and every now and again leant towards me and sniffed at my face. His claws scratched against the plastic as he moved around, uneasy, as though he knew we were getting to the end of something.

Fairbanks was so spread out it wasn't until we reached closed-up shops that I woke Fleur. She looked out the window, told me, 'We're here, we're home.'

A bleak place. Buildings that would have looked draughty in Seattle ran along both sides of the road, cheap blocks of flats behind them, a couple of big supermarkets. We turned off the main road into side streets lined with low wooden houses, taking a right, a left, another right then pulling up outside a house as narrow as a single room. Her parents' place. Hardly a real house at all.

I turned off the engine. Lights came on, shadows moved against the curtains and we climbed out of the truck into the cold night air.

I

II

The North

Fourteen

Home. Fleur's home at least. I woke up on a lumpy sofa in a house as long and narrow as a train carriage. At my feet the front door, at my head the dining table that stood half in the living room, half in the tiny kitchen. Three doors beyond: two bedrooms, and the bathroom.

There was nothing to that house. Skimpy walls, cheap double-glazed windows that didn't look up to keeping out a bad frost let alone anything more severe. I turned over and felt a weight on my legs. Bob. He looked up with his sad old man eyes, yawned loudly then laid his head back down, snout on my knee. Didn't close his eyes though and I couldn't blame him. When we'd arrived the night before the first thing Fleur's dad had said was, 'What the hell –?' as Bob rushed between his legs. The next thing he said was, 'Get that damn animal out of here or we're gonna have fleas everywhere.'

Bob hid under the sofa and Fleur's dad's arthritis was too bad for him to lean down far enough to poke him out with his stick. I put down my bags and watched him try while Fleur awkwardly hugged her mum, the best moment for that kind of thing having passed. Then her mum turned to me. 'Sandy?' she said and held her arms wide. Her dressing gown had fallen open and I could see the top of her breasts above her nightdress.

'Sandra,' I said, and stepped into her hug.

'Sandra. Thank you for bringing our girl home.' She hugged me so hard her bones dug into me, and I felt bad for some of the things I'd said to Fleur.

When she let me go she called, 'Earl? Earl? Why don't you come over and say hi?' but he was still poking around under the sofa. He dropped his stick. She picked it up and held onto it so he had to look at her.

111

He got to his feet slowly like a camel getting up, then straightened his dressing gown. 'You're late. You said Sunday, now it's Thursday. Are you telling me it took four days to get a water pump replaced?' His hair on one side was sticking out where he'd been sleeping on it. It made him look angrier.

'I expect Sandra wasn't used to the distances,' and her mum gave me a smile. 'You're from England, aren't you, honey?'

'The truck broke down in the middle of nowhere,' I said.

Her dad looked at Fleur. 'We were waiting. You knew that.'

Fleur looked too big for that tiny house. Already she'd stooped as though she was going to bump into things. 'We had to wait for a new pump – I told you that when I called. It couldn't be helped.'

'Never can be, can it? Not even when you have people relying on you.' He took his stick and with it stabbed his way back across to the bedroom. He shoved the door closed behind him.

Fleur's mum fussed in the kitchen until Fleur made her stop. 'I know where things are,' she said, 'leave it to us.' Her mum brought out a pillow and a blanket and laid them on the sofa, bent down to coax Bob out but he wouldn't budge, said, 'I'd better be getting back to bed too. Good to see you, girls, and we'll talk in the morning.' Then she pressed a kiss onto Fleur's cheek.

We sat in the kitchen with milk and sandwiches, keeping our voices down though there wasn't much to say. Besides, we were worn out and after so long on the road the stillness of the house was eerie. We yawned at each other then unzipped our bags. Her mum had made it plain who was to sleep where: Fleur got the spare room. I'd driven her all that way and I got the sofa, like an unexpected guest.

Now the morning sun scraped into the corner of the room and I sat up to guess the time. The further north we'd come the more the days had lengthened, and now I had no idea if it was painfully early or time to get out of bed. No one else was up. I lay down again and tried to fall back to sleep but my ankles itched, and when I sat up I saw a dark speck flick out into the air. A flea. I shoved Bob away, jumped off the sofa, batted at my ankles, the blanket, the sofa cushions with my hands. No more sleep.

I opened the curtains and looked out. A narrow street of small wooden houses, an intersection a few yards away, the dusty road pale in the early light. So this was Alaska. Poorer than Seattle, everything smaller and more broken, but otherwise not so different. A disappointment really.

The bathroom had an old man smell of dirty skin and piss, and the washbasin was speckled with grey bristles. I undressed and got into the shower but couldn't get the water to run hot. I was still shivering when I dried myself and sat on the toilet seat. None of this was what I'd expected: the house nothing more than a shoe box, Fleur's parents so old, her father so sour. She didn't look comfortable with them and I wondered why she'd come back all this way for a crummy job in a high school.

I hadn't locked the door and when it swung open I jumped. Bob. He sat in front of me and heaved a sigh. 'Not much of a place to have driven two thousand miles for, is it?' I whispered. 'And not much of a family either.'

I thought about home – whether Mum had decided to do the course in personnel management she'd been talking about for months, whether Matt and Ted had settled everything for him to buy into the practice. He'd always be around now. He'd bought himself into the family, which was what he'd wanted all along.

I dug out my warmest clothes but even in jeans and a sweater I couldn't warm up. On one side of the living room sat a fat-bellied stove. Cold. I opened the doors and ashes fluttered up against the sides. There was wood stacked beside it and matches. I had no idea how to light it so I curled up on the sofa with an old TV guide. I watched the woman across the road pack her three children into her car and drive off. And the whole time I thought, When can I get out of here? I'd have to call Jo, tell her I'd be a couple of days late because I wouldn't be able to leave Seattle now until Sunday or Monday. And that was only if I flew out of here tomorrow. I wondered what the chances were of that.

It was too chilly to sit around doing nothing. Bob followed me into the kitchen where I filled the coffee machine with water, found the coffee, looked everywhere for filter papers and couldn't find any so I sat back down. Waited. Turned on the radio and found the university station. At least it wasn't playing country music.

A while later a door opened and Fleur's mum nodded hello then closed herself into the bathroom. With her long hair down she looked like an ageing schoolgirl but when she came back out a few minutes later she had it combed and knotted back, making her face look big and empty like Fleur's. 'Well, you must be ready for breakfast, Sandy. I have bacon, pancakes and coffee if that'll suit.'

'It's Sandra. But yes, that sounds great.'

'Now,' she said, setting a frying pan on the stove, 'you must call me Hannah. And I want to tell you right now how much we appreciate what you've done for Fleur.'

'That's OK.'

'Really,' and she turned towards me. 'You're a good friend.'

'Well,' and I laughed, 'I could hardly leave her stranded.'

She pulled filter papers out of a drawer. 'Not everyone would drive a friend all that way. So if there's anything – *any*thing – we can do for you, you just let us know, you hear? We don't have much but you're welcome to what we have. I don't have to tell you how worried we've been. Things just haven't gone well for her – losing her job like that, then ending up in the hospital and all.'

'Yeah, it's a real shame about her arm.'

'If only it was just her arm, Sandy. But – well, I'm sure you understand why we've been so worried.'

'Right.' I wasn't sure I did understand but I couldn't say so, not right then. A good friend would have known.

'I wish we could have done something to help, but we were all so far away. She's found out who her good friends are in the last few months. That's just when you need them, when things aren't going right, but that's also when you find out most of them aren't there for you.'

There was nothing but the gurgle of coffee through the machine, the hiss of bacon as she slid it into a hot pan, the rattle of the radio beside me. Hannah said, 'When she got out of the hospital I wanted to head right down there and look after her, but we didn't have the money.' She poured pancake mix into a bowl with milk and eggs then whisked it all together. 'Anyway, she didn't want to see anyone. No one at all. I told her I'd call Ted but she got so angry I was afraid to. In the end I didn't call him until she'd already asked you to drive her home, so it wasn't a whole lot of use.' She sighed and watched batter drip off the whisk. 'She's so stubborn – you know how she can be.'

'Yes, I do.'

'They arranged counselling for her, but what use is that, talking to someone you hardly know?'

'Not much, I suppose.'

'That's exactly it.' She poured the batter into a pan. 'But she's home now, and that's what counts. She deserves friends like you. Ones who know her and'll stand by her. I can't tell you how much that means to us.'

'I'm really not sure how much help I am.'

She took my arm. 'More help than you can know,' she said, and I felt bad for not knowing Fleur well enough even to be sure what had happened to her.

When Bob came into the kitchen I crouched down to stroke him. Hannah asked, 'Are you taking him to the pound today?'

'I suppose. He's a nice little dog though.'

'It's for the best. Look at the state of him, poor thing. They'll get it over with quickly.'

I hadn't thought of that. I'd expected that we'd drop him off and someone would see how smart he was, take him home and within a few weeks he'd been clean and healthy. But this was Alaska. Small dogs couldn't stand the cold. 'You never know,' I said, 'maybe someone will want him. He's a Jack Russell. They're very bright.'

'I guess,' she said but she'd already looked away.

From outside came the hollow rattle of a badly tuned engine. With a hiss of gravel a car lurched across the intersection leaving a dark stain of exhaust on the air. Everything was old here, everything out of date, including the way people thought. I watched Bob sniff the lino and thought of him stretched out dead for no more reason than because no one wanted him. So much for survival. It wasn't the same as being civilised.

Hannah served up the bacon and pancakes, kept some back for Fleur and her dad. While she was fiddling around I slipped a rasher off my plate for Bob. He stared. 'Go,' I whispered but he just looked at it. I kicked it towards him, out of sight under the table, and Hannah set down her plate then changed the radio to some country station. We ate without saying much, drinking coffee so thin it hardly tasted of anything.

Afterwards she pushed her knife and fork neatly together. 'Well,' she said, 'you can't do better than a good breakfast.'

'Yeah, it's good to have some real food again.'

'Most diner food isn't much good these days,' and she dabbed at her lips with a tissue. 'And the prices they charge for it. It must have cost Fleur a small fortune to feed you both all the way up here.'

'Yeah,' and I concentrated on soaking what was left of my pancakes in a puddle of syrup.

When I finished I picked up my plate but she said, 'Leave it for now,' so I sat back down while she drank the last of her coffee. 'You've done so much that I hate to ask you another favour. Nothing gained by not asking though, right?'

'I suppose,' I said. As though it didn't matter, whatever it was.

She leant both elbows onto the table. 'It's been a long while since Fleur's been up to see us. Difficult to be close living so far apart, isn't it? So we don't talk about things the way we should. I'm not sure how she is – how she *really* is.' She touched my hand. 'You understand what I mean, don't you, Sandy? See, I think she needs to have someone around, a friend she can talk to. She doesn't really know anyone around here any more, so I wondered – would you stay a couple of weeks? Help her settle back in?'

I fiddled with my mug, said, 'I'd love to but I have plans. In fact, I need to get back as soon as I can.'

'I understand. You've got more important things to do.'

'I'm sorry – I'm moving and I have work lined up. It's all arranged.'

She leant closer. 'But you just think about it. You can do that without making any promises, can't you?' Before I could open my mouth she added, 'I knew I could count on you,' and smiled in a way that made me uneasy.

We were clearing the table when Earl came out in his pyjamas. One leg dragged, I noticed, and he held a hand out to the wall, just in case. Even with the door shut the sound of his piss rattling into the toilet came through to the kitchen. Hannah poured us both

116

more coffee then put bacon and pancakes into the microwave for him. I looked around for Bob but he was nowhere to be seen.

Now that Earl was up the house felt cramped. I retreated to the sofa and picked up the guidebook, though if I was leaving in the next day or two I wasn't going to have time to see anything. Some time today Fleur would buy me a ticket back and I'd be gone, down to Seattle then straight to Arizona. And she would pay my money back before my credit card bill came.

Earl sat down at the table with his pyjama top unbuttoned halfway down his bony chest. I smiled and said hello and he nodded, or at least I thought he did. Hannah slid his plate in front of him and he bent forward over his breakfast, neck stretched out like a tortoise's, mouth wide to catch the syrup before it dripped. His knife and fork scraped against his plate, his mug thumped dully against the table when he set it down. Hannah filled it up, came over with another of her smiles to refill my mug. Earl pushed away his plate and she called over, 'You always bolt your food. You're gonna give yourself indigestion.' He just shifted at the table, belched, rubbed his bristly chin as he looked out the window.

When the paper came I went outside to get it. Anything to get out of that house. The air tasted of earth and engine oil, autumn on its way though it was still only August, and I stood at the low gate breathing it in. Across the road more small houses like Hannah and Earl's, gardens full of dying flowers, grass grown long, colour sucked out of everything by the washed-out blue of the sky. I unrolled the paper. The *Fairbanks Daily News-Miner*. Made me imagine the town full of miners with unkempt beards and worn work boots who'd come in from working their claims in the bush. That's the frontier for you: you feel like you're caught up in a past that should have died years ago.

I took the paper inside and handed it to Earl who grunted and opened it up so that it screened him off. Nothing to do except pick up the guidebook again and hope Bob kept out of sight, but I sat there fidgeting and looking up from the book. Already I felt trapped: a house full of defeated furniture, the rusted pick-ups rumbling past, the radio station playing country singers so old even I'd heard of them: Johnnie Cash, Tammie Wynette, Dolly

Parton, Hank Williams. I thought about being here when snow had piled up all around and a brutal cold meant you couldn't go out for long. Nowhere else to go except Anchorage, and that was a good eight-hour drive away on icy roads. All you'd have would be this tiny house and Johnnie Cash. And that was more than people had had when they'd first come during the gold boom a hundred years before. A hundred years of lurching from boom to boom – gold, the railway and the Alcan, oil – but the settlers had survived and Fairbanks had grown. It didn't feel right though, this place in the middle of nowhere with its newspaper and university and super-markets.

When I put on my watch it said only half past eight. Must have been the light – it felt as if we'd already wasted half the day sitting around in that tiny house, Fleur's parents still in their nightclothes, me trying to concentrate on the guidebook. Eventually Fleur came out of her room in jeans and the same shirt she'd been wearing for days, hair mussed, face flat and grim. 'Morning,' she muttered, and shut the bathroom door behind her. Hannah got up and put Fleur's breakfast in the microwave then closed herself into her bedroom. Just me and Earl, and Bob hidden somewhere behind the furniture.

Earl put down the paper. He said, 'You Ted's wife's girl?'

'That's right.'

'He still pulling teeth?'

'That's right.'

'Bet he's doing well.'

'He's got a practice in a good part of town.'

'Figures. Ted always could sniff out money. Knew he was never going to be wanting for nothin'.'

'He's a good dentist,' I said. 'And he's worked hard.'

'We've all worked hard,' said Earl, 'but some of us end up with more than others. Isn't that right?'

'That's the way it goes.'

''Course that first wife of his nearly ruined him. That was his one big mistake, getting hooked up with her when he was so young. Mine was not getting out of here when I had the chance.'

'His first wife?' I said.

118

'Jeannie. I'm sure you know all about her.' He paused and watched me. 'Anyway, it didn't last long, but the way it was going it didn't need to. If he hadn't left her he wouldn't be where he is now, that's for sure.'

'Why's that?'

'She liked a good time, Jeannie did.'

I was stupidly relieved when Fleur came out. The microwave pinged and she took out the plate and sat by her dad. 'Sleep OK?' she asked me.

'Yeah, fine. Gets light early here though.'

'Not for much longer. You get to late September and it's dark longer than it's light.' She poured syrup on her pancakes and tugged a section of the paper out of the pile by her dad's plate. 'I need to get out and look at a few places,' she said through a mouthful of pancake. 'Students are gonna be back any day and the cabins'll all be gone.'

'OK,' I said. 'Any time you're ready. As long as we get to a travel agent sometime today.' Casual, as though it didn't make much difference to me when I was burning to leave – to get to a travel agent, book a flight, see how Fleur was planning to find the money to pay for it. If she asked her parents for a loan Hannah would know I didn't have any intention of staying. But then I'd already told her I couldn't.

The bathroom was still humid, the shower dripping, the toilet seat damp with condensation. I wiped it before I sat down and leant my head in my hands. Too much coffee. Too much of Fleur's parents and this tiny house. Why, I wondered, hadn't Ted ever mentioned he'd been married before? Had he kept it from Mum too? Chipping away the bits of life he didn't like to make a neat version to show the rest of us? But then what else can you expect from someone who chose to spend his life drilling and straightening to improve on the teeth people were born with and the damage they'd done to them since?

Earl was talking to Fleur. Through the door I heard him say, 'So when are we getting it? We can't wait much longer.'

'Soon as I can manage it.'

'And when's that supposed to be?'

'When I get paid.'

'You're telling me you ain't got nothing else? When you had that good job? Who you trying to fool?'

'I need to get Sandra a ticket home. It'll just be another few weeks.'

'Winter could've set in by then. What are you thinking, girl? How can we manage?'

'You've got the wood stove.'

'Don't tell me what we've got. I know what we've got. That wood stove can't heat water. And can you see me and your mom out chopping wood when it's forty below? Can you? You need to get yourself straightened out, Fleur. Can't mess around like this and expect to get anywhere. Can't let people down and think it won't matter.'

'I told you –'

'How we gonna get through the winter without a proper furnace? Bet you're not planning to get yourself a place with wood heat. Not good enough for you, I'll bet.'

I sat there with my jeans around my ankles. Didn't want to come out, not into the middle of that. Fleur on the defensive. Her dad pushing and pushing her when she'd told him *No*. A door creaked open nearby and Hannah said in a low voice, 'Earl, Fleur, this can be left for another time.' Not another word after that.

I heard Fleur calling the school to say she'd be in later – first she had to find a place to live. And I thought – even if she finds a place, how is she going to get to work every day if she can't drive? Is her dad going to help her?

They all looked up when I came out. I smiled a stupid nervous smile and poured myself more coffee for something to do. Eventually Fleur's mum said to us all, 'I phoned Ryan and Miriam. They're coming over tonight.'

'How about Cody?' said Fleur.

'Oh, Cody can't make it. Said to call around and see him when you have time.'

'How's he doing?'

'Just fine,' she said, 'his doctor's hopeful,' and even I knew from the way she was smiling that something had to be wrong.

'Cody's a fighter,' said Earl. 'He's not about to give up.' He folded over the paper to a new page.

Hannah looked up as I came past with my coffee and pulled out the fourth chair. 'Here, honey.'

'This cancer's not about to get him,' said Earl. 'Giving up's a sucker's game.' He glanced across to where Fleur was marking an ad in the classifieds. Her mum was watching her, expecting something I thought, but neither of them said a word. 'Gotta be tough on yourself out here,' and Earl looked at me. 'Alaska ain't a forgiving place.'

'So I've heard.'

'And you better believe it.' He gulped down some coffee, wiped his mouth with the heel of his hand. 'You're from England, aincha? There's nothing like this place in England, you can count on that.'

'No,' I said, 'nothing like this.' Bob crept out from under the sofa. Over Earl's shoulder I saw him walking towards us, his stub of a tail wagging. He must have remembered about the bacon I'd dropped for him because he dipped under the table.

'You've got history,' Earl was saying, 'but we *are* history. Look around you and you'll see.'

From under the table came a crunching, soft but distinct. 'How do you mean?' I said.

'We made this place with our bare hands. Practically in living memory. How about that for history?' He leant back to look under the table, smacked one hand against the tabletop. 'Who let that damn dog stay in here? Fleur? Get it the *hell* out or I'll take care of it myself and you'll regret it.'

Fifteen

It's hard to tell how seriously some Americans take themselves. Take Fleur's dad saying, 'We *are* history.' How did he mean it? Not ironically, that's for sure. Besides, given the way everything was so old and ramshackle I thought he had a point. Being in Alaska was like being dumped in the past: the dirt roads, the cramped houses, the dark cabin we passed being swallowed by the ground it stood on, its windows resting their chins on the earth and its doorstep gone from sight. Even the concrete low-rises downtown looked vulnerable, as though one day the permafrost was sure to get them too and the city would disappear back into muskeg.

As I drove through town I ate a sandwich I'd brought with me. Late morning but already I was hungry – after coming so far my body had lost track of time. Clouds were rolling in, making the light thinner and turning the air cold.

Fleur had put on a thick jacket, plus a handkerchief around her neck as though any minute now she'd have to lift it over her face. When she'd got into the truck I'd said, 'Hey, let's hit the trail,' but she'd just given me an annoyed look and folded up the page of classifieds. No hat though, not today, but then this didn't look like the sort of place where people wore Stetsons even for fun.

Fleur had five places to see and none of them sounded good. 'Think we'll have time to get to a travel agent?' I asked her.

Bob tried to climb onto her lap but she pushed him away. 'The priority's a place to live. Cabins go quick. Plane tickets don't. Besides, it's not like you have a job waiting.'

'Jo's lining up jobs for me. I need to get work as soon as I can – after all, I'm going to have quite a credit card bill.'

She stuffed the classifieds into her pocket. 'It's not like I've forgotten.'

'I know – but I won't be able to afford to move until you pay me back.'

Her face tightened up. 'You don't have to keep on about it. It's like you can't think about anything else.'

She was right about that. Having so much stacked up on my credit card bothered me. It bothered me too that her dad expected her to hand over what money she had for a new furnace. My credit card was close to its limit – I couldn't pay for a plane ticket, and I'd be stranded here. She'd promised too much: a furnace for them, a ticket home for me, plus all the money back I'd spent getting her here. She was going to have to let someone down.

I braked for a red light. 'Just as long as you don't forget.'

'Of course not.'

'Good,' I said, 'good.'

That morning the town looked small and lost with low cloud turning everything grey. We passed a supermarket, a small shopping centre, a bridge over a murky river with a sharp-spired church guarding one bank. This was the bridge I'd seen in the guidebook. In the photograph it had looked like the centre of a busy town: people strolling across, the church bright and hopeful. Now I drove over it from the small downtown to find a couple of down-market restaurants, a line of abandoned buildings where trains had once been loaded, a petrol station, a shopping centre so small it hardly deserved the name, then a massive new supermarket that dominated everything.

We drove out along the edge of town on College Road to a building that didn't look any better than Venice Mansions. Fleur got out to look at a flat; I stayed in the truck to keep an eye on all her stuff packed in the back. It was that kind of place.

She was only gone a few minutes. Then she got back in and slammed the door. 'Already rented,' she said. 'School must start early this year – all the university kids are looking too.'

We passed a campground and a sports shop, then turned off onto a road that was mostly dirt and gravel. Stones thrown up by the cars ahead clicked against the windscreen, dust poured out from beneath wheels. Farmers Loop Road. Not a farmer in sight but it did loop. Coming around a curve I braked hard but still came close to a man holding a stop sign. Just hadn't seen him in all that dust. Construction up ahead, and I hoped that meant they were laying tarmac. Bob stood peering out the windscreen and I wondered what he was looking for. Did he think we were taking him home?

I noticed the roads we passed: Madcap Lane, Army Road, Iniakuk Avenue, Sun Way, Wild Horse Lane, NRA Lane, Sunnyside Road. Nearly all of them dirt tracks leading off this dirt road, all of them bordered by the same scraggy trees. Spruce mostly, Fleur said, some birch. I guessed which was which.

We took a left along one of the roads through spindly trees and swampy ground with tall grass. We passed a dumping ground of broken fridges and old plywood, then reached a turnaround at the end. 'Sure this is it?' I asked.

'Yep.'

So I pulled up. A path of wooden pallets led through the trees and Fleur walked ahead, rocking on the pallets, ground soaked with water gleaming beneath us. We came out a few yards away on dry land next to a cabin wrapped in foil insulation, like something out of a hi-tech fairytale. An old sink lay propped against one wall. Nearby a couple of buckets had rolled into a hollow where a yellow dog sniffed then pissed on them.

'Hi there,' called Fleur. 'Anyone home?'

One edge of a curtain twitched then a man appeared at the door, lanky in tight jeans and a too-big leather jacket. He had a cigarette in one hand that he snatched a drag from as he looked us over. 'You here about the cabin?'

'That's right.'

He scratched his head, kept looking. 'Not sure it'd be your kinda thing, ladies.'

Fleur gave him a big smile. 'How about we take a look? If it's no trouble that is.' She sounded more hick than she had for days. Hokey charm, but it worked.

He smiled back. 'Well sure, you can take a look.'

More pallets, more water sloshing under our feet until we got to a cabin that looked dirty even from the outside. A green curtain clung to one end of a window that was bandaged with duct tape. The front door had dents where someone had kicked it. Inside it wasn't any better. The furniture leant at strange angles, and the carpet curled up from its tacks.

'Is there a stove for cooking?' said Fleur. As though she'd really take this place.

The man pointed to a one-ring electric hotplate. 'There's that,' he said, 'or whatever else you wanna use.'

Fleur just nodded. Maybe it wasn't so bad compared to Venice Mansions: no kids warring around on bikes, no music rumbling through from another flat. The thing was, when she'd said *cabin* I'd imagined something quite different: a log cabin with a steep roof, wood stacked against one wall, white smoke curling from the chimney, forest all around. The sort of place you see on maple syrup labels that's so sugary you just know the illustrator was told, 'Think cosy, think warm pancakes on snowy mornings.'

'The ad didn't say what sort of heat this place has,' Fleur said.

'Electric,' and the man gestured to one end of the room with his cigarette. 'If you want something else you can put it in and take it off of the rent. The landlord's pretty cool.'

Fleur nodded. 'And is there a loft?'

There was, up a flimsy ladder and through a trapdoor. Compared to the downstairs it was bright and clean-looking with the sun coming straight in over the tops of the stringy trees outside. Beyond them rose hills, and in the far distance the pale shape of mountains against the sky. 'A redeeming feature,' I said. 'Knew there had to be one. It'd be worth taking just for the view.'

'Yeah, and all that heat'll go straight through the window. Difficult to heat this loft, specially just with electricity. It'd be freezing.' She rubbed her face. 'This isn't gonna work, let's go.'

So we did, back across the pallets, out along Farmers Loop Road to the next place which turned out to have only a wood stove for heating, to a reeking place the size of a shed with furious dogs chained up in the yard. To get to the fifth out past the university I pressed hard on the accelerator and jolted us over bumps in the road because Fleur had only left us ten minutes to get there. 'Damn,' she kept saying, 'I can't believe I did that.' She blamed it on her dad talking while she was on the phone, on her mum interrupting to ask if we were staying for lunch, on hurrying because she didn't want Bob to piss in the truck where we'd had to shut him away.

'You just made a mistake,' I said, 'it happens to everyone.'

'I don't make mistakes like that,' and she pressed her hand against her knee. She was right: at least, she never used to screw things up, and the few times she did she took the blame and laughed about it. Now she glanced at her watch and leaned forward as though that would get us there faster.

Past the university the town disappeared. A railway line, a few cabins, stands of willow, scrawny birches, flashes of light from where water had pooled. Everything thin and poor out here where for half the year there wasn't enough light or warmth to grow. We roared up Goldhill Road and turned onto Cloudberry Lane. We nearly missed the turning onto Baines Drive, just a gap in the trees I had to reverse back to. A dirt road full of holes, cabins amongst the trees, a couple of dogs watching us pass.

The landlady was standing on the porch when we pulled up, one hand on her hip. Her hair was an uneven grey like a wolf's and her face sharp. Her skirt came past her knees, but it didn't stand a chance of looking feminine with her windbreaker and hiking boots. She called out, 'You must be Fleur. I'm Jonie.' Then, 'You're lucky – the next people haven't shown up yet.'

Fleur got out, told her, 'We got held up,' but Jonie was already pushing open the cabin door.

Although the sun had broken through inside the cabin was dark and chilly. The windows were small, the furniture shabby, the carpet worn threadbare in places. Depressing.

'The previous tenants left the furniture – keep it or dump it, as you like. Got oil heat, plus wood as a backup,' said Jonie. 'I pay for the oil, you buy the wood if you want it. Driveway gets ploughed every month, more often if there's a heavy fall. No pets, no redecoration without my say-so, one month deposit up front plus one month's rent. That's eight hundred, and if you haven't got it today I can't afford to wait: I have people lined up to see this place. Now,' and she moved towards the door, 'outhouse is down the path. Need to see it?'

'Sure,' said Fleur. That surprised me: this was the most expensive place we'd seen. What was the point if she couldn't come up with the eight hundred dollars?

The track was lined with last year's leaves that still hadn't rotted away. Some had been trodden into the mud that led to the shack, others were caught in the grass. Wood smoke hung on the air and noises came to us through the trees: a low bark, an engine starting up, the hollow ring of hammering on metal.

The outhouse didn't have a door. That wasn't what bothered Fleur though. She'd brought a torch and flashed it down the hole, her boots loud against the wood floor. 'This won't last the winter,' she said. 'It needs a new hole.'

'Dug one last year.'

'Well, take a look,' and Fleur stepped out of the way.

The landlady took the torch and peered in. 'I guess I can have a new one dug.'

'Long as it's before the freeze sets in.'

'You bet.' She shook her head, said, 'Can't believe how much some people crap. When I lived here the hole took years to fill up like that.'

A breeze picked up as we walked back to the cabin. Overhead branches slowly bounced and flashed the fresh gold of birch leaves on the turn. The three of us stood on the porch and Fleur said, 'They're predicting an early winter. Gonna catch a lot of people out.'

'Always does,' said Jonie. She pulled out a packet of cigarettes and lit one. 'We've hardly had any summer at all. Had a foot of snow in May, and that didn't melt until June. Don't think anyone's ready for another winter yet.'

'I've been in Seattle nine years. I'd rather have the cold than the rain.'

'Seattle?' she said. 'And you've moved back? You got family here or something?'

'That's right. Besides, I never did feel at home down in the Lower Forty-Eight.'

Jonie knocked ash off the end of her cigarette. 'I'm from Boston. Sometimes I'd give anything to go back. Can't afford to though – we bought in the boom. We'll be paying off our mortgage for the rest of our lives.' She glanced back as a car drove up behind

Fleur's truck. A man and woman got out, each carrying a young child. 'So, you taking this place?'

Fleur looked around and nodded. 'It's the best I've seen.'

Jonie went down to talk to the couple. Their heads bobbed, they looked at us, then they walked back to their car.

Fleur sat on a wooden chair at the end of the porch. She'd pulled a cheque book from her pocket and was writing carefully. So she did have money: she'd transferred everything to her account here. That made sense, though it didn't explain how she'd ended up in Venice Mansions. Still, I felt better seeing her hand over the money and the landlady tuck it into her skirt pocket. She'd said to trust her and I should have.

I sat on the top step and watched a squirrel skip along a branch. It leapt, and for a moment it was a dark ragged star against a patch of sky. Jonie came down the steps. 'Rent by the first of every month,' she told Fleur, 'deposited into my account. Any problem, call me straight away. They only get bigger if they don't get fixed.'

'You bet,' said Fleur.

Jonie had her keys out and was squeezing between Fleur's truck and her own when she turned. Bob was staring right at her. 'That your dog?' she shouted.

Fleur turned, mouth open. 'No, he's a stray. We're taking him to the pound this afternoon.'

'Good. Don't want no dogs stinking up the cabin and leaving hair everywhere.' She stood and looked from Fleur to Bob and back again. I thought she was about to say something else but instead she got into her truck and pulled the door shut.

'Damn,' muttered Fleur.

There was no point driving the truck back to her parents' house without unloading so I untied the tarp and started lifting out the boxes. With her broken arm Fleur wasn't much help. All she could do was push the boxes out of the way against the walls and rip off the plastic bags. I even managed to drag in her chest of drawers and her mattress, plus the bed frame that came in two pieces.

Light was edging in through one of the small windows by the time I had everything inside. It had taken most of the afternoon to unload, and now the air was turning chilly. With my jacket on I sat on the top step and drank the coffee Fleur had made. Bob nosed around us as though we had something for him but she shooed him away.

I said, 'This is a step up from Venice Mansions.'

'Sure is, and it's gonna look a lot better when I've unpacked.'

'So you've done it,' and I smiled. 'You've got back here, you've got a place to live, and you've got a job. Just like you wanted.'

'Right.'

The mug she'd poured my coffee into said *McArthur-Stone Inc*. The place she used to work. I held it up, said, 'So are you glad to have left? To be back here?'

She shrugged.

'It was a good job you had, wasn't it? I mean, you seemed to like it.'

'Yeah,' she said. 'I did.'

'So what happened?'

Resting her mug on her knee she looked off into the trees. 'I lost that job a few months back.' She slopped her coffee around in her mug, sending it up the sides and nearly spilling it out. 'The accident messed everything up. You may not think so but one moment can wreck the whole of the rest of your life.'

'Breaking your arm?'

'No, the truck wreck.'

'Must have been quite an accident.'

'I lost my Chevy and a whole lot else. And the funny thing is, I wasn't the one to come off worst.' She looked at her coffee then poured the rest of it away. 'You know, I just couldn't get it together afterwards. Couldn't get interested in what I was doing at work, couldn't even pay attention half the time, and that way I was bound to make mistakes.'

'Is that what happened? You made mistakes?'

'They couldn't keep me on – said I was too big a risk so my contract wasn't renewed. Can't say I blame them. In a way it seemed right for things to end up like that. Anyhow,' and she glanced at her watch, 'we ought to get going.'

The sun was out in all its glory, slipping down between magnificent clouds and sending out a rich light. It set the greens aglow and glared off pooled water like gold. Now the countryside looked pretty despite the dead cars in yards with the thrown-together cabins behind them. I let Fleur direct me back to town. I thought we were going to a travel agent but when we pulled up we were in a high school car park. 'They're expecting me,' she said and jumped out. 'Be back in an hour, OK?'

I drove away with the radio on. I sang to Bob and he yowled back, all the way to a McDonald's. 'I'll get you a cheeseburger,' I told him, and he wagged his stump of a tail. Afterwards I drove around looking for a travel agent and found one in a small shopping centre. Not that it did much good. The woman at the desk could give me times and prices – there were seats available for the next day but I'd have to pay right then. I sat there as she watched me. 'Oh,' I said, 'that makes sense. I'll be back later – my friend's paying.'

'It's the weekend – there are only two seats left for the early flight,' she told me, 'and all the other flights tomorrow are full. Then,' and she frowned as she tapped away at the keyboard, 'there's not much open for next week.'

I passed her my credit card with a hollow feeling in my chest. It was refused. I was over the limit, and probably had been for a while.

'Do you have another?' she asked.

'No, I don't.' I'd cut the others up when I'd left Matt. 'Never mind, it doesn't matter.' I took the card from her and walked out biting my lip.

At least I didn't cry. Instead I sat in the truck patting Bob on the head. 'It'll be all right,' I told him. 'Fleur will pay. She promised.'

But we didn't get back to the travel agent that day. There was no point, Fleur said – she had to make arrangements to get the money. I didn't ask what she meant because she said, 'Don't worry – OK? It's all under control. I just need a little time to sort things out. I mean, we only just got here, right?'

She directed me back through town, back to her parents' place I thought, but this time when we stopped we were at a fenced-in compound. I didn't notice the padlock on the gate until we'd walked up close.

'Damn,' said Fleur.

'One more day of freedom,' I told Bob. 'We're going to change your name to Lucky. How does that sound?' He ignored me and watched Fleur kicking at the dirt.

'My dad's gonna go nuts if we bring him back.'

'There's always the cabin. We could leave him there overnight.'

'He'll make a mess. Maybe Ryan could take him – he's coming tonight.'

I scratched Bob's neck, and he pressed himself happily against my leg. The tick had gone. I wondered where it was. 'I'll stay in the cabin with him. I don't mind.'

'Really?' she said. 'You'll have to drive back after the family dinner tonight, and you'll be on your own.'

I scooped Bob into my arms. 'Really,' I told her, 'I don't mind at all.'

*

If it wasn't for Miriam there wouldn't have been a family dinner that night. When we got back to Fleur's parents' place there was no smell of food, no bustle in the kitchen. Six o'clock and Earl was shouting out the answers to some TV gameshow while Hannah sat drinking coffee at the table. Fleur lay on the sofa and closed her eyes so I sat with her mum and waited. Eventually I couldn't stand it any longer and asked, 'Is there anything I can help you with for dinner?'

'Oh no, honey, that's all right. I couldn't think of a thing to cook that everyone would like so Miriam's bringing dinner with her.'

So we sat there listening to Earl yell out which was the longest river in Europe, and which was the first state to be created after the Civil War. Waiting for Miriam, and dinner.

Miriam was a lot like Fleur: tall, big-boned, hair the colour of dry grass. Miriam was older though and smiled easily. Everything about her was softer: her hair in curls down to her shoulders, her loose skirt, her sweater with flowers on it, her brilliant blue eyes.

She came in behind her husband Jim, a balding man with an upside-down egg of a head and ironed jeans. She hugged us all, including Earl who hardly noticed as he flicked through the TV channels to the news. 'We left the kids at home with a baby-sitter,' she said. 'It's impossible to talk with them around at this age.'

'Oh,' said Fleur. 'I thought I was going to meet little Sonia.'

'You will,' and Miriam slipped off her coat. 'But she gets cranky if she's kept up. Come over tomorrow for breakfast. How about that?'

Jim peered over at the TV, didn't even take off his boots but sat right down on the sofa. 'There's never much of anything on,' he said to Earl.

Miriam took the dishes of food she'd brought into the kitchen and peeled off clingfilm while she hummed along to old songs on the radio. Hannah, Fleur and I tried to help until she said, 'Go sit down, this is all under control. Come on now,' so we sat around the table and drank the coffee she poured us. 'I hear you're from England,' she said to me. 'Now that's a place I'd love to visit but with the kids we've just never had the money. If we go anywhere it's down to Georgia to see Jim's parents. You ever been there? It's as hot as an oven in summer, but just beautiful.' She popped open the microwave and slid in a dish, then came over and sat with us, laying one hand on Fleur's and saying softly, 'You're looking good.'

It wasn't true but Fleur smiled, said, 'I feel more settled now I've found a place to live. I just rented a cabin out towards Cody's old place.'

'You're stubborn,' her mum said. 'You know you could have stayed here, or with Miriam – she's got lots of room. What's the point of paying four hundred just for a roof over your head?' She turned to Miriam. 'Can you believe that? Four hundred for a cabin.'

'At least you found somewhere. I've been asking around for you but there's not much going this year.' She scooped one hand through her hair. 'I hope you're staying for a while this time. You know how we've all missed you.'

'You bet I am.' Fleur pushed her hands together on the tabletop. 'I'm here for good.'

Her mum and Miriam smiled at that. 'Well now,' said Miriam, 'how about that new job. Think it's a keeper?'

'Maybe. I haven't really started yet, but at least I have something while I keep an eye open for what else comes up.'

'That's right, keep those options open. And if you get restless, you just let me know and I'll get Jim to ask around and see if he hears of anything. You got that?'

Fleur nodded hard. She said, 'You know, it's strange being back here to live after all this time. It's like nothing's changed.'

'Well, of course. You just give it a few days and it'll be like you never left.' Miriam had a smile that broke right across her face. She propped her chin on her hand and gazed at Fleur. 'Good to have you home though.' Fleur just nodded again, took a long drink of her coffee, and Miriam stepped back to open the microwave. 'Just about ready,' she told us.

'Smells good,' I said. 'What is it?'

'Oh, just some beef stew. Served it up a few times in the diner last week and it's gone down real well.'

'Best food in town,' said Hannah. 'She's doing great.'

Miriam bunched her hair in one hand and sniffed the stew. 'We're doing pretty good,' she said, 'considering. Half the time with a restaurant you barely break even. Can't say we've made any money at it yet, but that hasn't stopped the other traders busting their guts telling me to get out of the business.'

'Why?' I said.

'Because they don't like the competition. But if you saw what gets served up in the name of food in some of these places you'd run scared, I tell you.'

'She taught herself,' said Hannah. 'Has a knack for it, always has.'

'I'm not afraid to try. You have that, you'll get to where you want. Right, Fleur?'

'Sure.' She didn't look at her sister but towards the window. A silver truck had pulled up outside. 'Ryan,' she said, and she jumped up, scraping her chair across the floor.

'Get beer,' Miriam yelled after her, 'you can bet he didn't bring any.'

'Get Canadian,' shouted Jim as she closed the door then sank back onto the sofa, both hands resting on his belt buckle.

Without even coming in they were off, engine roaring, a thin

133

cloud of white fumes melting into the air, Fleur and her beloved big brother.

'Well,' said Hannah, 'better get the table set.'

'How about that cloth I gave you for Christmas? Where's it got to?'

'Put away for best. It's so beautiful. You wait, I'll just get it,' and she heaved herself up from her chair like a much heavier woman and headed for the spare bedroom.

'This is one crazy family,' Miriam told me. 'You'd better believe it. Still, I guess you've worked that out for yourself. Now, let me tell you, we all really appreciate what you've done for Fleur, driving her up here like that. Maybe things will get straightened out now she's back home.'

'Let's hope so.'

'And it's such a help you being around.' She shifted closer, wiping her hands on a cloth and lowering her voice to just above a whisper. 'If it wasn't for that, who knows, maybe she'd have another go. I don't think any of us could stand the constant worry.'

I must have already guessed because it didn't shock me: she'd been in an accident, then sometime afterwards – in the last few weeks – she'd tried to kill herself. Solid Fleur, who always had an answer to everything, giving up hope. It didn't seem possible. At that moment, though, I wanted to put Miriam right. 'Listen, I can't stay –'

But she took my hand and broke in. 'Thank you for caring about my sister. We've all been so concerned about her, and she hasn't spent much time up here in the last few years. None of us really know how to help her.'

'I'm leaving very soon, but I'll do what I can.' As though that actually meant anything.

'Just helping her settle in is a big help.' She sighed. 'Fleur's one of those people – you can't help but love her, even if she does drive you crazy.'

*

The first thing Ryan did was turn up the radio so loud the murmur of the TV disappeared. Then he lit a cigarette and leaned back against the kitchen counter with it jammed between his lips while his hands worked the air as though there was a guitar between them. 'Oh man,' he moaned, 'he's so good.' Some song about *lonely roads* and *honky-tonk women*, one eye squinting under a thin scar and his dark hair swaying around his shoulders as he moved. He was a crow of a man: glaring eyes, a nose too long for his face, front teeth that sagged slightly to one side and threw his face off centre when he smiled. And he smiled a lot, mostly at himself.

Right then Fleur didn't look like someone who'd kill herself. She was grinning at us all like she'd just found something she thought she'd lost for ever, and maybe she had. This was the brother she adored, the one who'd sneaked her out to bars when she was under age, who'd nearly lost an eye trying to stop a fight, who'd taught her to love country music. I didn't count it in his favour.

Sipping a beer, I sat at the table and watched. In that tiny kitchen Miriam moved around him with her lips pulled tight. I heard her say, 'Come on, Ryan, out the way now, go watch the TV or something.' He just whirled around and bent his knees so that he was leaning back like a seventies rock star. A spoilt kid grown up into a show-off.

'He can't help it,' said Fleur, 'he's a showman. Aren't you, Ry?' and he nodded as he spun on a heel, coming close to knocking a dish out of Miriam's hands. She didn't say anything, just stood very still until, after another spin, he stepped out of her way then sat across the table from me.

'So, you drove little sis all the way home. That's mighty big of you.' It came out flat.

'Is it?' I said.

'Oh yeah.' He stubbed out his cigarette on the heel of his boot then dropped the butt into his palm. Just to show how tough he was. Fleur came over, sat beside him and fiddled with the edge of the tablecloth. He said, 'So sis, she a good driver?' and he jerked his head at me.

'She got me here.'

'Yeah, almost in one piece.' He bounced the wrinkled butt in his hand and watched me. 'Shame about the wing mirror, though.'

Dipping between us Miriam laid cutlery on the cloth. 'Now Ryan, Sandra was good enough to drive Fleur all this way.'

'Out of the goodness of her heart. Oh yeah,' and he laughed.

Miriam didn't. She plucked the fork he'd just picked up out of his hand and laid it back down. 'Be nice – Sandra had other plans but she did this to help out. And you're going to make it up to her, right, Fleur? Going to make being here worth her while.'

Fleur looked up, said, 'Sure.' She glanced at me, must have seen the frozen look on my face because she seemed about to say something else when Miriam put her hands on her hips and announced dinner was ready.

*

I didn't notice when Jim left. Sometime after dinner I realised he wasn't back on the sofa, that he wasn't anywhere.

'He had to go see someone on business,' Miriam explained. 'I could do with a ride home if you're going to the cabin anytime soon. The babysitter can only stay until nine.'

'Yeah,' I said, 'I can leave right now if you like.'

It took a while to gather up her dishes and wash them, then to say goodbye to Hannah who kept telling me, 'Honey, you can't stay in that cabin all on your own. Where's the sense in that when we've got room for you here?'

Outside town a blur of raw blue still showed between the hills. The night was cool and quiet, no radio, no traffic. 'Couldn't Cody come tonight?' I asked Miriam.

'No, he said he didn't feel up to it. Guess when we all get together we're too much for him.'

'He must be pretty sick then.'

She shifted in the seat, said in a different voice, 'Actually, we don't see much of him these days.'

'Don't you get on?'

'He's always arguing with someone. That's never mattered, but now he takes it all too seriously just when you'd expect things wouldn't matter so much to him.'

'Things like what?'

'Like money.' She paused, said, 'You can't blame him. His

136

treatment's expensive, and his insurance company is always putting up a fight – or so he says. When it comes down to it I think the problem is not the insurance company but the fact that he can't accept he might die. Who could, right?'

'Yeah, that's hard,' and I shifted gear for a hill. 'Fleur adores Ryan, doesn't she?'

'Ryan?' and she laughed. 'Oh God yes. Those two have always been close, listening to music and going out to hear bands. But he's the kind who always has his hand out, you know, *Gimme ten bucks, gimme twenty, I'll pay ya back.*' She had him down perfectly. That twang to his voice, the whipped-up hokey accent, just like Fleur's. 'There's one in every family, right?'

'Not mine,' I said, 'unless it's me.' I smiled at her in the dark. 'Apparently I'm always trying to squeeze money out of Mum and Ted – I tell you, dealing with them is like negotiating with the Mafia. God they're tough. And I never seem to have enough, no matter what.'

'Sandy, I've heard *all* the sob stories. I bet your job doesn't pay enough, and you have a car to run, and somehow there just isn't ever enough to last until the end of the month.'

'That's not so far from the truth.'

She laughed. 'And just what is it you do?'

'I'm a commercial artist.'

'Oh lord,' she chuckled, 'an artist? Really? Is there any money in that?'

Her house was quite a way from the city, out where the night was lit only by a giant moon hanging just over the hills like a huge silver dollar. It followed us along the lonely road we took, all the way up the steep hill and down the other side to the narrow valley where she lived. The truck bounced over the dirt road and when she told me to take a right into her driveway the truck died. I hadn't anticipated the slope, sharp as a roof. I jammed on the brakes to stop us rolling back and she said, 'Just imagine what it's like in the snow. Hell on earth. I'd move if the house wasn't so perfect.' She gathered up her bags. 'I can get out here. I'll see you and Fleur at ten tomorrow for breakfast, right? It's Saturday so you can't have anything else to do. Don't forget – the kids will be expecting you.'

Her pale jacket stood out as she strode up the driveway. I eased the truck back onto the road. When I started the engine and the lights dipped I saw how dark the night really was.

*

In the middle of the night I woke up with my bladder aching. Bob was so close I could smell him but in the dark I couldn't see a thing as I stumbled around trying to find the light switch, pulling on my boots, tripping over a box and hurrying outside in a T-shirt.

The wind was washing through the trees. It had picked up, not a gentle summer breeze any more but the sort of wind that hauls in a new season. Bob had followed me out and he gave a sharp yip at something in the trees before skittering off. Behind me a movement. I jumped. A branch reaching down.

I followed the beam of the torch down the path to the outhouse. Twigs caught my hair, and twice I stumbled on rocks embedded in the earth. In the thin light the outhouse was more rickety than I remembered, the hole horror-film dark. It took all my nerve to sit over it, to take a moment to wipe myself then pull up my underwear without rushing back out to the path, and as I walked away I made an effort not to look over my shoulder. In the end I glanced anyway and saw nothing but branches swinging low over the path. So much for strong nerves.

It came at me when I turned back. A glint of eyes, a big dark shape moving fast and knocking into my legs so hard I fell and dropped the torch. The beam shone uselessly against a tree trunk while I lay in the leaves with my hands up to my face, until I realised – it was gone. A dog. Some big black bloody dog.

Bob was on the porch waiting for me, stump of a tail wagging. 'No warning? Now I get it,' I told him, 'you're a traitor. That's why you were abandoned, isn't it?'

Sixteen

I woke up late, the cabin dim because of the small windows. Chilly too. At the sink a lopsided square of sunlight showed up the dust. I tucked back my hair and leant forward, turned on the tap, cupped my hands under it. Nothing. No pipes. No water. I'd forgotten.

In the container we'd used for camping there was barely enough water for me to splash my face, set out a dish for Bob and make a single cup of coffee. The place was bleak with all Fleur's boxes stacked by the blank walls so I took my mug outside and sat on the porch. From there I could see up the driveway to the dirt road, and to the lot beyond where a truck had pulled up. Two men stood talking beside the raft of a barely started cabin. Caps, jeans, work boots. Genuine Alaskan wear.

They turned when I came past in Fleur's truck twenty minutes later, looked before they waved. Half past nine on a Saturday morning but there was no traffic to speak of, no real buildings except a small store in a log cabin with petrol pumps out front. The town didn't start until close to the university where shops and offices began to line the road and the road itself spread to four lanes. University Avenue, Airport Way. Imagination had run out by the time they named the main routes through the town. Some shopping centres and businesses huddled along their roadsides, but not so far behind was nothing except trees and hills for hundreds of miles.

I found the right turning but went wrong just after I'd passed a small junction. All the buildings looked the same, downbeat suburban with dried-out gardens. Easy enough to reverse back half a block though. No traffic around except a boy in too-big jeans sitting astride a bike. He watched me as he chewed his gum.

Fleur was at the door before I'd even got out of the truck. 'We're gonna be late,' she said.

'Are we supposed to bring anything?'

'Nope, she'll have it all organised.' She climbed into the truck, saw Bob and said, 'What did you bring him for?'

'I couldn't leave him stuck in the cabin again.'

'Why in heck not? Did he make a mess last night?'

'No,' I said. 'It just didn't seem right.'

I shifted into gear and we passed the boy on his bike, passed the library then turned out onto the main road again. Fleur shielded her eyes against the sun and I asked, 'Why don't you wear your hat?'

'It's not the place for it, not unless you're in a bar. Makes you stand out like you just came up from Texas or someplace.'

'So why did you wear it in Seattle? It's not like it fitted in down there either.'

'I wasn't gonna fit in down there anyhow. But here, this is where I'm from. And if you're gonna wear a hat in Alaska you make sure it covers your ears or you get frostbite.'

'Well,' I said, 'don't you stand out here too? To me you sound like you were straight off the plane from Texas. So does Ryan.'

'Guess we picked up the accent from Mom and Dad and never wanted to lose it. Besides, up here there's no such thing as a local accent. People are from all over.'

'What I don't understand,' I said, 'is why you need that accent to sing country music. All of them have it, all those singers you listen to. They can't all be from Texas.'

'That's how most people in this country speak. Outside the towns, I mean. Or hadn't you ever noticed?'

'No, I hadn't ever noticed.'

She glanced at me, sighed, didn't say anything else as we drove out of town into the low hills. In daylight I hardly recognised the road: a turn-off with a long line of close-mouthed mailboxes and not a single house in sight, the gold of birch leaves gleaming in the sun against a sky of baby blue. Late August but it was autumn already. In a couple of months there'd be snow that would last until spring and temperatures so cold they could kill. Homes and

140

offices and cars would have to be heated so people could survive in pockets of warmth; everything else would be frozen. That morning it didn't seem possible.

Fleur had picked so much at the end of her cast that the end was a frayed mass. I changed down to second for the last part of the hill and said, 'When does that come off?'

'Another few weeks.'

'Because I was wondering how you were planning to get around without me here. If you can't drive how are you going to manage?'

'Haven't worked that one out yet. But I'll think of something.'

'Maybe you should stay with Miriam for the time being. You know, have someone who can look after you until you can drive again.'

'Nah.'

'Why not? It would be perfect. You'd have someone to drive you to work, and Miriam and Jim for company.'

Maybe I was selling it too hard. She said, 'It wouldn't be such a great idea.'

'But you get on, don't you?'

'Yeah. We get on well enough.'

'And you haven't forgotten about my flight home?'

'Nope,' she said. 'Haven't had the chance to forget about that. I'm working on it.'

'Good,' and I glanced at her. 'Because my credit card is frozen, and nearly everything's booked up for the next week.'

'You checked?'

'Of course I checked.'

She sighed as though she was disappointed with me. 'There's always standby. I've done it a few times.'

On our right were driveways cut into the hillside, and in the daylight I caught glimpses of houses above us that looked out over the low hills surrounding the city. Beautiful wooden places with picture windows that must have cost a fortune to build, let alone heat.

To get up Miriam's driveway I pressed the accelerator to the floor and the truck moaned all the way to the turnaround at the top. Jim was working on his car, and he stood and wiped his hands as we pulled up. 'She's inside,' he said. 'The kids have been playing up like crazy this morning.'

Behind him stood the house, the sort you dream you'll find in Alaska: an oversized log cabin with big windows, a sharp roof, a porch running along one side with a view over the valley. The real maple-syrup-label cabin – all it needed was lots of snow to tuck it in. No wonder Miriam didn't have any money to spare if she lived in a place like this, but it would be worth it, even if you had to struggle to pay for it. 'This place is beautiful,' I said. 'Just look at it.'

'Yup,' answered Fleur, 'it sure is.' Flat. The same way Ryan had spoken to me. She resented it, Miriam having this place while she could only afford a one-room cabin with no running water. And what must have made it worse was that she could have afforded a decent place of her own if she hadn't lost her job and given up on life down in Seattle.

There was wooden garden furniture on the deck and a book blown open where someone had been reading. Fleur came past me and opened the front door. We were both crouching to take off our boots when Miriam came through from the kitchen with a baby on her hip and a spatula in her hand. 'There you are. We were beginning to think you'd stood us up.' A little boy peeped out from behind the doorjamb, saw us and hid again. 'That's Lucas,' said Miriam in a bright voice, 'and this is Sonia.' Sonia blinked at us and when Miriam tried to pass her to Fleur she clung to her mother's sweater. Fleur clucked her tongue but the baby turned away and cried. 'She's teething. She's been cranky all morning and I can't do a thing with her.'

'Can we give you a hand?' I said.

She laughed. 'It'll be more than giving me a hand. Nothing's started. I just haven't had the chance to get around to breakfast with these two rascals.' She bounced the baby in her arms but she kept on crying.

She'd made coffee and measured the dry ingredients for pancake batter into a bowl, but that was as far as she'd got. Between us Fleur and I whipped up the batter, laid the table, made toast, made more coffee, sliced fruit for a salad and squeezed oranges. Or at least I did. Fleur did what she could with her one hand. The whole time Miriam perched on a stool with the baby on her lap. Little Sonia fell asleep but when Miriam moved she whimpered. The little boy was nowhere to be seen. 'How come you're not at the diner?' asked Fleur.

'My one day off. When Sonia was born I decided the place had to be able to run itself without me once a week so I could have some time with the kids. It's been hard though. You can't keep an eye on things if you're not there, and then you start losing money. It's not like I have people working for me who steal, it's just a matter of carelessness. Not checking what's in the fridge, that kind of thing. And Saturday can be a busy day.'

I poured pancake batter into a frying pan. 'So Jim doesn't work there too?'

'Good Lord no. We'd be under each other's feet. He used to work for the city but now he has his own business. Construction, mostly.'

'Did he build this house?'

'No,' she said, 'we bought this one in a hurry a few years back after we lost our last house. Still, if it hadn't been for that we'd never have ended up with this place which we love.' She smoothed the baby's hair then looked up. 'So, when do you start work, Fleur?'

'Monday morning, 8 a.m.'

'Straight into it. You cut it pretty fine getting here, but you made it and you found a cabin in no time. You're lucky. But then you always were.'

'That's not true. There's no such thing as luck. You should know that.' She didn't look at her sister, just kept her eyes on the sliced fruit she was tipping one-handed into the bowl.

Miriam gazed down into her baby's face as she rocked her. 'So how long are you staying, Sandra?'

'Only a day or two. We haven't bought my ticket home yet.'

She looked up at Fleur, eyes big with surprise. 'Oh,' she said. 'I thought you'd promised –' She caught herself then turned to me. 'I thought you'd promised Mom you'd be here longer than that.'

'No, no,' and I felt my cheeks getting hot. 'I told her I'd do what

I could – but I've got a friend lining up work for me down in Arizona.' The bottom of the pancake was done. I flipped it over and pressed it down.

Fleur carried the fruit salad to the table and muttered, 'I have to use the bathroom.' She disappeared upstairs. The bathroom must have been right overhead because I heard the boards creaking above us.

Miriam ran a finger along the baby's chin. 'Guess I'll have to break it to Mom that you're leaving so soon. Boy, I don't know what we're going to do with Fleur.'

'Couldn't she stay here? Just until the cast comes off?'

'I guess,' she said, but she didn't sound too sure.

I told myself it wasn't my problem, that I'd done more than could be expected. If I left they'd have to sort something out – Fleur could stay with Miriam, or with her mum and dad, and they'd manage, just for a few weeks. They'd have to.

Miriam pushed back her hair. 'You're going to need someone to drive you to the airport.'

I lifted the pancake onto a plate and covered it with a clean cloth. 'I suppose so.'

'If I'm not too busy I'll take you.'

'Thanks. At the moment I don't think I could even afford a taxi.'

'Oh,' and she raised her eyebrows. 'So you weren't joking last night.'

I ladled more batter into the pan. 'Getting us here has cleaned me out. If Fleur doesn't pay me back soon I won't be able to get to Arizona.'

'Pay you back? Like how much?'

'A lot – all the money for getting here. Plus the truck repairs, and a ticket home.'

She lifted the baby to her shoulder. Sonia's tiny hands curled up to her face, then she let her head sink down onto her mum's sweater. 'But Ted will help you,' Miriam said.

Footsteps above us. Fleur on her way back to the stairs. 'Yeah,' I told Miriam, 'they've promised me some money. But it's really –'

Miriam was on her feet, her head craned towards the doorway.

'Sorry – I'd better see what Lucas is up to. It's too quiet in there,' and she hurried into the living room.

I turned over the pancake then wandered into the living room myself. She wasn't there but Lucas was on the floor crouched over a sheet of paper. He had his tongue between his lips and was making a large square with a red crayon. 'It's a firetruck,' he said.

'Yes, I suppose it could be.'

'It's a *firetruck*,' and he peeped up at me. His brown hair stuck out at an angle, making him look surprised.

'It's a great firetruck.' I crouched for a closer look. 'So, do you want to be a fireman when you grow up?'

He shook his head. 'I want to be a dog.'

'Good for you. It's a lot less dangerous. But I have to tell you that the food's not great. Do you like dog food?'

He thought about it for a moment. 'Don't know,' and he went back to his drawing.

It was a beautiful room: log walls, a sleek beige sofa, an ornate quilt hanging by the stairs, and in a glass cabinet the sort of sophisticated sound system that looked like it could control the Shuttle. I couldn't even see the speakers but from somewhere came the quiet hum of a cello concerto.

I was on my way back to the kitchen when I caught the tail end of a noise from upstairs: an angry voice that had been hushed. For a moment I stood and listened. Loud words muffled by the floor-boards, then the shifting of feet. Lucas looked up too. 'Don't worry,' he said. 'Mom and Dad always fight.' But it wasn't his mum and dad, it was his mum and Fleur.

*

Fleur had looked sullen all the way through breakfast. She'd slopped syrup over her pancakes and bacon then poked at them with her fork, heaped fruit beside them and hardly took a bite. I'd barely finished when she stood up and announced, 'We need to get going.'

Miriam grimaced and I shrugged back, said 'OK,' just to suit Fleur.

We were turning out of the driveway when it started. 'You don't have to blab about everything,' Fleur said. 'I mean, it'd be good to have a few things I could keep private.'

'Like what?'

'Like what? You had to go and tell Miriam you paid for the trip up here? Did it make you feel good, like you're so much better than me?'

The sun was in my eyes. I pulled down the visor and glanced over at her. 'Christ – I drive you all this way, I pay for the trip, and you don't even say thanks. Instead you're all pissed off because your sister finds out you owe me money. I didn't know it was such a big secret. It just came out, OK?' Bob glanced at me, then jumped down, out of the way of our anger.

'Oh right,' and she jammed her foot against the dashboard. 'You have no control over your mouth, is that it?'

'Just like you have no control over your life? Isn't that why I'm here helping you?'

Yet another thing I wished I hadn't said. Maybe she was right – I didn't have any control over what I said. I looked over, told her, 'Sorry,' but she was staring out of the window and didn't answer.

The hill was magnificent with the glaring gold of birch leaves on the turn, but all I could think of was Fleur glowering beside me. We were at the bottom of the hill before she said, 'Why on earth did you promise Mom you'd hang around if you wanted to get out of here right away?'

'I didn't – I've got work lined up in Arizona, remember? She asked me to stay for a while and I said I couldn't.' I braked for a stop sign. A pick-up truck came speeding past, then a big submarine of an old grey car, all rusted and dented. 'They're worried about you.'

'I know it.' Bob jumped up, rested his nose on her knee. She gently scratched his head.

I pulled out and we passed a few houses half-hidden behind the trees then a bulldozer parked at a dangerous angle on the edge of a ditch. 'Fleur,' I said, 'what is this really about? So far all I've worked out is that you had an accident, you tried to kill yourself, you didn't go for counselling but instead decided to come home. I'm a bit short on details.'

'Reassuring you can be flip about it.'

It wasn't until I glanced over that I realised how much I'd upset her. Her face was red and she had a fist pressed hard against her chin. 'I'm sorry. But you won't talk about it.'

I thought that was the end of it but she twisted around on the seat until she was facing me and said, 'I planned to shoot myself, but I didn't have the nerve so I slashed my wrist. I only managed one because all the blood made me faint. Dumb thing is, I broke my arm when I fell. Broke the washbasin too and water sprayed everywhere. That's how come they found me. The neighbours' place flooded.'

'You should have told me.'

'Why? So you could keep an eye on me? In the end Mom called Ted though I told her not to. She wanted the whole damn world to know.'

'You know what Ted's like, he didn't tell a soul – he didn't even tell me, for chrissake. But then I didn't even know he'd already been married until your dad mentioned it.'

'Some things are private, Sandra.'

'He's my stepfather. You'd think he was some kind of secret agent the way he carries on.'

'Don't you have anything to hide?'

'Nothing worth knowing. Do you?'

'I guess,' she said.

'Like why you wanted to kill yourself?'

'Oh, that's easy,' and she looked away. 'Sometimes you just can't face the thought of another day. You know things will get better but you just can't wait that long.'

*

It was well after lunchtime when I called over to Fleur, 'We should get to a travel agent. It's already late in the day.' Bob squirmed on my lap, opened one annoyed eye because I'd woken him.

She'd been rummaging in the boxes I'd opened for her, carrying clothes one-handed over to the rod in the corner of the room that served as a wardrobe. Now she sat down on the bed with a green plaid shirt spread over her knees. 'Sandra,' she said, and I knew I was in for bad news, 'I can't buy you your ticket yet.'

147

I sat bolt upright, acting out a surprise I didn't feel. 'What?'

'It's gonna take a week.'

I stared over to where she sat in the shadows. 'I can't believe this. You promised.'

She smoothed the shirt with one hand. 'Just call your friend and say you'll be a week late. It can't be that big a deal.'

'Not to you, no. Christ,' and I pushed Bob off my lap and went and stood by the kitchen window. I wanted to say, *How could you? I wanted to tell her, You've let me down, you're just not the person you used to be*. But for once I kept my mouth shut.

Later, when the evening sunlight was stretched and thin, I called Jo. I explained that something had come up and I'd be late. She sounded all pissed off and told me how much trouble she'd gone to. She asked me what had come up but with Fleur beside me on the sofa all I could say was, 'It's kind of complicated.' Naturally she thought I was hiding something from her and snapped, 'You know, I really thought you were serious about this,' then hung up.

Seventeen

Lunchtime started at half past ten. Men in thick shirts and padded jackets slid into the booths and peered at the specials board while I hurried to finish refilling the salt cellars and pepper pots and get them back on the tables. One of the other waitresses came up beside me, said, 'Honey, we're never gonna be ready at that rate. Let me finish off and you take some orders.' Which was exactly what I'd been trying to avoid.

The chef kept shouting at me: Did the customer want whole-wheat or rye? What in hell did I mean by *S/L*? And how in hell was he supposed to get an order out if I put it at the wrong end of the rack? I lost my pen; I lost my order pad only to find it in my pocket; I forgot glasses of water and brought coffee to the wrong tables.

A couple of times I looked over to where Miriam was sitting ringing up bills behind the counter and shrugged. Later when she had a chance she came over. 'You're doing just fine, Sandra. That old bear in the kitchen growls at everyone but don't you mind him, he doesn't mean anything by it.'

'This isn't going to work. I'm just messing everything up.'

She poured me some coffee and put it on the waitress station. 'Listen – you're doing me a big favour here. Imagine how we'd be managing without you.'

She'd called a little after nine to say one of her waitresses had just walked out when she was already short-handed. Monday morning and she was desperate – could I come over? It wasn't as if I had anything else to do, and she knew it. No excuses to fend her off with except that I'd never waitressed before and to that she said, 'Heck, anyone can carry a plate to a table. Come on, Sandra, it'll be a great help to me and money in your pocket – it's not like you don't need it.' Of course it wasn't that easy. It had been busy

149

when I walked in just after half past nine, and since then the place had filled up so that every table was taken. Most of the customers were regulars and rattled off their orders at me. A few asked what I'd recommend, and I had to look over their shoulder to pick something off the menu.

When eventually the place emptied out Miriam went up to the office to put in her orders to suppliers. Half past two and I hadn't even had breakfast, just a cup of coffee before driving Fleur to work. One of the other waitresses came over – *Janice*, her badge said. She must have been in her early forties, her hair a little too red to be natural and her face starting to go soft around the edges. 'Sit down, hon. How about a plate of the beef stew?' She brought me fries and a Coke too, then slid into the booth opposite me with an ashtray in front of her. 'So how was it? D'you think you survived?'

'Only just, but I'm not sure about some of the customers.'

She blew out a thin jet of smoke. 'You should have seen Cindy. She couldn't even hold a plate straight. Some of the customers got their lunch right in their laps and boy, they were not pleased about that.'

The stew was scalding hot from the microwave. I dabbed at it with my fork, added salt, blew on it so I could eat. 'Is that why she walked out?'

'Well, I wouldn't have put it that way.' Her smoke drifted across the table. 'More like she got herself fired.'

'For spilling food on the customers?'

'There was more to it than that.' She slid over to make room for the chef as he came out of the kitchen with his lunch. 'Come on, Bud, sit with us and stop being such a grouch.'

Without his paper hat his bald head looked fragile. He was all stomach, legs too short, arms thick and tattooed. 'Any more of them mother-fuckers come in they can get their own goddamn lunch.' His knife and fork clattered onto the table. 'What was with them today? Low sodium bacon, free-range eggs – what do they think this is? A healthfood restaurant? Is that what it says outside, huh?'

'Those are the people with sad lives who don't know what real food is.' She winked at me.

Bud slapped ketchup from a bottle onto his bacon. 'That's right, so let's put a sign out front: *No losers, no freaks.*'

'That include staff?' asked Janice.

Most of the customers had gone. Gina was in the back loading dishes into the washer, and only Kelly was still working the tables. When she came past with her hands loaded with dirty plates she said, 'Who leaves a quarter for a tip any more? And it's always the ones who had you running all over for water and more coffee. Shit.' The kitchen door swung closed behind her.

'At least we've got you for a bit of class,' and Janice smiled at me. 'Don't you think, Bud?'

'It'd help if she got the orders straight. That'd impress the customers.'

'Come on,' she said, 'how many Brits do we get up here?'

He wiped sweat from his forehead as he ate and told her, 'Hell, you're such a sucker for accents, Jan. What was that last guy that ran out on you? Finnish?'

'Hungarian,' she said, 'and I threw him out.'

'Right,' and he speared a fry with his fork. 'Just like all the others.'

She rolled her eyes. 'The day *you* get laid, we'll have a party for you.'

'The day you don't they'll declare a national holiday.'

She stubbed out her cigarette. 'I'll bear that in mind. I could do with a day off.' She rubbed her face, looked at me and said, 'So what d'you think? You gonna be back tomorrow?'

'Tomorrow? Miriam said she needed help today.'

'Nothing'll be any different tomorrow, I tell you. Even with you we're a waitress short.'

Bud dunked a slice of bread into his stew. 'How'd she find you?'

'I'm a friend of her sister.'

Janice said, 'The one who tried to kill herself? That one?'

'Yeah. I drove her up from Seattle.'

Bud was grinning. 'Figures, don't it? Who wouldn't have a go with that family?' and he turned to Janice. 'Didn't you say you'd quit if Hannah and Earl ever came back here to eat?'

'Imagine being brought up by those two. One of them yelling

at you the whole time, the other one fussing around. No wonder the kids are all screwed up.' She grimaced and shook her head. 'Don't know why they hang around. I'd have been out of this state first chance I got. So her sister tries to kill herself then she wants to move back?'

'Must be crazy,' muttered Bud.

Janice lit a fresh cigarette. 'Why'd she do it?'

'I don't know.'

'You drove her here and she didn't tell you? You're a better person than me. I'd have wanted to know before I got behind the damned wheel. God, life's hard enough without taking on someone else's shit.'

'Don't worry,' said Bud, 'Miriam'll get it out of her. Then we'll all know.'

'What I can't figure out is why she'd want to come back. Christ.'

I slid a fry into ketchup. 'This is where she's from. She says she never felt at home in the Lower Forty-Eight.'

They both laughed at that. Bud choked on his food and had to put a hand in front of his mouth and cough hard. 'Jesus,' he said, 'give us some warning before you come out with a doozy like that.'

'Oh God,' said Janice. 'Me, I'd never get used to winters only getting down to ten below. I just *love* wearing a parka all winter and having to plug in the car before I go anyplace. Oh yeah, wouldn't swap that for the world. Stay here long enough and you think having class means a man that washes once a month.'

Miriam had come downstairs carrying a pile of cookbooks. 'You've said that so often you've convinced yourself. I can't see why else you'd still be here.'

'Why d'ya think?' and Bud pushed his plate away. 'It's the only state with so many guys per woman, and they're not picky. But then neither's Janice.'

'Come on,' said Janice. 'You've been playing the same tune for months. Give it a break, why don't you?'

Miriam glanced over at the clock. 'Let's get cleaned up in here. I'll be in the back,' and she went through to the kitchen.

'So much for half-hour lunch breaks,' said Bud.

'I should do like Cindy and move on.'

Bud stood and picked up his plate. 'No one's gonna pay you to take your clothes off.'

'She got in at Glimmers?'

'You bet she did. Why the hell else did she let herself get fired?' and he walked back to the kitchen.

'Look at me,' she said to me. 'I hit forty-three last year and all I can find is waitressing. Can't hardly live on what I make. There's just no money waiting on tables in a place like this.'

I finished my Coke. 'It was packed.'

'But it's not a place where big spenders come, is it? Can you imagine ever earning enough to retire on?'

'No, I suppose not. At least Miriam must be making money if the place is so popular.'

The skin around her eyes had turned dark from tiredness and she leant her head against her fists. 'Money pours out of this place like a leak that needs to be plugged.'

'How come?'

She looked up. 'You really don't know? Jesus,' and she laughed. 'That husband of hers, that's how come.'

*

Fleur must have told her dad to come over. When I pulled up in the driveway that afternoon there he was on the porch with Bob snapping and struggling in his arms. I yelled, 'Hey, wait,' but he dumped Bob in the back of his truck and Bob protested with shrill, angry barks. I came up close, said, 'Where on earth do you think you're taking him?'

He turned around stiffly and looked at me from until the bill of his cap. 'To the pound. Someone's gotta do it.'

'That dog's mine – he's not going anywhere.' I scooped Bob out of the truck but he snaked and squirmed until I put him down. He hid behind the front wheel and only came out to snap at Earl.

Bob was mine. One of those sudden decisions you hear coming out of your mouth before you even know you've made them. What was I going to do with a dog?

Earl pushed his hands into his jacket pockets. Underneath he wore two shirts and a grey undershirt that showed at his neck, as though it was already winter and he couldn't afford anything warmer. 'You ain't even got a place of your own. How in hell can you keep a dog?'

'It's not like I'm staying here.'

'That's not what I heard.'

'Only a week,' I said, 'that's all.'

'Goddammit. This is nonsense.' He coughed, spat onto the earth.

'What's nonsense, Mr Satchel, is taking a healthy dog to be put down.'

'There's always some soft-hearted fool wants a small dog around here.'

Bob's nose showed just beyond the truck's tyre. Earl kicked at him and Bob growled. 'What's nonsense,' I started again, 'is Fleur arranging this without even telling me. I stay here to help her out and she doesn't even tell me what she's up to.'

He sniffed hard, rubbed his nose with the back of his hand. 'What kinda friend are you? You help Fleur out and you think you can demand what you want? Well, let me tell you,' and he leant close, 'there are other people who've done a lot more for her than you ever will.' Stale aftershave and the flat smell of his breath. I didn't move. 'Now, why don't you move that truck out of the way so I can go pick Fleur up from work?'

I backed Fleur's truck out of the way while he got into the cab of his beaten-up old pick-up and careered out of the driveway. When I pulled in again Bob was nowhere to be seen.

For an hour I sat on the front steps as the shadows stretched out across the yard, shaking a box of dog biscuits, whistling, calling. 'Come on,' I yelled, 'I saved you, for God's sake. You're mine now.' But there was nothing.

When the sun swung away from me I zipped up my jacket. What kind of a friend was Fleur? She arranged for her dad to sneak Bob away while I was out. She wasn't any better than her family who gave me the sofa to sleep on, and didn't think I'd done anything much driving her two thousand miles home. So much for the big-hearted family I'd expected: all of the good nature had gone to Miriam. And Hannah? Even she wanted too much, asking me to stay, taking *I'm sorry* for *yes* because it suited her.

I'd forgotten about the groceries. Two bags packed full because there was nothing in the cabin except coffee and sugar and one carton of milk. My wages and tips for waitressing gone on food. I put it all away with the news on, some story about a mass killing back in England, bodies buried in the garden and neighbours who'd suspected nothing, said the man was quiet and they'd never had any trouble from him. As though the murders weren't trouble enough.

The weather included an update on how many hours of daylight Fairbanks was getting: more than twelve hours but, as the fore-caster said with a cheery smile, it was going down by six minutes a day. In a week we'd have lost half an hour. In another few weeks it'd be as dark as Seattle ever got in the winter, and more light would be worn away until by December we'd have a day that started at eleven o'clock and ended at three. We. As though I was still going to be here when the light had shrivelled to nothing and everything was frozen fast.

A movement at the window: Bob. He'd climbed onto the chair left out on the porch and was peering in like a nosy neighbour. I opened the door and he pushed past me only to stand with one paw melodramatically poised in the air as he looked around. 'Yeah,' I said, 'but then I suppose you've got a right to be suspicious.'

*

I phoned Mum and Ted before Fleur got home. Ted said, 'So everything went fine. Didn't I tell you it would?'

'Apart from having to get the truck repaired in the middle of nowhere. But we made it, yeah.'

'Are we going to see you back here anytime soon?'

'The end of next week, I hope.'

'So long?' He laughed and I heard him tell Mum.

She took the phone, said, 'We knew you'd love it, honey. Alaska's supposed to be just beautiful. Is it cold yet?'

'No, but it's autumn and the leaves are turning.'

'I'm glad Ted packed your camera for you,' she said. 'I hope

155

you take lots of pictures – I can't wait to see what it's like. Now, how's Fleur?'

'Well, she hasn't tried to kill herself, though I hear she had a go in Seattle.'

There was a pause, the sound of a hand over the mouthpiece, muffled voices. Ted said, 'I told you she was having a rough time. Maybe you understand now – she had to get home. So give her some space, Sandy – whatever this is all about it's something she has to deal with herself.'

'Space is exactly what we don't have.'

I heard him sigh. 'But hey, it sounds like the two of you are getting on just fine. Must have been like old times, driving around in that old truck of hers.'

I wound the cord around my hand. 'Listen, I had to lend her some money and I'm not sure she can pay me back.'

'That's already been sorted out,' he said. 'Don't worry. Now, have you met the rest of the family? How's old Earl these days?'

'Ted, I'm not even sure she can buy me a ticket home.'

'Of course she can,' he said. 'I put two thousand dollars in her account just after the two of you left – she said she needed a loan to tide her over. She can't have touched it until you got to Alaska.'

Mum said something in the background. I sat forward listening, couldn't make out what they were saying. Mum came on the phone again, said, 'Honey, it's all been arranged. Now, just relax and enjoy being there. There's nothing to worry about.'

But I was worried. Why couldn't she at least buy me my ticket home if she had all that money?

Eighteen

Thursday I had a day off from the diner: I got into the truck, drove downtown to see what there was to see. I cruised Second Avenue, Third Avenue, ran out of downtown a few streets later and parked in a dusty car park outside a boarded-up building.

I'd bought a lead for Bob but when we got out of the truck he chased around, trying to find what was dragging along his back and snapping at the leather. 'Oh, stop,' I said. 'I can't believe you've never had one of these before.' He wasn't content until he'd got the lead between his teeth so that he could patter along in front of me with it hanging out the side of his mouth. 'If you could only see yourself,' I told him, but he ignored me.

A lead: proof for Fleur that Bob wasn't going to the pound. On Monday evening when her dad brought her home she'd pushed the door closed hard behind her, said, 'What in heck is going on? You know we can't keep a dog here.'

I'd been thinking strategy: I told her I was taking him with me, and I'd be gone within a week, wouldn't I? Right then I'd known from the way her face closed up that she'd been hiding something from me. 'You've got the money, haven't you?' I asked. 'That two thousand from Ted?' I knew I wasn't going to like her answer.

She hunched down to unlace her boots, kept her face turned away as she dumped them by the door and straightened up to take off her jacket. She told me, 'Don't worry.' *Don't worry, don't worry.* Everyone telling me not to worry. That worried me in itself and I came closer, stood in her way so she couldn't scoot around me and switch on the TV until she'd said something more. In the end she told me, 'Look, I promised them the money for the furnace months ago. OK? I can't let them freeze.'

Her parents. Of course. 'Why couldn't you let someone else help them?' Meaning Miriam, of course, because if she could afford that beautiful big house surely she would have paid for the furnace if Fleur had let her. But good old soft-hearted Fleur who cared so much for her family wanted to show how big her heart still was. I said, 'So that's where the money for my ticket home has gone,' and she didn't deny it. 'You're broke, Fleur, you couldn't afford it. You're in debt. To me. And to Ted.' I got a sour look for that, then she sat in front of the TV and watched the news as though it was the most interesting thing she'd seen in weeks.

Bob trotted ahead of me now, yanking on the lead every now and again to tell me to keep up. We turned the corner onto the main street: a Woolworth's, a few banks, a cheap jeweller's. A shop selling thick clothes and ugly boots. Another selling souvenirs for the Yukon Quest – a sled dog race, as I found out by looking in the window. Mushing – the local sport.

I'd let her watch the news while I made spaghetti, dished it up, carried it over so we could eat and watch TV at the same time.

She murmured, 'Thanks,' and glanced up at me, said, 'If I have to I'll get a bank loan, all right? I'll sort everything out,' but it felt like yet another way of keeping me waiting. Who was going to lend her money when her credit cards had been cancelled? Soon I'd have to start making payments on all that money on my own card, and was she going to help me with that? I just didn't trust her any more.

I didn't have any choice but to call Mum and Ted again. If they could afford to lend Fleur two thousand dollars then surely they could pay to get me home. Besides, they'd got me into this, so they'd have to get me out of it. They'd have to see it that way. If they didn't I could be stuck here for weeks, in this town with its dingy downtown streets, its small shopping centres, its roads and houses that looked half-finished. And outside Fairbanks was nothing except smaller towns, military bases, trees and hills for as far as you could go.

Bob and I had turned up the next street: cars parked at an angle like needles on a pine twig, a man lurching across the road, a restaurant advertising jazz evenings, a bar, another bar with two men shouting into each other's faces in the doorway, a half-empty car park, a coffee shop. A good coffee shop, I realised, not at all what I'd expected in Fairbanks: through the window I could see wooden drawers labelled *Blue Mountain, Italian Roast, Spicy Java*. I tied Bob up outside and went in for an espresso. In Fairbanks, for God's sake. So much for Fleur's ideas about having to be tough to survive up here: you could get gourmet coffee and *biscotti*.

From a table by the window I got a view of Bob's back as he strained at his lead as though he could uproot the lamppost to follow passers by down the street. I sat there thinking, This is worse than being stuck at home. All Fleur cared about was trying to be the same old Fleur. But she wasn't. Hadn't Mum and Ted noticed it? Surely they'd suspected something when Ted had had to put two thousand dollars into her bank account. Didn't they wonder how she'd ended up broke after all the money she'd been earning with that job of hers? Maybe she'd given it all away: look at how she'd given in to her parents when they demanded a furnace, wouldn't say no because it wasn't part of that cowboy philosophy of hers of having a heart big enough to look after anyone who asked. Anyone except me, it seemed.

*

Even with me sleeping on the sofa and Fleur over on the bed we were never more than ten feet away from each other. I found out how she liked to watch TV while she flossed her teeth, how she pulled up her trousers with one hand by tugging the waistband in three places, one after the other. We had to wash in front of each other, and dress. The only privacy we got was in the outhouse, but as it didn't have a door it didn't feel very private.

Every day I asked her if she'd talked to the bank about a loan. Every day there was some excuse. She must have known she'd get turned down, and then there'd be no escaping what she'd done: she'd pulled my life off its path and sent it spinning out into the dark.

One evening I told her, 'Fleur, I'm going to call Mum and Ted and ask them for the money to get home. There's no other way.'

She was watching a *Star Trek* rerun, her broken arm resting on her chest. She sat up. 'Don't do this to me,' she said. 'I've asked you to wait – can't you hold out a little longer?'

Jean-Luc Picard was gazing out the window of the *Enterprise* at a planet far below. Troy came in, said, 'Captain, they're waiting for you down there,' and he nodded.

'I'm sorry,' I told her.

She glanced over at me. 'Sandra, it'll ruin everything.'

'But look what you're doing to my life.'

She turned back to the TV. Picard was on the transporter. His body broke up into thousands of fragments and disappeared. 'They trusted me,' she said.

'So did I.' It sounded so tragic, so final, like the last line of a film. But I picked up the receiver and dialled.

Ted answered. I told him, 'Fleur doesn't have that money any more. Apparently there was something else more important she had to spend it on.'

'Oh?' he said carefully. 'Is that right?'

I wound the cord around my hand. 'That's right. So I need the airfare or I'll never make it to Arizona. Jo's already all pissed off at me for not being there when I said.'

'Sandy, we were expecting you to hang around for a couple of weeks. Help Fleur out for a while, that sort of thing.'

'But you know Jo's waiting for me.'

'Don't you think you have a responsibility towards Fleur after the way she was such a good friend to you? You didn't know a soul when you first came over here – what would you have done without her?'

'That's got nothing to do with it. I've driven her all the way home, and lent her money, and now I'm stuck here. Am I supposed to be some kind of martyr?' I felt Fleur shift uneasily on the sofa beside me. I asked more softly, 'Isn't Mum there?'

'She's at her class,' he said.

In a dark cave Picard was standing over an alien who had the skin of a lizard, then both of them raised their hands as rocks began falling from the ceiling. 'Ted, it's not as though I got myself into this. You do realise that, don't you?'

'OK,' and he sniffed, 'we'll send you your thousand dollars tomorrow.'

'And the airfare?'

'The thousand dollars, Sandra. If you want to use it to fly home, you do that. But the rest of this is for you and Fleur to sort out. Understand? Between the two of you you've pretty much cleaned us out. We've done all that we can.'

My hand felt slippery on the receiver. 'But if I spend four hundred flying home, how can I afford to move to Arizona? Besides, she owes me well over a thousand for getting up here.'

'That's between the two of you, Sandra. You're adults, you sort it out.'

'Please, Ted, you know I've promised Jo, and I'm already late getting down there.'

'That's your problem, young lady. We can't keep coming to your rescue.'

I was on the edge of the sofa, one hand jammed between my knees. My voice came out tight and high. 'Talk about not taking responsibility – you and Mum got me into this mess.'

'When I was your age I wouldn't have had the nerve to talk back the way you do.' His voice had sunk and I knew he was holding in his temper.

'No, you were already married. Oh, I forgot – none of us are supposed to know about that – even Mum, right? Me and my big mouth.' I sighed. 'Look – you just have to get me home.'

He was silent so long I thought he'd dumped the phone on the table and walked off. 'Is this some kind of extortion? Well, forget it – I'll tell her myself. And you can forget about your money.' Then he hung up.

I stared at the phone. That wasn't what I'd meant at all. I just wanted to show him that he was no better than me, for all that he pretended otherwise.

Fleur turned around. 'You just had to, didn't you? Well, now he's pissed at both of us. That's really helped, hasn't it?'

Before she could say anything more I clicked my tongue and Bob came rushing over and stood at my feet. 'Time for a walk,' I told him in a shaky voice.

Twilight, the trees so close, the evening so still and blue-tinted it was like walking through a photograph. Fairbanks felt like the edge of things: if I stayed too long I'd turn into someone else, a waitress earning forty dollars folded into my hand as I walked out the door – hardly enough to pay off my credit card, or afford groceries since, as Fleur had pointed out, she didn't get paid until the end of the month. I'd end up dressed like her in men's jeans and men's shirts and not showering often enough, talking tough about Alaska as though it proved something about me.

And it would be her fault – and Ted's. And Mum's for always giving in to him. Between them they'd managed to send me about as far from Arizona as they could and now that I was broke and stranded they'd abandoned me. As though they'd had nothing at all to do with it.

I strode up the driveway swearing out loud with Bob running excitedly beside me. Damn all of them. There had to be a way out of here, and I'd find it.

Along the road the cabin's third wall had gone up. Wood stacked close by, a pair of work gloves on an upturned bucket, a man in a torn jacket sitting on what would be the porch with a thermos beside him. I looked over and he called out, 'Hi there.'

Bob trotted into the yard. 'Here, boy,' I snapped, but he didn't want to listen so I went running after him, face still stiff with anger. Damn Ted. Damn his secrets. To turn the whole thing back on me as though I was trying to blackmail him – how could he think that of me, for God's sake?

The man bent forward and grabbed Bob by the collar. 'Hey, little guy – you need to listen up.'

'Thanks,' and I took hold of him.

'You new around here?'

'That's right. We're living right there,' and I pointed through the trees to the cabin.

'Not such a bad place. There's plenty worse being rented out these days.'

'I know – I saw some of them.' Bob pulled away and sniffed around the wood stacked by the man's truck. 'So you're building this place on your own?'

'I am now,' he said. 'The owner's decided he's got better things to do. And he still thinks this place's going to be up before it freezes.' He had the rind of a sandwich in one hand and he stroked crumbs out of his beard.

'That gives you another few months – long enough, isn't it?'

162

'You aren't from Fairbanks, are you?' and he grinned. 'Could be ten below in another few months. Or next month, come to that.'

He looked as though he'd been living out in the bush. Long hair curling at his neck, bushy beard, clothes that had a shadowy look of dirt about them even in the twilight. 'You're not either,' I said.

'Fairbanks born and bred, but I've been working up near Barrow.' Bending down he clicked his fingers at Bob. 'Come on, boy,' he said, 'come on now.' When Bob came close enough he patted him hard around the neck and Bob growled deep in his throat, came back for more, barked when he stopped. 'Cute little dog,' he said. 'Skinny though.'

'We found him out in the middle of nowhere when we drove up here. Had to rescue him.'

'Oh yeah? Well,' and he rolled Bob over onto his back, rocked him around while Bob play-snapped at his hand, 'you'd better watch out old Mitchell's dogs don't get him. They're bred for racing, not being sociable.' He nodded to the cabin behind Fleur's. 'Used to run a team but now he keeps the dogs for the hell of it. Some of them are mean sons of bitches. Just like Mitchell.'

'Oh yeah? What makes him so mean?'

'Too long out in Korea, that's what. Really,' and he threw his crust off into the dark, 'you ought to watch yourself. Some crazy types come to Alaska – veterans, religious nuts from churches you've never even heard of, all sorts.'

'And how about the locals?'

'We're not so bad,' he said. 'On a good day.'

I asked him, 'Is this what you do? Build cabins?'

'When I get the work, but there's not much to be had in the winter. How about you?'

'I'm waitressing at the Aurora Grill.'

'Miriam Ruehl's place?'

'Yeah, that's the one.'

'Well,' he said, 'how about that,' and he nodded to himself.

'Do you know her?'

He ran his hand down his trousers. 'Know her husband. I did a job for Jim once. He's one of those people, always has some sort of project going, always making deals. Trouble is, he gets too busy to finish what he's started.'

'Yeah?'

'Yeah. Like taking a year to get around to paying people. Some sub-contractors in town won't do work for him now. Miriam though, she's hard as nails, so I hear.'

'Who told you that?'

'Well,' and he grinned, 'Jim, I guess.'

'She's been helping me out. I'd be even more broke if it wasn't for her.'

'Well, how about that,' he said. 'Maybe she's gone soft on the inside.'

Bob had left us, bored at not going anywhere, following a scent into some leaves further up the dirt track, getting near Mitchell's cabin. 'I'd better make sure he doesn't get torn to bits,' I said.

'You do that,' and he unscrewed the cap of his thermos. 'See you around.'

Mitchell's dogs strained at their chains as they barked and leapt and howled. Over a dozen of them in a small yard, each with a doghouse and a patch of earth padded flat by their feet and nothing much else. Bob pricked up his ears and glanced over at them. 'If you go over there you're on your own,' I told him, 'because I'm not going near those mean sons of bitches.'

But he was too sharp for that. He kept close to me until we were around the corner, and only then did he chase off into the trees, barking ferociously. I walked on slowly, past shadowy driveways and patches of electric light from cabins behind the trees. At this point we usually turned back, but this time I wanted to stay out, away from Fleur and her told-you-so attitude. More than anything she was annoyed I'd let Ted see what sort of person she'd become, as though everything would have been fine if only she could have kept it hidden.

I used to believe in her because she'd always come up with what she'd promised: that she'd take a look at my car, that she'd talk to Ted about my doing a degree in commercial art instead of the one in management he'd picked out. Mum wouldn't do it – she was too much in love and she'd slotted into Ted's life as though she'd never had one of her own because that's what he wanted.

My suede jacket wasn't warm enough for this type of evening. Now that the sun had gone the air had turned cold. I called out to

Bob and waited, my shoulders hunched and my hands deep in my pockets. My jacket still stank of smoke from our fires along the Alcan. I'd have to get it dry-cleaned – when I had the money to spare.

Bob emerged from the dark, a pale patch growing paler as he came nearer. 'At last,' I told him. 'It's too cold to be standing around. Let's go,' but he overtook me and trotted down the centre of the track. I went after him, and only when we passed the last cabin did I realise why it looked familiar: the road was a circle. We were back at Fleur's place, only now there was a silver truck in the driveway.

Ryan. Sitting with his legs splayed, one cowboy boot up on the arm of the sofa and a beer in his hand. 'Man,' he said as I came in with Bob, 'that thing doesn't need a walk. What you trying to do to it?' He hadn't taken off his leather jacket and it creaked as he leaned back to finish his beer. 'Right, sis,' he said, 'let's go.'

'We're going out,' said Fleur. She looked me right in the eye as if to prove she still could.

'Fine.'

He stood and threw the can from behind his back into the bin then spun around to face me. 'Country music. Not your scene, city girl.'

Fleur pulled on her jacket. 'Ryan and me, we need to talk.'

'I don't mind,' I said. But I did. She was leaving me behind with the dishes from dinner to clear up and nothing for company except the TV, and even though I was glad she was going out I didn't want to be alone in that cabin, so many miles from home.

I watched them leave, wondering if he'd just shown up or whether this was arranged and she hadn't mentioned it. His truck roared as he backed out into the road, headlights flashing across the cabin windows, then the place was utterly quiet except for some TV advert twittering away.

'You and me, Bob. We've got the truck, we could have a night on the town too. How about it?' He cocked his head. 'Yeah,' I said, 'but we don't know a soul.'

Except Miriam. And she'd said to call around, any time.

*

Lucas had a train set out, a lumbering plastic locomotive with carriages that rattled along their thick yellow track, round and round until he shoved a dumper truck in the way. Then, with a crash of plastic, the locomotive lay on its side, grinding away like an angry insect.

Miriam lifted another slice of cheesecake onto my plate. 'Months back,' she said, 'she promised Mom and Dad shc'd pay for their new furnace, so they've been counting on her.'

'But things have changed since then. I don't get it – why does she think she has to pay for it?'

'There's no way Mom and Dad could afford it themselves. Neither of them paid into a proper pension plan. Dad used to work laying dynamite in the gold mines just outside town. It was a real small operation, and he never earned much. Mom did this and that, mostly looking after us kids.' She reached over and grabbed a biscuit the baby had dropped, dusted it off and put it back in her hand. 'This year they put their dividend cheques towards getting a decent used truck. You wouldn't think people could be badly off in a state that pays you for living here, but a lot of Alaskans can't afford to live the way people do down in the Lower Forty-Eight. And who knows how much longer the state can afford to pay out the profits from the oil. If they stop it's going to hurt a lot of people.' She made a face at the baby who grinned back. 'I'd have gone down to Seattle when Fleur was in the hospital but we didn't have that sort of money lying around. None of us do.'

'I didn't even know what had happened – no one told me.'

'Fleur's proud. Always has been. She didn't want anyone to know what she'd done – she was furious at Mom for telling Ted.' She went over and got the coffee pot and refilled both our mugs. 'You know, even if she could have paid to have her stuff shipped she'd probably still have wanted to drive back up here – that's the way she's always done it.'

'Except she wasn't doing the driving.'

She put the pot back on the warmer then sat down at the table again. 'That trip means a lot to her – as though it proves something about her.' She pushed back her hair, same gesture as Fleur. 'Now she's overstretching herself but she won't back down: she promised herself she'd do the trip back, so she did, even though it meant you had to drive her. She promised you your ticket home and that she'd pay you back, but she couldn't because she'd promised Mom and Dad their new furnace.' She leant her elbows on the table, poked at her cheesecake with her fork. 'Before she could live up to most of what she promised. Now she can't and she won't see it. I can tell you, it's worrying us all.'

The cheesecake was creamy and delicious. I scraped the last of it from the plate and sat back. Too much food. 'More?' she asked.

'Don't tempt me.'

The baby was restless in her highchair so Miriam lifted her out and curled her into her lap. 'She should at least have asked you out tonight. That's pretty mean-spirited, leaving you home.'

'I don't think either of us would have been in the mood for it. It's not like we've ever spent that much time together – I hadn't heard from her in months before she phoned and asked me to drive her here. And now we're sharing that tiny place. I don't know how long we'll be able to put up with each other.'

'Well,' and she smoothed back the baby's fine hair, 'at least she has you for company and to help her out. She went ahead and rented that place before she thought things through – what would she have done if you'd gone home? How would she have managed?' She sighed. 'Poor Fleur – I don't know what's gotten into her these days.'

She hadn't drawn the curtains and the moon showed behind branches that were slowly dancing in the breeze, the only light in the sky apart from a few scattered stars. I said, 'I still have no idea why she tried to kill herself. I came right out and asked her but she was all vague about it.'

'You too, huh? Makes you feel used, doesn't it? She has a right to her privacy, but she's asking a lot from us and won't give anything back, like we're not worth it.' She pulled her cardigan tighter around her. 'And she still thinks she's so independent when we all have to help her out. Oh God,' and she sighed again, 'it's too bad. But maybe she'll pull herself together now she's back home with us.'

She unrolled a colourful mat with flaps and bells for the baby who lay on it like a swimmer trying to get her bearings. Jim was out again. Often was, said Miriam, and didn't tell me more about it though I knew from the way she said it so lightly that it must have been a problem between them. She changed the subject and we talked about Ryan and how he'd been trying to make it big for years, and this house that she'd spent all her time on before she had the idea of opening the diner.

Somewhere around half past nine a key turned in the door. Jim. A little drunk, I thought, but looking pleased with himself because he had, as he told us, pretty much got in on some project to renovate a building for a new nightclub. Miriam nodded, said, 'That's great, honey.' She crouched and scooped up the baby, and I understood it was time to go.

At the front door I crouched to pull on my boots and said, 'Thanks. You know, it makes such a difference having someone to talk to.'

'You bet,' she said. 'And please, call around whenever you want, you hear? You know, I'm a member of a group of business-women here in town. We meet for lunch once a month, and we're getting together tomorrow. If you want I can ask if there's any illustration work for you. I know it's more your thing than waiting on tables. Just to tide you over until things get sorted out.'

'That would be great.' Tears prickled in my eyes so I didn't look up. Ridiculous to be so moved but I was.

'Fairbanks isn't such a bad place. You might even like it – you said you wanted to move out of Seattle, right?'

I stood up. ' I was thinking of somewhere warm and sunny.'

'It can be pretty warm and sunny here in the summer.' She touched my arm. 'I know you're disappointed, and angry at Ted for not helping you out. Just give it a little time – everything will work out.'

'Yeah,' I said, but I didn't sound very sure, even to myself. 'I'm sure it will.'

She smiled and I realised I'd expected more – that she'd suggest that I come and stay with her, or offer to lend me the money to get home. Stupid ideas. But I felt cut off up here, as though the rest of the world was so far away it would pass me by.

Outside it was chilly and the wind had picked up. I zipped up my jacket as I went down the steps, and when I looked back I saw

Miriam standing in the doorway with the warm light of the house all around her and the baby in her arms. 'Thanks for everything,' I called, and she waved and closed the door.

Nineteen

Between dropping Fleur at work at seven and going in for the lunchtime shift I had just enough time to finish the paintings. A hundred dollars for some corny watercolours to be printed up as cards tourists would buy: ravens flying over a frozen lake, moose grazing among willows, bears snatching salmon out of a river, birch leaves a flame yellow under a low sun and caribou hiding among the trees like ghosts. Greeting cards for four seasons, the woman had said, though Fairbanks really only had two: winter and summer. Thing was, she'd explained, you can't sell two seasons – it doesn't seem complete.

This wasn't what I'd envisaged: fitting painting into the time left over from waitressing and driving Fleur around. The work wasn't enough to give up the diner, not when this was the only job Miriam had found me, and not when she'd had four women come in asking for work. She took on one of them, a skinny older woman with a bony face and a voice hoarse from too many cigarettes, and the others she told to come back in a week or two.

I'd got the waitressing down, could reel off the specials, could slide a glass of water onto the right table while I was taking four breakfasts to another and still remember to clear a table on my way back. I knew for Bud *B* meant bacon and *W/F* meant with fries; I never forgot to ask how the customers wanted their eggs or gave them brown toast instead of white. I'd turned into a waitress, and to sit down and paint again felt awkward at first, as though my muscles had realigned for holding plates instead of a brush.

A couple of times Jim had come to the diner and sat at a table by the kitchen door. Miriam would go over and lay a hand on his shoulder and serve him herself. Afterwards he'd go up to the office with her and Janice would grimace. 'Trouble,' she'd say or,

'Here we go again.' Jim and his schemes – renovating a downtown building for office space no one wanted, investing in a bar that was already on the rocks. 'He's a born fool,' she told me, 'and so's Miriam for staying married to him. I hope to God this place is in her name, and the house.'

'What do you mean?'

'They lost their last place – or hasn't she told you about that?'

'She told me all right – but I thought they lost it in a fire or something.'

She smiled. 'No, though that's what she always says – "lost it". They sure did lose it – just not the way you might imagine. It got repossessed by the bank. One of Jim's business deals went wrong, and he'd used the house as collateral.'

But somehow Miriam must have salvaged enough for the new house, had borrowed and scraped and done God knows what else to buy that magnificent place. Wouldn't you have to be as hard as nails to do that? But it just didn't fit her – Miriam in her pinafore dresses and bright sweaters, her soft hair and wide smile.

I had to sit at the kitchen table to get enough light to paint though it was cold so close to the window. I put on a sweatshirt; I put on one of Fleur's quilted shirts, wrapped a scarf around my neck. I thought I'd escaped this: painting in the cold with stiff hands, drinking too much coffee to stay warm. 'Damn you, Fleur,' and I whisked my brush in a jar of water.

The temperature had dropped. Forty Fahrenheit by the thermometer we'd put up by the window, one which went all the way down to sixty below. Mid-September and too early for winter, according to Fleur, but the air had an icy bite to it and the corners of the cabin felt chilly despite the oil heater.

I got up and switched on the radio, found the college station, put more coffee through the machine. We were running low on water already. Twice a week we had to go to the launderette to fill up, wash our clothes, use the showers, and in-between time had to take care that the bucket under the sink full of stinking waste water didn't get too full and run out onto the carpet. That was Alaska, not the ravens and moose and caribou I was painting.

I added another willow to the right of my moose and laid the painting to one side to dry: three attempts to make the moose look ruminant rather than just sullen. Summer finished, spring and autumn almost done. Winter needed more shades to suggest uneven snow, and a spectacular sun just above the horizon – half an hour if I worked fast, and that would give me time to make my autumn caribou look wilder than deer, to paint in more skinny trees like the ones all around the cabin.

Dab into the water, dab into the paint then a couple of swift strokes across the paper, dab into the water again. I didn't stop until I'd got some caribou I was happy with and only then because I heard boots thumping on the porch, looked up in time to see the door swing open. Ryan. Bob jumped up from his blanket, barking unhappily because he'd been caught out too. 'Well hi,' Ryan said, standing there in the doorway with his knees a little bent, balancing himself on the heels of those cowboy boots of his.

'Hi.' I didn't smile, didn't put down my brush, and that made him grin as he closed the door.

'Fleur's at work. She won't be back until half past five.'

'Jeez,' and he strode over to the radio, 'what sort of bullshit music is this?' He fiddled with it, found a country station which he turned up loud then sat on the sofa with his legs crossed and one foot beating the air. His boots were worn down at the heel, the toes scuffed to grey. He sniffed then said, 'So how's it going, Miss Seattle?'

'It's going.'

He flicked back his long hair and rubbed one hand along the thigh of his jeans. 'Got some work to keep you outta trouble?'

'That's right.'

'Helping out in the diner too, I hear.'

'Yeah, I'm short of money.'

He held his head at a strange angle, as though he was looking over the top of something. 'It's an obsession of Miriam's, thinking she has to help everyone out, finding them a job. So now I bet you're going to hang around. Got work, got a place to stay, got a truck to drive around.' He gave a smile that lifted slyly at one end. 'Got it made, haven't you?'

'Oh yeah,' I said, 'this beats having steady work and living in Arizona. I was wasted as an artist – I was born to waitress.'

He pulled a packet of cigarettes from his pocket and lit one.

Soon the room was full of smoke and a song about how *a little country music is good for your soul* that he hummed along to. I went over and turned the radio off but the quiet made every creak of his leather jacket louder as he tipped his ash onto a plate, leant back and spread his arms along the top of the sofa, legs wide, feet splayed. I put down my brush – just couldn't concentrate with him sitting there in the middle of the room.

Everything about him was sharp, from his nose to his jaw to the tips of his boots. Nothing like Hannah, nor like his sisters who both looked like her, the same flat faces, the same pale lashes. If he looked like anyone it was his dad: the dark hair, the small chin, the same mean lines bunched together on his brow. Both men thin as sticks.

I made a show of rinsing off my brush and wiping it clean. 'Did you just happen to be passing, or was there something you wanted?'

He opened his eyes. 'You could do with a dog, out here all on your own.'

'We've got one,' I said.

'I mean something to protect you. There are one hell of a lot of crazies up here.'

'So I've heard. The state's overrun with them.'

He grinned. 'That's about right. Take your neighbour, for instance.'

'Mitchell? I've already heard about him.'

He leant forward with his elbows pointing out over his knees. 'Used to live out in the bush. Now he races his dogs off and on, does a bit of this and that. His mind got screwed up in Korea. Keeps a shitload of guns in his cabin.' He rubbed his chin and paused. 'A few years back when he was living in the bush his wife disappeared. He says she took off but no one's heard of her since. Shot one of his neighbours through the leg too, right here in Fairbanks. Accidental, they said, so he didn't do any time for it.'

I poured myself more coffee. 'So do you think I should do some target practice with Fleur's gun? Or should we be stockpiling Uzis in case things turn really nasty?' He put his feet up on the coffee table and beckoned for me to give him my coffee. Instead I sat back down at the kitchen table. 'Listen, I've got work to do, so if you're just visiting, thanks but I'm busy.'

'Whoa, little Miss Seattle hasn't got five minutes to spare. Wants to throw me out when I just sat down.' I picked up my brush again and whisked it through the water though I wasn't planning on doing any more painting with him sprawled out on the sofa like a spider.

He reached over and switched the radio back on. 'The two of you must be pretty close, you and Fleur.'

'Not so close,' I said.

'You'd drive someone you hardly know two thousand miles? C'mon.'

'She's practically family.'

'Uh huh, about as much as me, and I bet you have plenty of brotherly feelings for me.'

Even the DJ on the radio station spoke with a slow country drawl. I imagined him sitting in the studio with a Stetson crammed down on his head and a string tie around his neck. Probably someone who'd never been near a cow but if you asked him he'd call himself a cowboy, or at least think it. Ryan, though, was someone I could imagine being a cowboy, one of the old Hollywood sort – not the hero who comes galloping into town to save everyone but the mean son-of-a-bitch who drifts from town to town with the law just behind him.

From somewhere close by barking started up, turned to howling. Mitchell's dogs probably. Ryan heaved himself up and got himself some coffee, lit a fresh cigarette and came over to the table where he sat right opposite me with one hand around his mug. He breathed out smoke through his nose, two trails that parted, blurred, disappeared. For a moment he looked at the end of his cigarette, then tapped the ash off into my coffee. 'There's nothing for you here, city girl. Count on it.'

'I wasn't planning on staying.'

'So you've said. Still here, though, aren't you?'

'That's right. You should ask Fleur to explain that,' and I looked up. I hadn't noticed his eyes before. They were the colour of muddy water, impossible to catch the depth of. He leant forward with his elbows on my paintings.

'You still haven't said why you're here,' I said.

He laughed at that, spewing out a big wobbling cloud of smoke that caught the sunlight and fogged the air around us. 'Not so sharp, are you? You come up here and think you know it all. But you don't know shit.'

'That's what you came to tell me?'

He made a face as he gulped down some of his coffee, sat smoking his bloody cigarette and flicking his ash into my mug and hardly took those mud-brown eyes of his off me. 'Look at you,' he said at last, 'all dressed up – your designer jeans, your make-up, your hair in a fancy braid. Think you can bring Seattle up here? Think Fleur wants that?'

I stood and dumped my coffee down the sink. 'Tell me, do you think Fleur would be better off on her own? I mean, given that she tried to kill herself less than a month ago. Then there's her arm – she can't drive with that cast.'

He took a drag on his cigarette. 'How much did you ask for?'

'For what?'

'To drive her here.'

'She's broke – I did it for nothing. I'm driving her around for nothing. I cook and wash up and clean for nothing. I get stuck up here because I brought her home.'

'You think she's got sucker written all over her, don't you, but you haven't wised up. She has though. You won't get any more out of her.'

I said, 'What the hell are you talking about?'

'You and your demands for money.' The words came spitting out at me.

'All I want is to get down to Arizona like I'd planned. For chrissake, she *owes* me for getting her up here!'

'You should let her alone. She has enough worries.'

'I can't afford to.'

'Oh really?' And he caught my eye, lifted his coffee, tipped it, sent it cascading down onto my paintings, splashing into a mass of dark drops that bounced onto his jacket, the table, the floor, went rolling and trickling and dripping until the cup was empty and the coffee lay in dirty pools all over the work I'd spent days on. Then he pushed back his chair.

175

'Did *you* know she killed someone?' he hissed at me. 'I mean, I just wanted to know what you thought about *that*.'

'Get the hell out,' I told him, but he was going anyway.

*

After work I drove to Fleur's school and waited in the car park with the engine running, my hands between my knees because the heater barely worked. Since lunchtime the temperature had slid down another ten degrees and the air had turned icy. 'Gonna snow,' Bud kept saying, and everyone moaned back at him that it couldn't, it never snowed this early, that the leaves hadn't even fallen yet.

He was right though. Tiny flakes skittered down the windscreen as I sat in the car park wishing I'd packed a longer skirt because even with my wool tights my miniskirt didn't do much to keep my legs warm. But it wasn't just the cold that made me sit with my hands jammed between my knees – Ryan's visit had turned the whole day ugly. Fleur must have been complaining to him that I was asking for money, but I didn't understand it – why was he so furious over me wanting my money back? Did he think I should just forget about it because Fleur was broke? Well, I couldn't, even if I wanted to. And so he'd ruined my paintings. Now I'd have to spend every free moment redoing them.

Janice and Bud were right: there was something wrong with this family. Earl and his temper. Hannah thinking I'd stay when I'd told her I couldn't. Fleur telling me to trust her when she'd spent my fare home on a furnace for her parents. And now Ryan furious with me because he thought I was being too demanding when all I wanted was to get home and get on with my own life.

I revved the engine, as though that would make the heater work any better. Barely any warmth was coming out of the vents. As I sat there shivering I wondered – was it really Ryan's fault? Or had Fleur twisted the truth around so he wouldn't think less of her? She hadn't liked Miriam finding out she owed me. Maybe she hadn't told Ryan the whole truth – just enough to make me look bad instead of her.

But underneath it all I kept coming back to what he'd said: that

176

Fleur had killed someone. I told myself he'd said it for effect but that didn't ring true. All lunchtime as I took orders and carried plates I kept thinking about her truck accident, and no matter how hard I tried to concentrate the thought of it kept snagging my attention. What if someone had died? Was that why she'd tried to kill herself?

When it got to five o'clock and people started coming out of the main school building my hands pressed more tightly into each other as I sat very still, waiting for Fleur. I realised I expected her to look different, as though I'd be able to see some sign of the truth on her face. But she looked the same, her bland face, her thick shirt, her rolling walk as she crossed the concrete talking to some bloke then nodding goodbye and glancing around for the truck. I'd brought the laundry along and it sat lifeless between me and the passenger door. When she got in she shoved it along the seat to give herself more room. 'Let's get out of here,' she said.

I headed towards the small huddle of shops by the university with a stream of snowflakes bursting towards the windscreen. What did I usually say? I could have asked if this was winter starting, and how about stopping at the bookshop while the laundry was on, and guess who'd called around that morning, but I didn't trust myself. My voice wouldn't sound right, and then she'd know something was wrong.

She guessed anyway, said, 'What's up?'

'I didn't think I'd still be here when winter started.'

'This isn't winter. Just a few flakes. They'll melt, you'll see.'

'I hope you're right or I'm going to freeze.'

She glanced at my miniskirt, didn't comment as I flicked on the indicator and slowed. The wind chased the flakes across the road in feathery strands that billowed and broke and rejoined. So much for melting. If anything it looked as though the snow was searching for a finger-hold.

'Have a good day?' she said at last.

I should have said, *Yeah, nothing special* and kept it at that, but instead I heard myself saying, 'No.'

'Why's that?'

I pulled into a parking space outside a shop selling local arts and crafts. Hand-thrown pottery. Paintings of birch trees and snow. Carved stone earrings in the shape of polar bears and ravens. The intricate webs of dreamcatchers made from leather, thread and polished stones. My cards would fit right in here – when I finished them. 'Your brother called around,' I told her. 'Just before he left he spilled a cup of coffee all over my paintings. They're ruined, every single one of them.'

'He always was clumsy.'

I turned off the engine. It spluttered and lurched forward. 'It wasn't an accident.'

'Course it was. Why'd he want to do a thing like that?'

'Because he thinks I'm taking advantage of you.' I pulled the keys out of the ignition and looked at her. 'Now why would he think a thing like that?'

'C'mon now, that's crazy.' She dragged the laundry bag towards her and opened her door. The wind caught it and pulled it wide open.

I called over, 'Then maybe you can put him right.'

She held onto the door. 'Why are you making such a big deal out of this? I'm sure he didn't mean it. I know you put a lot of work into those paintings, but you've got time to do them again.'

I got out and zipped up my jacket all the way to the collar. The wind was gusting around us strong and raw, and the snow stung my skin. As quickly as I could I lifted our water containers out of the back of the truck and followed her towards the launderette. 'Fleur, you don't get it. He *poured* the coffee onto my work. It was to get back at me – he thinks I shouldn't want the money you owe me.'

The wind blew her hair back from her face, and she looked smaller, paler.

'What have you been telling him?' I asked her.

'Look,' and she turned to me in the doorway, 'it's a shame your paintings got messed up, but you can't pretend like it was on purpose. What kind of guy would do that? I mean, come on – he's my brother.'

I had the words right there in my mouth: *He said you killed someone.* I wanted to spit them out but she pushed open the door and dragged the laundry bag in after her. Too late. All I'd done was

178

complain about my paintings. Not enough guts to come out and ask her if it was true.

The launderette smelled of hot soap and damp clothes, its carpet full of strands torn loose by a vacuum cleaner. A woman in tight sweatpants came past with her laundry in a rattling supermarket trolley. We took the machine she'd just emptied. Nothing for it but to put our clothes in together, my small pink and black panties next to Fleur's that must have reached her waist and came in colours I'd never wear: beige, pale green, yellow, a few dingy whites-turned-blue. She dumped in less soap powder than I would have and turned the machine on warm. I switched it to hot. Not that warm had bothered me the last time.

Over at the sink by the far door I slipped a couple of quarters into the slot and filled the water containers. They were so heavy I could barely carry them, their weight wrenching my arms as I tried to hurry, shoving open the door with my back, half-sliding them across the concrete. It was almost more than I could do to lift them into the back of the truck. One of them leaked and the water numbed my leg in the cold wind.

I brought in my towel, soap and shampoo but all three shower cubicles were occupied. Instead I bought a can of Coke and sat in one of the plastic chairs away from the TV with my pad on my knee, my watercolours and a jar of water on the low table. Fleur came over and sat beside me reading an old *Newsweek*. When she glanced at my painting I angled the paper away from her. My moose still came out stiff and flat with a rack like a row of coathooks.

'Not bad,' she said.

I told her, 'It's a piece of shit. There's no life to it.'

'OK, it's a piece of shit then. I'm sorry you have to do this over, but hey, it's not my fault, right? And now you're making it worse by trying to do it while you're still mad. So quit because you're gonna drive us both crazy.'

I wasted three more sheets of watercolour paper painting moose that came out flatter and deader with each try. And the whole time I was thinking, Is that what's been eating away at her? That she killed someone? Was it her fault?

When she tapped my knee I jumped. 'Shower's free,' she said.

179

By the mirror a stocky man in shorts and a T-shirt that said *I live at North Pole* was combing his straggly hair. He nodded as I came close. 'That felt good,' he told me. 'I haven't been near running water in months.'

I said, 'I can't imagine,' and he laughed. 'It must feel good to be clean again.'

'Oh, I ain't clean yet. Just scrubbed off the first layer.'

Which explained the smell in the stall, the hint of sweat and dirty feet on the warm air. Taped to the wall was a notice: *No shaving No spitting and No dogs in the showers PLEASE*. When I stepped over the strands of hair on the floor and closed the door the smell got stronger. Fleur was still having strip washes at the cabin. One more week until the cast came off and her hair looked dull with dirt. For some reason it didn't seem to bother her. But at least she didn't have to deal with this.

The jet of hot water didn't feel as good as I'd hoped. The shower stall looked so grimy I kept my eyes closed, but that just meant I saw Fleur walking across the car park towards me again, mouth a hard line, her broken arm crooked across her chest. I realised I didn't feel the least bit sorry for her. All those secrets she'd stacked up around herself, just like Ted, as though she could disguise who she really was.

After I'd fixed up my eyeliner and rubbed my hair dry I went over and said to Fleur, 'I could tie a bag over your arm again.'

'It's OK.'

'Your hair looks like it could do with a wash, you know.'

She shrugged, went back to her magazine until a woman in a fleece jacket came over. Long hair, a knitted hat on top, a round face wide with surprise. 'Fleur? I didn't expect to see you here. Why haven't you called around?'

Fleur sat forward with her cheeks turning red. 'I only just got back.'

The woman stuffed her hat into her pocket and ran her hand through her hair. She looked better without it. 'How long you staying this time?'

'Oh, I'm back for good. Got myself a job as a high school lab tech and I'm renting a cabin out by your old place.'

'Really?' She sat down. Pink fleece jacket. Jeans. Hiking boots.

180

Alaskan chic. 'I had no idea – I thought this was just a visit. No one tells us anything. Isn't that just typical?'

Fleur slid the magazine back on the table, said, 'How's Cody doing?'

'He'll probably have to go back in for more treatment. At the moment though he's doing good. He'll be here in a minute. He's getting gas right now. You know, he's been feeling down – your family haven't been too supportive. I know they don't get along, especially him and Miriam, but he's made such an effort recently. And what happens? It's like he's not even part of the family. No one told him you were *moving* back.' A thin man with a long-tailed red hat had come up behind her and she turned, gave a quick smile. 'Look who I found in here,' she said.

But he didn't smile back. 'How long have you been in town?'

'Three weeks,' said Fleur. Her fingers knotted together, as much as they could with the cast.

He nodded and the end of his hat bounced. 'Figures,' he said. He'd brought in a bag of laundry and now he moved away to one of the machines and loaded it in.

His girlfriend shrugged, said, 'Guess we know how things stand then,' and went over to help him.

Fleur picked up the magazine again but I knew she wasn't reading it. 'What was all that about?' I asked, but she didn't answer.

Twenty

I curled up against the cold and pulled the sleeping bag tighter around my neck. Still couldn't sleep so I lay there listening: no hum from the heater, and when I sat up and couldn't see its small green light I reached for the lamp. Nothing. A power cut. I'd have lain there longer but my bladder was aching. No choice but to hunt in the half-dark for a sweater and leggings, hopping around in my hurry to pull them on because the air was turning my skin to gooseflesh, Bob dancing around me because he needed to go out too.

When I opened the door, though, he shied away. Snow. Fluttering down in big unwieldy flakes, dropping slowly onto the handle of a shovel, on a nail sticking out from the porch, capping everything with white party hats. I pushed my feet into my boots and went outside. Snow had slopped onto the porch in untidy heaps, swamping the steps, the path, the trees, and it was still coming down. My boots weren't much good in this kind of cold. That was a shock – the way the cold came right through their leather soles as I stumbled going down the steps, feet disappearing, snow filling my boots and squeaking against my socks.

Soft white clumps sagged on trees as though they'd slid whole out of the sky. Everything disguised, including the path to the outhouse. Now it was just a slight depression blocked off by broken branches and trees bowed towards the ground by the weight of the snow. Leaves had frozen fast to twigs, had given the snow more of a hold. Now the clumps of snow were freezing onto the branches. And it was only mid-September. Snow as big as cornflakes clinging to whatever it touched, my sweater turning white as I tramped towards the outhouse, my feet and hands scalded by the cold.

I'd have managed to get through except for a broken spruce. Its snapped branches were too heavy to move so I crouched right there and pulled down my leggings and underwear. My piss burnt a yellow hole beneath me that I kicked snow over. Heading back was worse, my feet going so numb I fell and the snow stinging my hands. Nothing I had was any good for snow: not my boots, not my thin leggings. I wasn't prepared for this; I was supposed to be in Arizona.

At least after being outside the cabin felt warm. When I sat on the sofa and kicked off my boots chunks of snow pressed hard like polystyrene fell off the soles. Lumps clung to my socks and I brushed them off. Then the pain started as warm blood forced itself back into cold skin. I pressed my feet together and tucked my hands into my armpits, surprised at how much it hurt. Bob came over and sat in front of me. He tried to lick my face but I pushed him away. 'Yeah,' I said, 'you're a lot of help but no thanks.'

It must have been ten minutes before I moved again, and then all I wanted was coffee. The power was off but we still had gas so I filled a pan with water and sat at the kitchen table. The ghostly shapes of the snow that had fallen off my boots' soles still hadn't melted thanks to the cold leaking in. I could feel it around my feet, finding the damp patches in my socks. Before long the cabin was going to be as cold as outside. I put on another sweater, one of Fleur's, and pulled my jeans on over my leggings. It made sitting down hard but I felt a little warmer, for the moment at least.

The smell of coffee woke Fleur. She sat up in bed with her hair sticking out and said, 'Why're you up so early?'

I picked up my watch from the table. 'It's not so early. It's half seven.'

'Jesus,' and she leapt out of bed, 'why didn't you wake me? I'm late for work.'

'So's everyone else.'

She stood beside me and looked outside. 'But it's only September. We never get snow this early.' Then she looked at me sitting there with a mug of coffee, said, 'And I bet you didn't think to do something useful like shovel the driveway. We're gonna have a hell of a job getting the truck out – it's not even winterised yet.'

'I'm not winterised yet either. I nearly got frostbite just going to the outhouse.'

'I've gotta get to work. I'm late as it is.'

'And I want to keep my toes.'

'Christ,' she said, 'Christ almighty.' She went over to one of the boxes she'd stacked by her bed and ripped it open. 'Here, these'll keep your feet warm,' and she dropped an ugly pair of thick brown boots beside me. Insulated with felt, warm even in much colder weather than this, she said. But they were too small. It had never occurred to me that her feet could be smaller than mine when everything else about her was bigger.

She sat down and took the coffee I passed her, said, 'You won't get frostbite in the time it takes to shovel the driveway, not in this weather.'

'Temperature's down to fifteen. I've already been out once and my feet still hurt.'

She rubbed her face. 'Goddamn.'

'Fleur,' I said, 'I haven't got any winter clothes.'

She ran a finger around the rim of the mug, found a stain and worked at it with her fingertip. 'This won't last.'

'Look,' and I tugged at her arm. 'Look out the window. It's winter.'

'Maybe you should apologise to Ted – he might still send you that thousand bucks.'

'I've already tried that. He's still all pissed off.'

For a moment I thought she was going to give me more of her advice but she just sipped her coffee and said, 'I'll sort something out. Miriam must have some spare clothes.'

'Well,' I said, 'I'd appreciate it, but it would be a lot easier if I could just fly home.'

'Sorry,' and she gazed out the window. 'Guess I've screwed things up for you.'

I measured out some food for Bob and called out, 'Go!' but he just ambled over as though he was feeling down too. I'd only drunk half my coffee and didn't feel like the rest. I dumped it down the sink.

'Why aren't I worth helping?' I said. 'I helped you, didn't I?'

'It isn't like that.'

'Then what is it like?'

'I've got other commitments. It doesn't matter what I do, someone's gonna be pissed at me.'

'But why me?' I went and stood in front of her. 'You've made too many promises, and I have to pay for them. It isn't fair – it isn't even close to being fair.'

'It isn't out of choice, Sandra. Sometimes promises are demanded of you, and there's nothing you can do.'

'You can say no,' I said.

'Sometimes people just won't understand no.' Then she went and washed her face at the sink while snow rushed past the window.

*

Ryan didn't come in. He hit his horn and Fleur left in her heavy boots that thumped across the porch until the thick snow muffled them. We'd found a candle and in its shifting light I knelt at the stove screwing up newspaper, laying smaller pieces of wood over it, then larger pieces, balancing it so the whole lot wouldn't keel over. Perfect, only there was no way to get a match to the kindling in the centre. That was the trouble with never having been a Girl Guide. I built it again, this time with gaps for a match to fit through. The paper caught straight away and yellow flames sped along its edges then disappeared. I tried with another match. Same result. So much for that.

So far north the sun moves more sideways than upwards. Even if you wait for an hour the light will hardly change at all, especially on a day with fast-falling snow. Time slows right down until you'd swear it had stopped altogether. That's how it felt that morning. I abandoned the fire and stood by the window. Miriam would be by later to pick me up. If I didn't get the fire going we'd come home to a cabin as cold as outside, our water frozen, Bob frozen too.

In the worn light flakes as light as ash drifted past. Nothing else moved. Easy to believe that now winter was here it would last for ever, to feel the miserable weight of it as snow kept falling. And down in Arizona Jo must have had to keep the air conditioning up high to stay cool.

I had to finish those pictures. The light wasn't much good but I got out my paints anyway, had to because time was running out. I'd finished the moose's rack when I noticed the flames licking from the stove that I'd left open when I gave up trying to light it. Smoke coming from the carpet. And the smell: burnt nylon. I grabbed a boot from beside the door and beat out the flames. A piece of burning wood had fallen out. Shit.

It was hard to concentrate after that. I kept glancing over my shoulder at the stove though I knew the door was shut now. I made tea to stay warm, dug out Fleur's mittens, went outside in my damp boots for more wood and had to dig under the snow for it. Odd-sized blocks left by the previous tenants, nothing like enough to keep us warm for more than a couple of days, and who knew how long the power would be off. I found an axe at the end of the porch and swung at a few pieces of wood, chipping off just enough for kindling if we needed it but not managing to do much else, then came in and fed the fire. Old-fashioned chores, I realised. Ones I'd never done before.

By half past nine the temperature had dropped to ten degrees Fahrenheit. I peered out at the snow piling up on the porch in light heaps like desiccated coconut. Sinister, the way it accumulated without a sound. It muffled Miriam's footsteps as she came up to the porch hunched against the cold, two bags weighing her down. When I opened the door she gave me a big smile from inside the ruff of her hood, said, 'Bet you weren't expecting winter yet, huh?'

It took her a couple of minutes to undo her coat, take off her boots, tuck her mittens into her pockets, unwind her scarf from her neck and drape it onto the hook behind the door. 'This is the earliest,' and she fluffed out her hair, 'the very earliest I've ever had to get out my winter clothes. And it's only September – can you believe it? Plus the forecast says it's just going to get colder. You've got to be prepared.'

'Yeah, but we're not. Not even close to it.'

'That's what I figured. Got enough here to kit you out for the whole winter. Most of it's just been hanging in my wardrobe waiting for a good home, and it looks like you're it.' She lifted one of the bags onto the sofa and pulled out a parka, pale blue with a fur ruff around the hood plus a trim of flowered ribbon along the zip. It looked like an Eskimo costume, not a coat. 'Had this made when I was still in school but it's got another few years of wear. Here,' and she passed it to me.

Inside it I felt big and clumsy. Miriam reached over and put up the hood then zipped the parka up so it covered most of my face. Already I was sweating. She said something. 'What?' and I pushed back the hood.

'It fits.'

As though something the shape of a sack wouldn't fit. I unzipped it, said, 'Yeah, it does.'

'Keep it. I have some other things for you too.'

Thick mittens, a hat like a tea cosy, a hand-knitted scarf in scarlet wool, three pairs of thick socks. Ugly things, all of them.

'Alaskan wear,' I said.

'That's right. Somehow you just didn't look as though you had anything for winter. And boy, in that miniskirt you weren't going to last long. The only thing I don't have for you is boots. How about we swing by a store downtown after work? You got eighty bucks to spare, or are you going to need an advance?'

'I don't have anything to spare.'

'Right,' and she unfolded a pink sweater with a snowflake design and held it out to me. Not my sort of thing at all. 'You know,' she said, 'you should think about phoning home again – maybe Ted has calmed down by now. You don't really want to hang around – what's there in Fairbanks for someone like you? Besides, you've done more than you said you would. You've stayed to help Fleur out.'

I took the sweater from her and put it on in front of the mirror. Hard to see anything in the candlelight, but up close it looked like a cushion cover. 'I already tried. Ted's still furious.'

'That's too bad,' she said. 'It's not like him to be mean. And it's not your fault you're stuck here, is it? He'll change his mind.'

I pulled off the sweater. 'I doubt it.'

'You'll have to do something unless you want to spend the whole winter here.' She pulled her parka back on. 'But to be honest, I don't see how Fleur's going to pay you back on her wages.'

'Me neither.'

She reached up above the stove and turned a small handle on the flue that I hadn't even noticed. 'There. That way it'll keep burning low and the cabin will be warm when you get back.'

'And Bob won't freeze to death. I'm beginning to think he's a Florida dog. He won't go out in the snow.'

'Bad news for a dog in Alaska,' and she smiled. 'You're gonna have to get him a kitty litter.'

'You hear that, Bob?' and I put on my boots. He opened one eye and watched me. 'If you don't toughen up that's your fate. You'll never live it down.'

When I stepped outside in Miriam's clothes the cold didn't hit me as it had before. Instead it just gently seeped in where I hadn't pulled the cuff right down to the mitten, and between the scarf and my neck. My feet were still a weak spot: walking through deep snow in thin, damp boots wasn't much better than going barefoot. By the time we got to where she'd left the truck at the end of the driveway I couldn't feel my toes.

Miriam brushed snow from the windscreen saying, 'Exactly how much does Fleur owe you?'

'Quite a lot.'

'Quite a lot like how much?'

I hesitated but I felt awkward, standing there in her parka and her mittens and her scarf. I muttered, 'Over a thousand on my credit card. Plus the ticket home.'

'God,' she said. 'So much?'

I climbed into her truck and had to take off the mittens to do up the seatbelt. The metal was icy against my fingers. 'I don't know if she'll ever pay me back.'

'You can't help but be disappointed with her after something like this, but you're right, you can't count on her. You've gotta look forward – earn enough to get home then start over. Forget about what she owes you. You can't wait around for her to get herself back together, can you?'

She twisted around to reverse out, her long hair spread over the hood of her coat. Snow squeaked under the tyres and she steered through the billowing mist of the exhaust. Then we were off, up the dirt road that had been ploughed but was already covered with an inch of snow. Above us branches drooped to make a tunnel. Some had broken and dangled down, or lay pushed to the side of the road. It looked like the sky was crumbling and falling, turning the whole world a bland white. Only the stop sign stood out: a spot of vibrant red.

'All of a sudden,' Miriam was saying, 'Fleur's just let everything go to heck. You have to understand something about her. When she was little she was so tough. You know, the sort of little girl who refused to cry over anything. It was like she closed herself up inside and all we saw was the sort of person who'd give you her last dollar if you asked for it. But you never knew what was going on in her head – if she minded helping you out, or if she resented it but wouldn't say so. Somewhere along the line she changed. She'll still give you whatever she has, but there's a price to pay. Know what I mean? She won't let you forget it. And we could never help her – oh no, not her, because she was so together.'

Ahead of us a snowplough moved along the road shoving the snow aside. We overtook it on a road more white than black.

She adjusted the heat blasting out of the vents. 'She's changed, and we don't even know why. Something's happened, and it's killed off a part of her.'

'This is going to sound crazy,' I said, 'but Ryan came by the other day. He said something about her killing someone.' Stupidly I laughed like it must all have been a joke.

'What?' She slowed and glanced over. 'What did he say?'

'That she'd killed someone. I wasn't sure if he was serious.'

'Lord.'

'But you know what? It explains it all – writing off her Chevy in an accident, being so depressed. All of it.'

'You're right, it fits. Oh God,' and she sat back, hands loose on the wheel. 'So she killed someone, huh?'

'I don't know if it's true.'

'And the only person she told was Ryan. Isn't that just typical? What's he ever done for her?' She braked for the traffic lights, bringing us slowly to a halt, and we sat watching headlights gleam at us through the falling snow.

189

Twenty-one

The cold had settled in. In the days after it snowed the temperature stayed stubbornly well below freezing, and nearly a week later out in the hills some people still didn't have electricity. We'd been caught out, but then so had everyone. In the space of a couple of days we'd had to have the truck winterised, buy a cord of wood, have Ryan come over to chop it, and cut down an old sweatshirt for Bob to wear outside. I had to learn not to count the money I was spending, not to leave the groceries in the truck while I was at work, not to spill the water from our kitchen slopbuckets onto the porch where it would freeze, not to drink from a can while I was outside if I wanted to keep the skin on my lips. Going anywhere took twice the time: we had to plug in the truck's block heater in advance, we had to put on parka and boots and scarf and mittens, we had to shovel the drive if more snow had fallen.

Driving Fleur home from the hospital when she had the cast cut off: that was reasonable. Driving her to work for the next couple of days, picking her up, dropping her at her parents' – I didn't mind because her hand was still stiff. By the sixth day though, a Sunday, when she said to me, 'I need to get to Sourdough Sally's by nine,' I didn't get out of my sleeping bag. 'Did you hear me? I'm meeting Ryan for breakfast,' she called over.

'I heard you,' and I cupped one hand over Bob's head as he settled down on my chest.

'At this rate, I'm gonna be late.' She stood over me in her ugly beige T-shirt with her arms folded across her breasts. 'Ryan'll be pissed if he has to wait.'

'You have to start driving sometime.'

'You're invited too, you know.'

'I don't want to come. Besides, being in diners reminds me of work.'

'Look, he said he didn't mean to mess up your paintings. Why are you so stubborn?'

I scratched Bob behind the ear. 'All I want to do is lie here in the warm for as long as my bladder holds out.'

'I just don't get it. If you don't go out, what are you going to do all day?'

'Nothing. Nothing at all.'

A few minutes later, while she was standing at the sink washing herself, she had another go. 'If you gave him a chance you'd like him. I know he can be kinda abrupt, but that's the way he is. He doesn't mean anything by it.' She ran her washcloth over her face, under her arms, squeezed it out. 'You can't keep this up. He's about the only person I see much of here.'

'So get him to pick you up.'

'He'll have left already. I told you, we're late.'

'Then drive yourself, Fleur. You don't need me.' Back to where we'd started. I slid further into my sleeping bag.

It was still awkward for her to hook up her bra behind her back but she managed, then pulled on a clean T-shirt, a shirt, a pair of long underwear and her jeans. 'Well, I do need you, Sandra, for the moment I do.' She folded her towel and hung it over the back of a chair. 'The thing is, I'm kinda nervous about driving after writing off my Chevy.'

I rubbed Bob's head hard. 'Must have been quite an accident.'

'Yeah,' she said, and she crouched to pull on her boots. 'It was. Believe me.'

I sat up. 'Someone died in that accident, didn't they?'

Her face went still. 'Yeah.'

I got out of the sleeping bag and stood watching though that just made her shift uneasily on the chair as she fumbled with her laces. 'What happened?' She took a breath and I waited. I asked, 'Was it your fault?'

Then she pressed her hands onto her knees. 'You could say that, yeah.'

*

She didn't tell me about it until I pulled into Sourdough Sally's.

191

The car park was crowded and I drove around on the compacted snow until I found a space we could squeeze into. All the way there I'd been waiting for her to say something more about the accident, had given up because instead she was telling me stories about getting locked out of a cabin in the middle of the night, how one summer when they were just kids her brothers had tried to set up a still in the shed. Then as I swung the truck between a low-slung red car and a pick-up she said, 'His name was Ronnie Caprio. The guy who died.' She gave a small laugh. 'Strange that. I couldn't remember until just now. How could I forget something like that?'

'Ronnie Caprio? Sounds like a Mafioso. No wonder you had to get out of town fast.'

'Yeah, I had to get out town all right.' Somewhere in the middle of saying it her voice tripped.

'What happened?'

In her mittens her hands covered her knees entirely. She said, 'I was coming back from town one night, a Thursday. It'd been raining all day and I was going pretty fast. I was coming up to a junction and the lights changed. Guess if I'd stamped on the brakes I could have stopped, but the road was wet. Besides, there wasn't much traffic around. So I didn't. I went through on the tail end of orange and I got right across the intersection and kept going. Didn't see the car coming out of the gas station just ahead. Suddenly he was pulling out right in front of me. We slammed into each other and my truck spun around, went up on the sidewalk, hit a wall broadside. I was all shaken up but not hurt and I got out. His car was in the middle of the road blocking both lanes. The horn was going because he was bent forward with his head right on the steering wheel. I thought I saw him moving so I tried to get him out. In the end someone stopped me. By the time the ambulance got there he was dead.' She tapped her mittens on her knees and watched them. 'He'd hit his head so hard he dented his skull. Caused a giant haemorrhage and they said that's what killed him. Just his head. Nothing else was hurt.'

'Except you.'

She turned to look at me out of the hood of her coat. 'No, I was fine. Just a couple of bruises. I had my seatbelt on and the Chevy had air bags. He was driving an old thing, and the seatbelts were all frayed.'

'That wasn't what I meant.'

Despite the sun coming through the windscreen the cab felt cold. A beautiful day with a sky the blue they paint swimming pools and snow a dazzling white. 'They said it was his fault because he'd been drinking. I can't stop going over it though. If I'd been going a little slower, if I'd seen him earlier, if I hadn't gone out that night. Stupid stuff like that. He was gonna get married, you know. Had the date set and everything.'

He'd had plans. He'd been loved. All those ugly snapped ends. 'And maybe,' I said, 'he was a little shit. Maybe *he'd* have killed someone with his drinking and driving. He's messed up your life, hasn't he?'

She was watching cars slide past on the road. 'His family invited me over.'

'And you went?'

'I met them all. And his fiancée. They took me for dinner and told me it wasn't my fault. That was just after the funeral. They said they didn't want me to worry, that one life ruined was enough. His fiancée still had the ring. She was wearing it and kept twisting it around her finger. She hardly said anything to me. His dad was the one that talked the whole time. About Ronnie and how him dying was God's will. Said if there was anything to forgive it would be forgiven if we all prayed.'

'So did you?'

'Right there in the middle of this Italian restaurant. They prayed for me too because I'd been touched by the hand of God, I'd been the agent for carrying out his will.' She wiped at her face with her mitten. 'You know, it hadn't been so bad up to then. But after that I kept thinking about what he wouldn't ever do, like getting married and having kids, and how I'd wrecked his fiancée's life. It's the biggest thing you can do, taking away someone else's life like that. Even if you believe it'll all get less painful, you can't wait that long. That's the problem – trying to get through one day when all you can think about is how you screwed up so many lives. Nothing else matters so you end up making dumb mistakes, and you get scared to do anything because maybe what you do will screw things up in ways you can't even imagine. I went out to see a movie and I killed someone. I keep going over it, like there's a way to go back and fix it all.'

'It's going to take a while to get over something like that. But you're getting your life back together.'

'Am I? I thought I could be like I was before and make everything OK.' She reached for the door. 'Things just aren't working out that way.'

Twenty-two

All night long a car engine churned away on the edge of my sleep. I woke up several times, saw Fleur by the window, went back to sleep. Later I heard a noise and said, 'You OK?' but there was no answer.

When Fleur's alarm went off I woke up from a dream of a man with his head flattened on one side, his eyes blank as eggs. Bob was scratching at the door so I unzipped my sleeping bag and put on a sweater and leggings. Outside the temperature had dropped far enough for the hairs inside my nose to freeze stiff, making me sneeze as I led the way along the path we'd trodden through the snow. The engine was still rumbling somewhere close by but I didn't look around for it, just hurried to the outhouse past the broken branches we'd had to move, sat down on the polystyrene seat while Bob crouched outside. Then I kicked snow over the yellow stain he'd left and we raced back to get out of the cold. Inside the door we both stood panting. Already my hands were red. At my feet Bob was shivering and nipping at the snow caught between the pads of his paws.

While I made coffee he perched on a kitchen chair and stared outside, got down and sniffed at his bowl, barked a couple of times by the door. Days at a time cooped up in the cabin, shifting from his bed of old sweatshirts by the heater to the sofa to the kitchen chair and back again, round and round. No life for a dog. 'You picked the wrong people to hitch a lift with,' I told him as I poured two cups of coffee. 'We were heading north. Still, it could have been worse. You could have ended up in Barrow. They don't see the sun for months at a time up there.'

'One month,' corrected Fleur. 'Only one,' and she took the coffee I'd just poured.

Of course I drove her to work that Monday morning, even though it meant I had two hours to kill before I needed to get to the diner for my shift. Couldn't insist she drive herself, not after what she'd told me. I was treating her differently, careful not to argue or even disagree, or to use words that had anything to do with death. As though it would upset her when she'd been living with what had happened for months. Ronnie Caprio dying, head smashed in by his own steering wheel. I hadn't even been there and I kept seeing it, coming back to it as though I could change things so that he wouldn't pull out in front of Fleur, so that his fiancée wouldn't be left twisting her ring around her finger, or Fleur lose her job and decide to come home.

While Fleur finished getting her things together I went back out and unplugged the truck's block heater. The cord was so long I wound it around my arm then left it at the bottom of the steps. Then I started the engine so it would warm up enough not to choke. It took four tries for it to catch and between scraping ice from the windscreen I had to dart back into the cab and press my foot onto the accelerator to keep it going. The whole time I felt watched. I swivelled left then right to see out of the funnel of my hood, then went back to scraping. Ice flaked off the glass onto my mittens. Colder today for sure. Already my thumb was turning numb and despite my lined boots I could feel the cold of the snow under my feet.

I didn't see them until I dropped the scraper. Four of them creeping up on me with their bodies bent low and their front legs reaching across the snow. Not wolves, surely, but as close as you could get in Fairbanks, some wolf-sled dog mix. Fur a mixture of whites and greys, faces sharp, bodies tight curves ready to spring away. Beautiful animals but the moment I moved towards them they scattered across the snow. I waited but they didn't come back. Instead Fleur came out of the cabin in her parka and plodded across to the truck.

As we pulled out of the driveway I told her, 'I just saw some dogs. Well, not dogs, more like wolves, creeping up on me.'

'Yeah?' she said, but she was looking at the truck in the yard next door. A feather of white exhaust fumes twisted from it in the slight breeze and drifted past the shell of the cabin.

'Yeah. They must have been half wolf. You should have seen them.'

'He's sleeping in his truck,' she said. 'The guy who's working on that cabin.'

'At least he doesn't have to drive to work.'

'It's crazy. One morning he's never gonna wake up. The carbon monoxide builds up and you don't even notice, you just feel sleepy, then you die.'

'Maybe he hasn't got anywhere else.'

She fiddled with the radio, found a song about cowboy life, about how things were *nuthin' like Hollywood* what with cold nights and flooding rivers and worse. 'People come up here, they don't know how to deal with winter,' she said, 'then they die from blocked heater exhausts or misjudging the cold.'

'But he's from around here, Fleur. He told me.'

'You talked to him?'

'He's from Fairbanks, he does carpentry. Says he did some work for Jim a while ago.'

'Well, how about that? This city is so small.'

We were almost at the main road when she said, 'Stop. We should go back and check he's OK.'

'Oh come on, Fleur.'

'We have to.' So we did. I reversed the truck along the narrow road, trying to keep it on the hard-packed snow and out of the softer layers along the sides. Then we sat there looking at his truck. 'Guess I'll take a look,' and she got out. I did too, for no better reason than to see what on earth she was going to do.

She marched right up and rapped on the window. Not much more than a soft thudding with her mittens on. The windows were so frosted you couldn't see a thing through them. She pulled off her mitten and gave another rap then yanked open the door. There, lying over the length of the seat, the man I'd talked to wrapped in a sleeping bag, mouth open, eyes shut. Not moving. 'Shit,' and she reached out and shook him.

He sat up so fast he banged his knee on the steering wheel. 'Fuck,' he yelled, 'fuck, what the fuck?'

'You OK?' she asked anyway. 'I heard your truck going all night –'

197

'What the hell right do you think you have? Haven't you ever heard of privacy?'

'We were worried.'

'Worry about yourselves,' he said and hunched forward to grab the door and pull it closed.

Our boots crunched on the snow as we walked back to her truck. 'Well, looks like he's all right,' I said.

'Might not have been though. He might have been dead.'

'And there wouldn't have been a thing you could have done about it.'

She wiped her nose on the back of her mitten. 'You gotta try. You can't just let people die.'

'And you can't make up for what's happened. Come on,' and I got into the truck, 'you can't pester strangers like that.'

She buckled her seatbelt. 'You don't understand – that's what Alaska's all about – looking out for other people.'

I shifted the truck into gear. 'Well, apparently some of them don't appreciate it.'

*

Janice came past with an armful of loaded plates. 'Heard the news yet?'

'No,' I said. 'What?'

'Got me a job working as a clerk for the city. Start in a month.' She grinned and walked to the table with more of a sway in her hips.

A customer in a red checked shirt said, 'Hey now, Jan, you going to tell everyone? Why don't you just put a notice around your neck to save your voice?'

'Yeah,' said another with a drooping moustache, 'anyone would think you were glad to get away from us.'

'That's about it,' she said. 'Won't have to put up with this kind of shit.'

'Yeah, it'll be a whole new kind of shit,' he said, and they all laughed.

It was a busy lunchtime but then Mondays always were. Everyone wanting to shake off the gloom of starting another week at work, treating themselves to hearty platefuls of mashed potato, gravy and chicken pot pie to keep out the cold, then blueberry cobbler or apple pie with whipped cream sliding off the top. Nadia, the new waitress Miriam had hired after me, the one with the raspy voice and bony face, didn't say much more than, 'Ready to order?' and 'More coffee?' She moved stiffly and whenever she could she sat down with a cigarette at a booth in the back.

'Nadia's hardly moved her sorry ass off that chair all morning,' said Janice. She nodded at where she sat flicking ash from the end of her cigarette. 'Earlier Kelly handed her a menu and asked if she was ready to order. That didn't go down too good but at least she got up and cleared a few tables.'

When Nadia did get up she moved so slowly Bud shouted at her, 'What's the matter? Getting lost between here and the table? Want me to draw you a map?'

She said, 'Fuck off,' so quietly I barely heard it.

The rest of us had to cover her section. Not much choice when her customers were leaning out of their booths to snag us and ask, 'That roast beef special is on its way, right?' or 'How about that pie I ordered?' Nadia carried the coffee pot as though its weight was slowing her down. The customers watched her with their fingers tapping the tabletops and their cups shoved out to the edge so she'd see them. Often she walked right past.

Miriam didn't come down from the office until lunchtime was almost over. With her order pad slapping against her leg Janice passed me and leaned onto the counter. She spoke to Miriam with one finger jabbing the countertop while Miriam nodded, hardly looking up from the receipts she was sorting through. I heard Miriam say, 'She'll get the hang of it. I'll have a word with her and it'll work out, just you wait and see.'

I followed Janice into the kitchen with a pile of dirty plates that I dumped by the sink. 'Glad I'm on my way out of this place,' said Janice. 'I can't put up with this kinda nonsense any more.'

Bud flipped over a burger and pressed it onto the grill until it sizzled. 'Uh huh,' he said.

'I mean,' and she took a sip of the coffee she'd poured herself, 'what's the point in taking on people that just make more work? It

199

gets the customers pissed when they see how many of us are serving and it still takes ten minutes to get them a cup of coffee.'

'You got it,' said Bud. 'But then,' and he cracked an egg onto the griddle, 'Miriam doesn't have a whole lot of choice.' He looked up as the egg bubbled. 'If you know what I mean.'

Janice sighed. 'Thought we'd seen the last of those.'

'The last of what?' I said.

'Her charity cases. Well,' and she put down her coffee, 'this place isn't going to get cleared up if we don't do it,' and she went back out with the door swinging behind her.

'Was I a charity case too?' I asked Bud.

'You bet. Difference was, you could hold a plate straight.' He turned the egg over then slid the burger onto a bun lined with lettuce and tomato. He had a rag hanging from the string of his apron and he used it to wipe his face. 'Nadia's never going to move fast unless someone sticks a firecracker up her ass, and that someone won't be Miriam. Now,' and he handed me the plate, 'get this to table nine before they pass out from hunger.'

It was past two when we took a break, Janice taking long drags on her cigarette, prodding her hash browns with her fork, watching Miriam at the counter, breathing out her smoke noisily from the side of her mouth and telling me, 'Sorry, hon, got to have a cigarette or I'm liable to hit someone.' I ate my burger without saying a word. Nadia was moving between the tables with the coffee pot though no one needed coffee and three tables were waiting to be cleared. When Miriam went out to the kitchen and Nadia sat down and lit a cigarette, Janice said to me, 'I've had it here. Really had it. You should find yourself something else too. Maybe the university takes on people to teach art and stuff – and they have to pay better than this place.'

'Too late for that – the semester's started. Plus I'd be stuck here until December.'

She shrugged. 'You're stuck here anyway. Besides, there are worse places.'

'And better ones.'

With a laugh she squashed the rest of her cigarette into the ashtray. 'I guess you're right about that.'

Kelly was working the floor on her own and Janice called over to her, 'Need some help there?'

'Yeah, sure could use some,' she said. They both looked at where Nadia was sitting in a back booth.

'Nadia,' said Janice, 'Kelly could do with some help.'

'Help her yourself,' and she walked off to the kitchen.

They didn't bother to wait until she was through the doors before they laughed. 'Hear that?' said Kelly. 'Anyone would think she was expected to do some work around here.'

'Haven't had one as bad as her since what was she called? Brenda?'

'Brenna. Miss Nail Polish. Couldn't do a thing while that polish was drying, and couldn't do a thing while she was painting on another layer. Man, I wanted to clip those nails of hers so bad.'

I pushed away my plate. 'I don't get it. This is a business. Why's Miriam taking on people like Nadia?'

Kelly walked away with a wink and Janice propped both elbows onto the table. She glanced behind her before she said, 'It's like this. Jim gets himself into debt and can't pay people. They show up here, or their wives do, and they tell Miriam they can't make the rent or they can't feed the kids. Whatever. True enough, most of the time. So she takes them on so they won't sue him, or so they won't spread it around, or because she feels bad. Who knows.' She shook another cigarette out of her packet. 'Thing is, everyone in town knows what Jim's like so only the ones who can't get anything else work for him. Means if he doesn't pay them they're really in the shit. That's why they show up here.'

I didn't say anything and she said, 'Don't look so shocked. He's a nice enough guy, but he's dumb. He has no business sense, none at all.'

'And Miriam ended up with him?'

'His family has money,' said Janice. 'Not that any of it comes his way these days. And Miriam always did have grand ideas about how life should be lived. Just look at that house of hers. Who else has a place like that? Some people brought up poor don't think they can do any better and don't try. Then you get the ones like Miriam who put everything into raising themselves up, whatever the cost.'

'That's not the way she seems to me.'

'Yeah? Well, I'll tell you something, Sandra. You watch her and make up your own mind.' Then she got up and took her plate back to the kitchen.

She was right about one thing: I needed to find myself something else. After the cards I hadn't had any other art work come in, and at the end of my shift I mentioned it to Miriam again and she squeezed my wrist and told me she'd keep looking around but winter was always tough. When I mentioned the university she said she had contacts there, she'd see if they had anything. It didn't sound promising.

I pulled on my parka telling myself what an idiot I was to let Ted get me into this in the first place. And now I was making it worse by helping to pay to have the truck winterised so we could keep using it in the cold, buying myself snow boots, waiting for Fleur's pay cheque only to have her tell me she was still broke and couldn't pay me back for the cord of wood I'd bought let alone anything else. Miriam was right – the only way I was going to get out of here was if I cut my losses and bought my own ticket home.

I sat by the door to pull on my boots and Kelly glanced over, told me, 'Cheer up. Things can't be that bad.'

'Yes they can,' I said, and she walked away laughing.

Twenty-three

October, and Bob had taken to pissing in a corner of the cabin instead of the litter tray. The smell hung around though I cleaned up as best I could and bought some spray from the supermarket to keep him from doing it again. The can had a big sloppy cartoon dog on it that wrinkled up its cute nose at the smell of the spray. Bob didn't like it either but it didn't make him use his litter. After scratching at the door then deciding it was too bloody cold to go out he'd piss on the doormat, the sofa, anywhere I hadn't sprayed yet. I couldn't blame him – he was shut up in the cabin all day because it was snowy and well below freezing outside. Hardly the sort of weather for a small short-haired dog bred to go down holes.

There wasn't much warmth to the sun now, and daylight was shrinking by seven minutes a day. The dark hung on for longer in the morning, and cut off the evening so that as we ate dinner the sky was already deep violet.

Fleur didn't say anything about the smell. No *I-told-you-so* or *What-are-you-gonna-do-about-it?* Even when the landlady called around and Bob jumped up to bark at her, Fleur didn't tell me that it'd been a stupid idea to keep him though it took both of us to persuade her not to give Fleur notice, that if there was any sign of Bob in the cabin when Fleur left then she'd forfeit the whole deposit. Jonie didn't look happy about it but she agreed. No more friendly conversation though. She kept what she said to curt questions and left.

Every morning I drove Fleur to work then either headed straight to the diner or home and waited for the lunch shift to start. One lunchtime when Miriam asked why she wasn't driving herself yet I shrugged, told her that Fleur hadn't got her nerve back. Looking through the bills she had spread on the counter she said, 'But come on, Sandra, you're not going to stay here just to drive her around, are you? Besides, she needs to get back on her feet again.' And she was right, except that I couldn't force Fleur to drive herself around. Or rather, I wouldn't, not now that we'd come to some sort of truce that meant treading more carefully around each other.

As it got closer to her last day Janice stopped trying so hard. Sometimes she sat down before all the tables were cleared and lit a cigarette that she smoked staring out into the traffic. It was left to me and Kelly to clean up, what with Nadia moving so slowly between the tables that she just got in our way. I thought Miriam was going to ask me to take on some of Janice's hours when she left but instead she took on a woman called Lilia with a turned-down mouth and a thick plait of orange hair. I had so little coming in that once I'd bought groceries and petrol there was hardly enough to cover my credit card payments. Little chance of more work now though: Miriam said she'd asked around but there was nothing going and nothing likely to be at this time of year. One afternoon while she was bagging up the money we'd taken she told me, 'You need to save what you can. Surely it can't take that long to get four hundred dollars together for the fare home.' When I shrugged she said, 'How come? I mean, what in heck can you be spending your money on? You're not still bailing out Fleur, are you?'

'Just buying the groceries and helping with the bills. She's always short.'

'That's Fleur,' she said, 'she never could manage her money. Well, it's your loss. I doubt she'll ever pay you back, but then I guess I've already told you that.' The way she looked at me with her mouth pulled to one side I got the feeling that if only I'd been more careful I wouldn't be stuck here without enough money to get home, that all this was somehow my fault.

'Am I supposed to refuse to help her?' I said. 'Buy food for myself and tell her to buy her own groceries?'

'You're not helping her,' and Miriam leant onto the counter. 'Can't you see that? She's not going to change unless she's left to do things on her own.'

'It's more than that. Her money's just evaporating and she won't tell me what she's doing with it.'

'It's like this,' said Miriam. 'She takes on more than she can handle. Promising to pay for the furnace, promising to pay some of Mom and Dad's bills, and to help out Cody with his medical expenses. Heck, she's probably told Ryan she'll give him the money to get back in the studio. She just can't say no.'

'She can to me,' I said.

She closed up a small bag of quarters. 'You're a pushover – that's the problem, Sandra.'

*

I didn't quite believe it, and that irritated me. Like having something stuck between your teeth and your tongue can't leave it alone. I wanted to know: was she really still helping out her family when I was having to buy groceries so we could eat?

So one evening when Ryan took Fleur out to The Wild Dog Saloon I looked through the drawer where she kept her papers. Right on the top sat her bank statements neatly paper-clipped together. Wage deposits twice a month that were far more than I earned. Withdrawals for ten dollars, twenty dollars, a cheque for four hundred dollars for the rent. A withdrawal for a thousand dollars. Every month. No wonder she was broke. I took out the rest of the papers and leafed through them with my heart thumping but there was nothing to tell me where the money was going so I shoved the whole lot back in the drawer. Couldn't sit down again though so I put on my parka and my boots without even knowing where I was going. Bob opened one eye to watch. 'Don't wait up,' I told him, 'this could take a while.'

It occurred to me as I drove out onto the main road that the money could be going to Ronnie Caprio's family, or to his fiancée. Maybe Fleur had made them the sort of promise it would be difficult to break. Still, that wasn't something I could find out unless I talked to Fleur, and I had no idea how to get to The Wild Dog Saloon. So instead I turned into town towards Hannah and Earl's place. Miriam had as much as told me Fleur was helping them out, and maybe she was giving them more than fifty or sixty dollars to help with bills. But what did they need with a thousand dollars a month? I didn't know what I expected to see: perhaps a brand new truck parked outside their house, a flashy programmable VCR perched below the TV, one of those microwave ovens that can roast and brown your food as well as just getting it hot. Signs of decadence.

Apart from the times I'd dropped off Fleur I'd hardly seen Hannah and Earl since we'd arrived. I'd been avoiding them: Earl with his bad temper, Hannah with the way she stood a little too close or took my hand and squeezed it as she told me that Fleur deserved friends like me who stood by her. She'd never mentioned the fact I was still driving Fleur around weeks after she'd had the cast taken off, as though it wasn't worth noticing when surely she should have been worried by it.

That evening with snow slopped over its roof and piled up against its walls their house looked smaller than I remembered. I knocked and stood in the arctic entryway tapping the snow off my boots as I waited. Hannah opened the door and looked over my shoulder. 'Well, this is a surprise,' she said. 'You girls don't call around often enough.'

'It's just me. Fleur's gone out to hear some band.'

'Is that right? Gone to hear some band?' For a few seconds she stood there with one hand on the door until she caught herself. 'Look at me keeping you standing in the cold. Come on in, Sandy.'

The house smelled of boiled potatoes and fried meat. At the table Earl was sitting over a dirty plate reading the paper. He lowered it as I pulled off my mittens, unzipped my parka, unwound my scarf, and hung all those outside clothes by the door. 'Well, how about that,' he said, 'I recognised the parka but look who's inside. Ted's wife's girl.'

'I was passing so I thought I'd call in.' A thin excuse but he didn't tell me so, just picked up the paper again.

'You're welcome any time,' said Hannah, 'you know that. Let me fix you some coffee. It's bitter out there, isn't it? This just has to be the worst winter we've had in a long time, and it's barely started. I haven't seen anything like it in years.'

'You say that every year,' said Earl. 'It's like you still expect it not to get cold. You'd think after forty years up here you'd be used to it.'

Her smile twitched, and she said, 'Let's just hope it doesn't get any colder. Not for the moment.'

Earl leant back. He was wearing glasses but he stared at me over the top of them, said, 'Still got that dog, have you? Hasn't got frostbite yet? Bet you're having a hell of a time getting it to go out for walks in this cold,' and he grinned like it was the funniest thing he'd heard all day. Then he folded the paper and moved over to his armchair where he sat with his feet up on a stool and the TV remote held high, flicking through the few channels until he got to the weather.

'Must be hard for that little thing,' said Hannah. 'What do you do with him all day?'

'He stays in the cabin.'

'Poor thing. It's not fair on them to be closed in all the time, is it?'

'No,' and I leant against the counter, 'it's not. But then I thought I'd be gone weeks ago.'

'I'm sure you did, honey.' She moved over to the coffee pot and poured me a mugful. 'Now, I have some apple pie – Miriam brought it round yesterday. Or if you like there's some zucchini bread.'

Food instead of sympathy. Still, I told her I'd have the pie, and as she cut me a slice she said, 'Funny thing about having grown-up children. They feel they have to take care of you. I was the one taught Miriam how to make pie, and now she's bringing me pies like I had no idea how to make them myself. I guess it's having her own children that does it. It's sure brought out the best in her. Now she gives us a hand any way she can.'

'Didn't she do that before?'

'Oh,' and she sliced hard into the pie, 'I wouldn't say that. But you know how it is when you're young and you only have yourself to think about – you just aren't considerate in the same way.' She lifted the pie onto a plate. 'Now, though, she'll help anyone, even when it doesn't do her any good. Some of those women she takes on at the diner, I think she goes too far.' She sat down across from me, the electric light making her skin paler, her eyes a flat grey. 'At least knowing so many people in town she's been able to fix up all that drawing work for you. That must make quite a difference, having that money come in.'

'It was just one small job.'

She patted my hand. 'Even though I know this isn't your kind of place, you've stayed to help out Fleur. Bless you for that, honey, but isn't it time for you to be heading home?'

I put down my fork. 'I was supposed to be in Arizona weeks ago. Had work lined up and everything.'

'Yes, and I really appreciate you staying on. But is there much more you can do?'

'I'm still driving her around,' I said. 'She hasn't got her nerve back.'

She stirred sugar into her coffee. 'She used to be such a go-getting little girl. You'd hardly know it now. Maybe she needs some time on her own.'

'Maybe,' and I speared another piece of pie. 'Thing is, I can't leave just yet.'

'Sure you can,' and she put down her cup. 'She's changed, but I don't think she's going to try again. Do you?'

'No –'

'It breaks my heart I don't have a clue why she wanted to kill herself. It makes you realise how cut off from each other we all are, that you can never really get through to the life we make for ourselves inside our heads. In the end we're all on our own, aren't we?'

'Yeah,' I said. 'I suppose we are.'

In the chatter of the TV I caught myself glancing around the house. No new TV, no new fridge-freezer. Nothing that hadn't been there before. But that didn't mean Fleur wasn't helping them. Maybe she was paying their electricity bills, or their house insurance. The kinds of things that don't show. I said, 'You know, the one thing that does worry me is that Fleur never seems to have any money. I don't understand it – I still have to help her out. It's like her wages just disappear.'

She leant back and looked at me. 'Well, I have to be honest now, Sandy. If Fleur's paying rent and keep for two people, it's not hard to see why her money's disappearing fast. Alaska's more expensive than you might expect, so if you want to stay it's only right she'd ask you to pay your way.' She pushed her cup away, her mouth pinched in and her eyes blinking. 'I'm sorry, I don't want to sound hard, but I know you've had your problems with money, Sandy. Ted's been good to you, but now you need to look after yourself.'

'But Fleur owes me. I'm stuck here because she can't pay me back.'

'That doesn't sound like her,' she said, then she sighed. 'But anyway, we can't help you out – we hardly have enough to live on ourselves.'

'I'm not asking you to help me – I just want to know where her money goes.'

'I don't know, Sandy, I really don't.' She looked toward the window as a car pulled up outside. Then she was out of her chair telling me, 'That'll be Cody and Teresa.'

They came in bundled up in coats and mittens and scarves. Hannah said, 'Sandy dropped by. Isn't that great?' A big smile as she turned towards them, too big to be natural. If they noticed they didn't show it, just came over with their faces still red and their noses running from the warmth. I could smell the frosty air from outside on them as they sat down at the table. Cody's cheeks looked more angled, his nose sharp as a fin in his thin face. He sat at the kitchen end of the table and called out, 'Any coffee, Mom?'

'Sure.' Hannah brought over the pot with the rest of the pie, then the zucchini bread and a box of chocolate chip cookies. She took her time filling the mugs, draining all the coffee and turning back to put on more. No one said a word. From the TV a jingle for toothpaste was cut off as Earl flicked to another channel. Some sitcom with a family crammed around three sides of a table, as they always are on TV.

'Well now,' and Hannah sat down, 'how're you feeling? Been in for more treatment?'

Cody poked at his slice of pie. 'Not for a while. Anyway, we've been having trouble with the insurance company.'

'Again?'

'Yup,' and he stabbed a piece of the pie then pushed it into his mouth.

Teresa sat forward. 'They're dragging their feet over every-

209

thing. Don't want to pay up until they have to, telling us we have to pay a higher deductible, telling us some of the treatment isn't covered. Stuff like that.'

'But you must go in for your treatment,' Hannah said. 'Cody? You will go in, won't you?'

'Yeah.'

'Because if it comes to it we'll sell this place. You know that. You can ask us for whatever we have and we'll give it to you.'

'I know, I know,' and he ate more pie. 'But I'm doing good for the moment. Really.'

Hannah looked at Teresa who said, 'He's better than before – thank God, because the rest of our savings are gone. Anyway, Dr Cortez thinks it's gone into remission. He still needs some more tests to be sure though.'

'So you have to have the tests, Cody.' Hannah pressed her hands onto the tabletop. 'You don't want to get bad again.'

'It's OK, Mom. Quit worrying so much.' He took a noisy slurp of his coffee and wiped his lips with the back of his hand. He turned to me and said, 'So, what have you been up to?'

'Nothing much.'

'Still working at Miriam's place?'

'That's right.'

'But Miriam's found her some illustration work,' said Hannah. 'She has so many contacts with the business people in town – you want something done, you just need to ask her and she'll know someone.'

'It was just a small one-time job doing some greeting cards,' I told Cody.

Hannah was still talking. She said, 'Miriam's got herself into this association of businesswomen in town now. That's how come she could find work for Sandy. They all help each other out. Isn't that great?'

'Surprised they let her join,' said Cody. He smirked, added, 'Given what Jim gets up to I'd have thought they'd have black-balled the whole family.'

Hannah's smile flattened and disappeared. Cutting another slice of pie for me she glanced over at Earl. He'd fallen asleep, paper spread across his chest like a blanket, remote loose in his hand like the pistol of a dead gunfighter.

'After all,' said Cody, 'he must have just about the whole city pissed at him by now.'

'Now you know that's not true,' Hannah told him.

'And Miriam sticks by him. Now why would she do that? Helping to clear up the mess he makes, like she was his fucking mother or something.'

'Cody.' She put down the knife and he looked up in time to catch the way her face had gone hard. He nodded and took another bite of pie while Teresa sat beside him sipping her coffee and not looking at anyone. But Hannah didn't look away. She said to Cody, 'I will not have any more of this. You hear me?'

He laid his arms flat on the table. 'Why do you listen to her? Don't you want to know what's really going on?'

'We're a family,' said Hannah. 'We help each other. We look out for each other. What else are we good for?'

He snorted. 'Just don't ever ask me to help her out again. Understand? Not ever. When she's having a rough time everyone has to pitch in, but when we're having a rough time she couldn't give a damn.'

Not a sound except applause rattling out of the TV. The click of the coffee machine turning itself off. The low hum of the fridge. Nothing else as we sat around that table with Teresa picking her zucchini bread apart and Cody and his mum glaring at their plates. The three of them knowing what all this was about and me still wondering.

When the sitcom ended Hannah stood up and cleared the plates. Teresa gave her a hand, said, 'That was great zucchini bread. Really.'

'Yes, it was.' Hannah turned the taps on full and loaded the plates into the sink.

'My mom was a lousy cook. Your kids are lucky.'

'I guess,' said Hannah.

I could feel Cody watching me. When I turned he said, 'Just think of it like a kind of theatre. Or maybe,' and he flicked crumbs off the table, 'like the zoo. You know, all the animals going nuts because they're caged up.'

211

'And which animal are you?'

'Oh, I'm one of the hyenas. Always making a racket about something. You'd have to be a snake though.'

'A snake? That doesn't sound very flattering.'

'Quite the opposite – you're up there hanging around in your tree, looking down on what's happening on the ground. Thing is, you could get shaken off your branch by all the commotion.'

'Don't worry,' I told him, 'we're renowned for holding on tightly when we have to. Very tightly, in fact.'

He laughed. 'Point taken,' he said.

Twenty-four

I told Janice it was a waste of time but she insisted: she'd met some bloke who worked in the university fine arts department, she'd give him my résumé and if there was any work going she'd make sure I got it. I told her Miriam had tried, that there wouldn't be anything this late in the semester, but it didn't do any good. A parting favour she called it because – and this came out on a scornful breath of cigarette smoke – she wasn't going to be back around the diner again, no way, no how.

Without Janice the hours at the diner dragged. November started and customers sat silently over their food, watching the slow dawn though it was halfway through the morning. We took orders, carried plates, served coffee, bussed tables, all of it with hardly a joke to change the pace of things. Bud snapped at us for letting customers have combinations not on the menu, as though it was something we'd never done before. Shovelling in a lunch of chilli and fries at two in the afternoon he would say things like, 'What kind of a life is this, standing over a hot grill all day?' and mean it. He didn't even shout at Nadia any more and she took even longer to take orders to the tables.

Some of the regulars didn't come by so regularly and the ones who did ate and left without hanging around drinking coffee and ordering slices of pie the way they had before. New customers came, people who quietly ate their breakfast or lunch and left small tips. I hardly saw Miriam to talk to any more. She didn't pour the two of us coffee and say, 'So, how are things?' She didn't ask about Fleur or tell me to call around some evening. I can't say it bothered me though. In the end her help had always come down to telling me it would be better to go back to Seattle where there was more work. It made me wonder if there was some other charity case she wanted to give my shifts to.

Not long before Thanksgiving I got a call: could I teach a couple of drawing classes for the university? The instructor had been taken ill, was very ill in fact. But they needed me that night, and every Tuesday and Thursday night until mid-December. Of course I said yes. The pay was much better than what I got from Miriam, and on top of what I earned from waitressing I'd have more than enough for a ticket home by Christmas. I hadn't called home in weeks, and even then I hadn't said more to Ted than 'Hi,' and 'I'm sorry, but you got me all wrong.' Rather than say something meaningful back he'd passed me to Mum. This time was the same. He handed the phone to Mum who said, 'That's great.' I heard her put her hand over the mouthpiece and tell Ted the news. He said something I couldn't catch and she came back on, said, 'You know, if that's what you wanted you could have got teaching work here.'

'It's not what I wanted. It's all I could get that pays well.'

'You don't sound very excited about it,' she told me. 'But teaching will be good experience for you.'

'I know, Mum.'

She must have guessed something had gone wrong between me and Ted because she made him take the phone again. He said, 'So I guess we're not going to see you for Thanksgiving.'

'No,' I said. 'I'm stuck here, remember?'

'I hadn't forgotten,' he said with a nervous laugh.

'Is Mum still there?'

'Yes.'

'Have you told her yet?'

Silence.

'Well, at least say something when I apologise. How many times do I have to say I'm sorry?'

'You went too far, Sandy.'

'You got me all wrong. It wasn't like I was going to tell her. Why would I do that? She'd probably be as furious at me as at you.'

He coughed, said, 'OK then. OK.' Then his voice went low and serious. 'Well, if you're not coming down I might as well tell you anyway. I hope you won't take this badly, but you should know: Matt's seeing someone else. I've no idea if it's serious.'

'Tell him congratulations.'

He laughed again. 'Oh,' he said, 'we don't see much of him these days.'

'Why's that?'

'I guess he thinks it doesn't feel right to spend so much time here, and neither do we, not if he's seeing someone else.'

'Don't you see him at work? I thought he was buying into the practice.'

'Well,' he said, 'you see, things are a little different now, aren't they? We've had to rethink the situation, see if it's really best for everyone.'

'You thought we were going to get back together, didn't you? That's why you wanted him in the practice.'

'What were we supposed to do?'

I knew he must have a finger raised to tell me not to answer yet but I broke in anyway. 'You should keep your word. It's not like he's done anything wrong.'

'He wasn't very open about it.'

'He probably guessed how you'd react.'

'I don't like it,' he said. 'I don't feel I can trust people who try to hide things.'

'Right,' and I didn't say any more, didn't have to.

He sighed. 'Anyway, we can talk about all that another time.'

'All right,' I said, 'but in the meantime, I'm sure Matt would appreciate it if things were back to how they were. You know, back when you wanted him to be a junior partner.'

'I'll see about that,' he said.

*

Fleur had gone to her parents' for dinner straight from work so I didn't see her before I left to teach my first class. When I got back she was watching TV with her feet up on the coffee table. 'Hey,' I said, 'what do you think? Do I look any different?'

'Why?'

'Because you're looking at a new part-time temporary instructor of drawing.'

215

'Well, hey,' she said. 'You do look smarter than usual. Bet you were freezing in that outfit though.'

'Turned out most of the students were older than me so it didn't make much difference what I wore, some of them were never going to listen. What do I care? If they want to ignore perspective that's their problem.'

I hung my parka on the rack and scooped up Bob who'd been dancing around my feet since I came in. He tried to lick my face and I turned away, held on tight as he wriggled in my arms then I put him down and rolled him over to rub his belly. That was something he loved, but I noticed: he was getting fat from too much food and not enough exercise. I'd have to force him outside no matter how much he hated the cold and the sweatshirt we'd cut down for him. It made him walk as though he had a heavy load on his back, glancing back at me, resentful.

When I got up and filled a pan for tea I found Fleur watching me, grinning. 'What?' I said.

'Don't *I* look any different?' she said.

'Why?'

'I drove all the way home.'

'In the dark? My God. What made you do it?'

She shrugged. 'Dunno. It just felt right, no one telling me I had to do it. I told Ryan to get in the passenger side of his truck and he did. Didn't say a word, just passed me the keys and off we went.'

'Well, that's great. How was it?'

'Scary,' she said. 'It didn't help it being dark. And it felt different from how I remembered. All this time I believed that I couldn't do it. It seemed too much, having to think about shifting gear and braking, and watching out for other traffic at the same time. But when I pulled out it wasn't like that at all. You just do it, like your body automatically knows the moves.' She hooked her arms around her knees. 'Anyhow, heck, it's over with. And you can take that water off the stove – there's a six-pack in the fridge to celebrate.'

So we sat on the sofa listening to some CD Ryan had bought her, sipping our beers and telling each other stuff about our day, and it felt fine, like I remembered it had sometimes when she'd come over for barbecues and we'd sat in the garden watching Ted

216

brush sauce on steaks. Early days. Back before Ted decided to push things, nagging me to call Fleur, asking how come I didn't ask her along when I went out with my college friends. Trying to make me relieve his guilt at not spending so much time with her since he married Mum. But sitting there with Fleur that evening even the music felt right, some growly voice that curled up at the end of lines. Clint Black I guessed, and for once I got it right. A song about loving and leaving and people being wrong for each other but hoping for love one day that didn't say much new but wasn't trying to. That, I realised, was what I'd been missing all this time: that none of the songs were supposed to say anything that hadn't already been said, or tell it in a way that hadn't been tried out. I could guess the next rhyme, and it made the songs seem familiar – *start* going with *dark*, *find* going with *behind* – corny as heck if you expected something more surprising, but comforting if you didn't. Songs about a world people wanted to believe in, one with broken hearts and love gone bad, true enough, but where love could be put right in the end, where food meant home-cooking, and people worked hard on the land in jeans and Stetsons and loved it no matter how tired or dirty they got. Not my world, but Fleur's somehow, no matter that she'd gone into chemistry not ranching. When she sang along she looked more settled, as though she'd found the answer to what she was doing with her life in these songs about love and cowboys.

But by the time I'd finished my third beer that feeling of goodwill and contentment was fading. I stared out into the night, feeling the dark stretching out from the windows and away into the distance, wondering what it was that was bothering me until I remembered: Matt had taken me at my word and found someone else. That love wasn't mine any more, I'd turned it down, and now no one loved me the way he had. I felt it, that loneliness that comes after being loved, when being free means being adrift.

Corny songs on top of a few beers and I'd lost all sense of proportion. Still, as I sat there on the sofa with Bob dozing in my lap and Fleur telling me about some record company interested in Ryan's band, moving to Arizona felt beyond possibility, and when I thought about living there it felt lonely too, down south where I hardly knew a soul.

Twenty-five

When it snowed again the temperature soared to five below –
Fahrenheit of course – and for the first time in weeks it felt warm.
At the supermarket the man in front of me was in shorts and a
T-shirt, his legs a ghostly white against his green wool socks and
his bare arms all goosebumped from the cold. He whistled as he
unloaded his trolley at the checkout: tins of pork and beans,
individually wrapped breakfast rolls, cheese slices, pop-tarts, a
towering carton of orange juice. 'Not gonna be warm for long,' he
told me, 'so you might as well make the most of the heat wave.
This is one real mother-fucker of a winter, I'll tell you that.'

'Isn't it always?' I said.

'I guess so. Last year we had a snow drought and everything
was ugly as hell, year before that we had so much snow I didn't
get to see out of my windows until May. Shit, that was depressing.'

He was right about the cold. Two days later when a foot of snow
had fallen the cold came back and set it hard. It crunched dully
under my boots when I took Bob for walks, me bundled up in
parka and mitts and him in his cut-down sweatshirt. Fleur had got
him some booties, the sort mushers put on their sled dogs to stop
ice freezing between their pads. If I didn't keep him walking he'd
try to gnaw at them, and I couldn't blame him: green sweatshirt,
pink booties – he looked ridiculous. It didn't stop him from
yelping out threats to old Mitchell's dogs though, telling them to
watch out, that he was out and about. Typical small dog mentality,
taunting bigger dogs, a new habit he'd developed no doubt because the other dogs howled back so angrily, chained up as they
were. I'd expected more of Bob and put it down to cabin fever.

Sometimes I'd see Mitchell in his stained overalls dishing out
food to his dogs, or loading a dog sled onto his truck. The yard

must have stunk in summer with all those dogs but in the cold there were no smells at all. No scent of resin from the spruce, no odour of the earth, just the cold prickling the inside of my nose.

The bloke working on the cabin next door to ours was rarely there now. He'd come back a few times to work on the inside and a radio had blared during the day, his truck had rumbled through the night, then he was gone. I was glad. I couldn't sleep well wondering if I should go and check if he was slowly suffocating from carbon monoxide leaking into his cab. Fairbanks felt more dangerous as the days wore away to a few hours of light and the cold froze everything solid. I noticed the deaths in the *Daily News-Miner*: in accidents from driving too fast on ice, from suffocation after using a gas heater in an unventilated cabin, from collapsing drunk by the side of the road on a day when the temperature was eighteen below.

On my few days off from the diner Fleur drove herself to work and I was left stranded in the cabin, no way of getting anywhere because there was nowhere to walk to. I got up when the sun came up halfway through the morning and fiddled around washing the dishes that had built up over the past few days, emptying the slop buckets under the sink, thinking up exercises for my students, using a cookbook of Fleur's and baking different kinds of bread for the hell of it – an all-day occupation if you did it properly and let the bread rise twice, but then I didn't have much else to do. In a way I enjoyed it. Lazy, fragrant days with the warmth of the oil heater and the smell of dough, brief trips to the outhouse or to take Bob for a walk, then back inside where I kept the radio on for company. So much quiet. The only movement from squirrels and small grey birds, branches bouncing under their weight, small showers of loosened snow glittering as it fell.

The day before Thanksgiving I hefted the slop buckets across the cabin to the door. Leggings, sweater, boots, just enough to keep me warm for the couple of minutes I'd be out. The smell of the water was nauseating and some spilled over the edge as I struggled out the door. I pulled it closed then hauled the buckets down the steps, through the snow to just beyond the outhouse with Bob in front of me snapping up mouthfuls of snow and licking stray flakes from his nose. The scummy water ate through the snow steaming like acid. In minutes it would be frozen but I didn't stay around to watch, just whistled for Bob and hurried back to the cabin because it was colder out than I'd expected. I pushed the door. It didn't budge. I tried again but it was no good: the lock must have broken because the handle went round without releasing the catch, shutting me out in the harsh cold in my thin leggings with Bob shivering at my feet.

Thirty-six below that day. You can drown in a cold like that. It swamps you and no matter how much you jump up and down and stamp your feet or hold your dog close to your body you can't keep it out. You realise you can't feel your hands, your feet, your ears. Soon your face goes too, and your thighs. You disappear bit by bit, like Bugs Bunny rubbing on vanishing cream. I thought about breaking a window with the shovel, but cold air would stream inside and then how would I stay warm? I hugged Bob closer and he shoved his snout into my armpit. He was shaking hard.

Someone had to be home close by. There were cabins around after all, and I stumbled up the drive and onto the road. No vehicles in driveways, but I went up and knocked on doors anyway. At the one place with a car parked out front no one answered except an angry dog chained up in the yard. I called out, 'Someone help me. Is there anyone there?' but my shout just faded away.

Bob was shaking so hard I tucked him inside my sweater. I walked on, stumbling on my frozen feet, and he started struggling. I hugged him to me more tightly and tried to run, falling this way and that, stopping and turning back, going crazy from the cold. I thought about trying to make it to the main road. It wasn't far, not if you were in a parka. But dressed as I was it might as well have been miles away. I realised: I could die. Right there, right then. It seemed too pitiful for words.

I'd come almost full circle. Only one place left and that was Mitchell's. Truck parked in front of the cabin, dogs howling as they saw me coming towards the door. Before I had time to knock Mitchell was in the doorway with one hand against the doorframe and his bulky body blocking my way. He stood there in his brown overalls and thermal undershirt with a grim look on his face, one

220

hand moving just out of sight as though he was reaching for something. 'Please,' I said, 'I'm locked out and freezing.'

I didn't wait to see if he minded. I just walked right up the steps and stumbled past him into the cabin. Warm air clogged with the smells of dogs and food and burning kerosene. A lamp hanging in the middle of the room, an old bathtub by one wall propped on bricks. Even as I sat down on the only chair not piled with junk I thought it was strange: a bath in this tiny place where without a doubt there wasn't any plumbing. But already the heat was prickling my skin and Bob was going frantic inside my sweater until, struggling with my frozen hands, I managed to set him free.

Mitchell had been staring. As Bob jumped out onto the floor he let out a roaring laugh, said, 'What the hell – ?' as Bob darted under the table. Maybe the cold had knocked some sense into him because he didn't come out and didn't make a sound.

The warmth scalded me. I pressed my hands into my armpits, my face against my knees, and my feet against each other. None of it helped. My blood burned as it pushed back into cold skin. I don't know how long I stayed with my head down listening to Mitchell moving around the cabin: ten minutes, maybe longer. It felt longer.

When I sat up I found a cup of coffee in front of me. Mitchell was sitting across the table with a cigarette jammed into one corner of his mouth and a newspaper folded in front of him. The lamp above us hissed like a gas leak and the shadow of its base swung gently over the table.

My hands were so stiff and sore I dribbled some of the coffee down my sweater and had trouble putting the mug back onto the table. I had no idea if Mitchell noticed because he kept reading his paper, one hand smoothing his beard. From the way it spilled down over his overalls it couldn't have been cut in months. What surprised me most was that he wore glasses. Plastic-framed ones that could have done with a wash because even from where I was sitting they looked cloudy.

He kept on reading, I struggled with the mug, and from under the table came a quiet crunching. Bob chewing something. Could have been anything because the place was full of harnesses and rope piled by the bed, fishing line in tidy spools on a low table, pieces of rod, reels, and old tin cans by the door, gaping sacks of dog food by the stove, rolled up furs on shelves beside small metal pots with lids jammed on at an angle, a box with bullets peeping out of it, containers of water, cans of food. A gun hanging by the door. That's what he'd been reaching for as he stood in the doorway watching me come close.

He poured me more coffee from an enamel pot grimed brown, and after he'd put it back on the stove he came over and lifted my face. I jumped though I didn't mean to. Something about him getting so close. I shut my eyes while he prodded my skin with his thick fingers. A fusty smell came off his overalls and his breath stunk of cigarettes. 'Got yourself frost-nipped,' he said.

'I got locked out.' It came out too quickly. Those stories I'd heard, that he'd gone crazy in the Korean War, that he'd shot his neighbour in the leg and killed his wife, they unnerved me now.

'Should cut yourself a spare key and hang it outside some-place.' As he sat down he bent under the table to drag Bob out. He cradled him in his arms to look at his paws, his ears, his nose. 'Didn't do him no good either,' he said. 'Ears got frozen. He doesn't wanna be out for long in this kinda cold. Could kill him.'

'The lock's broken. That's why I couldn't get back in. I only expected to be gone a couple of minutes.' Too much explaining because I still couldn't believe it had happened: I'd gone out, I'd shut the door, I hadn't locked it, hadn't done anything out of the ordinary and now it was broken.

But he wasn't listening. He was tugging at the skin around Bob's eyes, then he pulled his mouth open and was craning his head to see his teeth. He said, 'Had it rough, aintcha boy? What kinda troubles have you had?'

I didn't notice he had two fingers missing until he picked up his mug. It made him look sinister, capable of killing his wife and hiding her body so no one would ever find it. It didn't help that his hands looked worn, as though the skin had frozen and thawed more times than it could recover from. In places it had cracked, and the cracks had filled with dirt that looked like it would never come out. I said, 'I hear you used to live out in the bush.' Then I wished I hadn't said it. His wife had disappeared out in the bush. Maybe he'd think that was what I was getting at.

222

He looked up. 'Who d'ja hear that from?'

'The bloke who was fixing up the cabin just down the road.'

'Well,' he said, 'you won't be hearing any more from him.'

'Why's that?'

'Truck went off the road out towards Ester and they didn't find him till too late. Froze to death. Was in the paper a few days back.'

I didn't know what to say, but it didn't matter because he went back to his paper. In the end I said, 'Did you know him?'

'Just his name.'

I hadn't even known that. The cold had killed him and you'd think from the way old Mitchell said it that it was just one of those things. Maybe he was right. This far north the climate was brutal and a mistake could cost you dearly. I sat there with my hands and feet and face still throbbing, wondering what I'd have done if Mitchell hadn't been in. Would I have gone back to the cabin and smashed one of the windows? Maybe the cabin would soon have been as cold as outside with all the heat leaking out. Maybe I'd have cut myself on the glass and been too cold to notice until too late. Would I have headed out to the main road on my numb feet and waited for someone to come past, more skin and muscle freezing the longer I was outside? I didn't know. I wasn't prepared. I could have died, Bob too.

It looked like Bob didn't trust me any more. He'd curled up by Mitchell's feet as though the way he'd picked him up and looked him over had been enough to win his loyalty. Mitchell knew what he was doing. I didn't, and it showed.

The afternoon sun was sinking. Already it had sloped from one side of the window to the other and now it was too late to send more than a few weak rays between the trees. Soon it would be gone. I should try to call Fleur, I realised, warn her that the lock was broken and we couldn't get in. 'Can I make a call?' I said.

'Nope,' and Mitchell looked up. 'No phone.'

So that was that. I sat there with my coffee wondering how long it would be until Fleur got home. My watch was in the cabin, and there was no clock in Mitchell's place. No clock, no phone. No electricity. I tugged out one of the old papers on the table and read through it but the whole time I was thinking about the bloke who'd been fixing up the cabin and the way he'd frozen to death. He'd

223

gone off the road not far from Fairbanks with its malls and coffee shops, with its McDonald's and Wendy's and big, bright super-markets. Outside town there was nothing but snow and trees and the biting cold he hadn't been able to survive.

*

Fleur was furious. Not about me giving myself and Bob frostnip, nor about the fact that I'd frozen the door shut with the water I'd spilt in the doorway. What she was angry about was my telling Miriam she'd killed someone. I tried to explain it had been weeks ago, and that I'd only been guessing. None of that made any difference. She slammed around the cabin telling me that now I had a decent job I ought to get a place of my own, that I was using the fact she owed me to stay in her cabin for free. There was no point showing her the huge gaps in her logic because she wouldn't listen to a word. Instead she stood in front of me brandishing the TV remote like a weapon, red blotches showing up on her face, raging at me out of all proportion to what had happened.

Bob wouldn't come out from behind the sofa. A sensible tactic. She was still furious when I took the keys from the windowsill and told her, 'I'm going out, OK?' Of course it wasn't OK, it was her truck and she told me that three different ways but I went anyway.

Even though I wrapped myself up the cold hurt me more than it ever had before. All the flesh I'd frost-nipped stung again, and more than anything I wanted to stay in the warm. Impossible though with Fleur in that kind of mood. I had no plan except to drive, and when I came to an ice cream shop near the university I pulled up. Jazz coming over the speakers. The smell of fresh coffee. Most of the tables full of people in fleece jackets and hiking boots. I sat in the corner with a magazine and in the three hours until they closed I had a bowl of chilli, garlic bread, a chocolate sundae, a slice of carrot cake, and three coffees. The man behind the counter said things like, 'You eating for two or what?' and 'When did you last have a decent meal?' By a window frosted with thick ice I spooned up the food and watched head-lights coming past. I could still hear Fleur's voice telling me I'd betrayed her, that she'd never forgive me, that she'd never forgive

Miriam either because this was typical of her, to turn on her after all she'd done to help her, that everyone took advantage of her, that she was going to start taking my share of the rent out of what she owed me because that was only fair, and why hadn't I suggested it myself? A whole catalogue of hurt coming out as though this was the first time she'd added it all up and seen how much she'd been wronged.

One thing was certain: I needed to move out, but if I moved out I'd have to buy a car, and if I bought a car I wouldn't have the money to leave. Back to where I'd started when I'd sat in Marco's that wet Saturday in August wondering how to find the money to get down to Arizona. Except now I was even further away and in debt.

I'd saved Fleur from herself and now I had her life weighing me down. I imagined myself slinking along like Bob in his sweatshirt, belly close to the ground and head down. A pathetic sight.

Twenty-six

I'd never quite got the hang of Thanksgiving. To me it was like a trial run for Christmas with no decorations or presents, the whole day focused around eating because that's all it was when it came down to it, a celebration of food. Turkey. Cranberry sauce. Corn. Sweet pies made out of vegetables. Ted always made a big deal of it so every year we'd spend most of the day in the kitchen basting a turkey far too big for six people, chopping vegetables, Mum peering at a recipe for pumpkin pie though she'd never quite got it right. Thanksgiving morning I'd drive over early with Matt, stopping off somewhere for him to buy chocolates for Mum. A couple of hours later Fleur would show up in a new shirt with a bottle of white wine she'd jam into the fridge, then she'd roll up her sleeves and start on the pots in the sink. 'Don't let me touch the food,' she'd say, 'not unless you want it ruined.' Ted would put on a CD of Frank Sinatra, and we'd make soup, salad and gravy dancing around each other to 'They Can't Take That Away From Me'. That's what these holidays are: doing the same thing year after year, making up your own traditions as you go along.

At Miriam's, though, everything was already done. Barely eleven o'clock and the turkey was in the oven, the vegetables peeled and ready for boiling, the pies baked, Miriam herself in a pinafore dress with her hair in a loose plait and the baby peering over her shoulder as she moved about the kitchen. Hannah took the wine we'd brought and slid it into the fridge while Fleur looked around. No pots to wash. Everything put away except a plastic bowl of porridge on the baby's highchair.

It would have been easier if there had been things to do. Instead Fleur and I moved around each other in that beautiful kitchen with its sleek wooden cabinets and framed autumn leaves on the walls, trying not to meet each other's eyes. When I'd come back the

226

night before she'd either been asleep or pretending to be. On the sofa where I slept I'd found a note: *Amount owed Sandra* and beneath a total of the money I'd paid for getting us here with a calculation subtracting half the rent for September, October and November. Into the shadows at her end of the cabin I'd called out, 'Have you forgotten that it's your fault that I'm here?' There was no answer. Just Bob staring up at me from his bed of old sweatshirts by the heater.

I thought we'd have a chance to sort things out before we went to Miriam's but she'd got up late and dressed and drunk her coffee without a word. I'd tried saying, 'Look – you got it wrong,' and 'It's not at all what you think – I mentioned it to Miriam before you told me. I was only guessing.' She simply turned away from me and switched on the TV. I stood in front of it holding her note and said, 'And this is beneath you, Fleur. How mean can you be?' Without looking up she told me, 'But you're earning good money now. You can afford to pay your share.' As though I'd been living off her all this time.

At half past ten she'd pulled on her parka and boots and I'd done the same. She took the keys from the windowsill and stomped outside, unplugged the truck and wound up the cord, would have left without me, I think, except I wasn't going to let her. I wasn't going to sit at home all day because it suited her, even if Thanksgiving didn't feel like a real holiday to me.

The baby was chewing on a teething ring, her eyes wide and staring as she watched us from Miriam's arms. Miriam had set out mugs and was pouring coffee for us. Fleur was standing by the window, trying her best to ignore me, or that's how it seemed. She took the coffee I passed her and blew on it, all without taking her eyes off the shallow valley beneath us with its bare birches and glinting snow. I was about to turn away when I noticed something move: a moose. A massive creature down on the slope, long legs wading through the deep snow, its nose down to sniff for food. I was sure she'd been watching it. Hadn't bothered to point it out to me, though she knew I'd never seen one. 'Oh yeah, thanks for telling me,' I told her under my breath. She didn't say anything back, and I stood beside her until she moved away.

The sun was still low because it never got that high these days, and the sky had a bruised look as though it hadn't quite finished with night. The lights were still on in the kitchen and they made the warmth of the house more real: golden light reflecting off the wood of the table, the cupboards, the walls with their garlands of dried leaves and ribbons Miriam had hung up. A picture-perfect Thanksgiving scene.

'Come on now, don't just stand around,' and Hannah tried to herd me and Fleur out of the kitchen but neither of us moved more than a step or two. 'Ryan's out back chopping wood, and Cody and Teresa said they'd be here just before lunch.'

Miriam said, 'The only reason they always get here just before lunch is because we always wait for them. I don't know why they don't bring her grandparents over here.' She tickled the baby to make her smile. 'We always have plenty of food, and it'd beat us waiting. Besides, it can't be any fun Cody and Teresa spending the whole morning in the kitchen, then driving over here without even eating. Where's the sense in that?'

'Well now,' and Hannah took the baby from Miriam, 'her grandparents are getting on. They don't want to go out at Thanksgiving. It makes their day that Cody and Teresa go over and lend a hand. I think it's good of them.' Looking up into Hannah's face the baby stretched her legs and kicked happily.

'We'll end up having our lunch halfway through the afternoon again. All I want is to eat the food when it's at its best, that's all. The turkey gets all dried out if we eat late,' and Miriam turned back to the sink where she rinsed the coffee pot and refilled it.

From the living room the TV chattered. Through the doorway I could see Earl with his feet up and the remote on the armrest, Jim on the sofa with a glass in his hand, Lucas on the floor with his toys: his train track laid out, blocks scattered as though there'd just been an explosion. No one saying a word except some TV sports reporter talking about a football game that hadn't even started yet. At least if I went and sat with them their silence wouldn't be full of ill will like Fleur's; we'd all just sit there and stare at the TV and not mind each other.

The back door opened and Ryan came in stamping the snow off his boots. He told Fleur, 'Hi sis,' then smiled and told me hi too.

The meanness I thought I'd seen in his thin face had gone. A few weeks before he'd even said sorry for ruining my paintings – not when Fleur was listening but in the few minutes it took her to go to the outhouse, as though he was embarrassed by what he'd done. Maybe he was – Fleur had refused to believe he could do a thing like that on purpose, and I doubted he would ever admit it to her. I asked him, 'But why did you do it?' and he bent his head to light a cigarette, said on a breath of smoke, 'No one takes advantage of my little sis.' I told him, 'But I wasn't – you know that now, don't you?' As Fleur's footsteps thudded on the porch he looked me in the eye, said, 'Yeah, well –you could have been. All that talk about her owing you because you'd driven her back here.' Then he'd sniffed and turned to watch the door open as Fleur came back in.

Miriam was laying newspaper on the floor and he dumped the wood on it, then pulled off his hat and gloves. 'Cold enough out there to freeze your goddamn balls off.'

'Ryan,' and Miriam pointed at his boots as he started across the kitchen.

Thick snowboots – no cowboy boots now because his toes would have frozen and the slick soles would have been deadly on ice. He unlaced the boots and dropped them by the door then sat down heavily, took a gulp of Fleur's coffee, said, 'So, Miss Seattle, how you getting on in this cold? Looks like you've got yourself frost-nipped.'

I touched my cheeks. Lumpy, as though in places the skin was still frozen. I'd put on foundation but it wasn't much use to hide the red marks. 'Yeah, I got locked out.'

Fleur told him, 'She went out in a pair of leggings and a sweater. Took the dog as well and the two of them could have frozen to death – can you believe it?'

'You gotta dress properly for this cold,' Hannah told me. 'You can't take it lightly.'

'It wasn't like I was planning on being outside for long.'

'Door froze shut and she didn't think to force it,' Fleur explained. 'She ended up spending the afternoon at old Mitchell's place.' She shook her head, as though I'd done something idiotic.

'You did?' and Miriam leant forward with a cloth to wipe the baby's chin. The baby reached for her, spreading tiny hands as her necklace dangled close, and Hannah had to hold onto her tightly.

'Yes, I did,' I said.

Across from me Ryan was laughing. He made a show of wiping his eyes. 'And you got out alive? Hey, you must have scared him half to death, showing up on his doorstep like that. Didn't he try to shoot you?'

I smiled. 'He went for his gun but I was quicker, slid right past him and into his cabin.'

'Bet it was a fun afternoon. You and old Mitchell, huh?'

'Yeah, we drank coffee and read the paper. Very companionable.'

He grinned at me. 'He's one mean sunnavabitch.'

'I could see it in his eyes. Each time he poured me more coffee I thought to myself, *He's a mean sunnavabitch*.'

Ryan got up and brought over a jar of chocolate chip cookies, slid it onto the table and helped himself. 'You know,' he told me through a mouthful, 'I'm not kidding you. Mitchell's all fucked up.'

'That's right,' said Hannah. 'Korea messed him up. He used to be one of those men you thought would really make something of himself. Look at him now. Once his wife disappeared he just couldn't cope any more.'

Ryan grabbed another cookie. 'Guilt. That's what's eating him up.'

'That's nonsense,' and Hannah took a sip of her coffee.

'Still, you shouldn't have gone there,' Miriam told me. 'He's a strange guy. Spends all his time with his dogs. All he cares about is racing, not that he even does much of that any more.'

'It was dumb,' said Fleur. 'The whole thing was dumb.'

'It was that or frostbite. It wasn't as though I called in for a chat. I went all around the neighbourhood trying to find someone who was home before I ended up next door at his place.'

'Next door?' said Hannah, and she looked over at Fleur. 'Is that true?'

Fleur blinked fast. Then she spat out at me, 'You know what? You haven't learnt a thing about surviving here.'

'Now, Fleur,' and Hannah rocked the baby in her lap, 'Sandra does her best.'

Fleur propped her elbows on the table. 'Mom, she has no idea. I feel responsible. She does dumb things like freezing the door closed and burning the carpet.'

I didn't think she'd noticed the carpet – had never mentioned it in the two months since the power cut. 'It's OK,' I said. 'I won't hold it against you if I die of frostbite.'

'But Fleur's right,' Miriam told me. 'It's risky being here if you don't know what you're doing, and if you don't take care.'

'Might get eaten by a bear,' Ryan said, 'or stomped by a moose. Oh yeah, man, you gotta watch it here or you're dead meat.' Fleur glanced at him, then back into her coffee. Ryan said, 'Hey sis, ain't I right?'

'Sure,' she said, but she picked up her coffee and took it into the living room.

Outside the window wind chimes swayed gently. The baby took hold of Hannah's finger and tried to put it in her mouth. She'd dropped her teething ring somewhere. Hannah eased her finger out of the baby's grip and said, 'Ryan, I can't believe you didn't tell me she was living so close to old Mitchell.'

'Hey, it's her choice if she wants to live near some wacko.'

'Thank you for caring,' said Miriam, 'I'm sure she appreciates it.' And with that she took the baby from Hannah's arms and carried her upstairs.

Ryan looked across the table at me. 'Hey, Thanksgiving morning and already half the family's sulking. That's what it's all about.'

*

Cody and Teresa didn't get there until after two. The rest of us had ended up in the living room watching an old John Wayne film, sipping beers and picking at peanuts until Miriam said, 'Hey, at this rate no one's going to want lunch. Come on now.'

Jim didn't take any notice. He scooped up another handful of nuts and chucked them into his mouth one after the other while Lucas sat on his knee trying to catch them and squealing with laughter. Fleur sat at the other end of the sofa from me. She kept her face turned towards the TV as though she couldn't bear to turn my way, even when I went to fetch her a beer from the fridge. Unforgiving, and it got to me because she hadn't bothered to listen to my side.

When Earl fell asleep Ryan plucked the remote out of his hand and switched over to the Country Music Channel. Golden summer scenes of horses galloping across pasture, a round-faced man in a barn singing a sad, slow song, a woman in a Stetson climbing out of a pick-up while a man sang about *hope and longin'* in a voice that started each line so low it growled.

That was when Cody and Teresa arrived, just in time to save us from more corny videos and finishing all the snacks. They took off their coats and boots then stood by the door and gazed at us until Miriam said, 'Well, come on in. Everything's about as cooked as it can be. Why don't you guys go sit at the table? I'm sure after spending all day in the kitchen you want to sit down.'

'Nana and Pops wanted us to stay and eat,' said Teresa. 'It was difficult to get away.'

Miriam was already on her way back to the kitchen. 'I'll need a hand in here, Fleur, Sandra, Ryan. Come on now, let's get this lunch on the table before it gets to be dinnertime.'

So we trooped in after her and uncovered vegetables and put them in the microwave, stirred sauces as they reheated and carried everything to the table at the end of the living room. I uncorked the wine while Ryan poured beer into a jug, and by that time the sun had already slanted far enough across the sky for the day to feel as though it was winding down. Golden light, glistening snow, in the distance spruce dark against the hills. From Miriam's house the outside world looked perfect, as though none of the snow and cold could hurt you. And inside – well, inside was perfect too if you liked the pioneer look of quilts, bare wood and rag rugs, the cosy cabin feel that was supposed to mean something about being American, and down-home, big-hearted values. Except, of course, quilts cost a fortune and any cabin worth the name would have had no plumbing.

Earl had dozed off again and had to be woken to come to the table. The bowls of soup were steaming, the smell of warm bread floating out. He sat at the end of the table and poured himself a beer, said, 'Well, another Thanksgiving. They're coming around faster and faster.'

Hannah added, 'And for the first time in years we're all together. That's something to be thankful for.' We clinked glasses at that. Bright sounds of glass against glass.

Teresa spread her napkin on her lap and said to Miriam, 'There was hardly room for the four of us to sit down at Nana and Pops'. I don't know why they moved into such a small place.'

'You should bring them here next time,' Miriam told her. 'We've got plenty of room and we could put another leaf in the table – it can sit twelve.'

Teresa looked around, as though working something out. 'Yes, you've certainly got the space for a big gathering like this. And the furniture.'

Jim reached over for the jug of beer. 'You bet. Well, if you work hard for something, you get it in the end. You just have to believe in yourself.'

'It's an amazing place all right,' said Teresa, but her voice sounded hollow.

Hannah was sitting beside her. She told Teresa, 'And she's done such a wonderful job of decorating it. This place is like something out of a magazine. I think that every time we come here.'

Miriam reached for the rolls, felt to see if they were warm, passed them around. 'When you have a house like this you have to make the most of it. What would be the point otherwise?'

'Yes,' said Teresa, 'I guess.' She picked up her spoon and concentrated on her soup.

I recognised it: same as we'd been serving all week in the diner as part of the Thanksgiving special, tomato and oregano soup that went with a roast turkey dinner served with mashed potato and followed by a choice of two pies. The place had been crowded from ten all the way through until three every day, no chance of getting off early and hardly time to get home, changed and back into town to teach my class. As for real daylight, I didn't get to see much of that except through the diner window. The tips had improved though, and even Nadia had been making more of an effort. Janice had called in one lunchtime, dolled up in a tight skirt and make-up, and sat at a table by the kitchen door with a man in a suit and a sulky expression. There wasn't much chance to say more than hello. She poked at her food and lit a cigarette while the man talked at her with his head crooked to one side. When I asked about her new job she said, 'Well, it ain't heaven but it's better than this place.' I wasn't sure I believed her. She looked lost sitting there in her office clothes.

Ryan got up to change the music, and as he came back to the table he said, 'Just listen to this. This is gonna be the one to make me famous.'

Some song about *leavin' home is tough on the soul* and how *it's the only way when love's gone*. 'This your band?' said Teresa. 'Really?'

'Sure is,' and he leant back in his chair. 'Got a record company calling us and asking if we can come down to Seattle to talk about a contract. Can't miss a chance like that.'

'Well now, how about that?' said Hannah. 'You can be near Cassie and Michael. A little boy like him needs to spend time with his dad.'

Earl scraped up the last of his soup. 'You going to be away long? What about your work?'

'Hey Dad, this is the big time. I'll tell Daggart to go screw his job.'

'You're throwing everything away,' said Earl. 'You get yourself a job then you chuck it in to chase some dream.'

'Don't you worry,' said Jim, 'I can always fix you up with something if you need it. Just let me know,' but Ryan ignored him.

Miriam was stacking up the dirty soup bowls. 'So this is for real? You're not kidding this time?'

'Why would I kid you about something like this? Ain't it great?' and he nudged Fleur but she only nodded and dabbed her mouth on her napkin, looking all pissed off. I wondered if she'd moved back because Ryan was here, her favourite brother – her favourite person in all the world.

Cody leant back. 'So you're gonna be in Seattle?' He turned to me, said, 'Isn't that where you're from?'

'Hey,' said Ryan, 'just think, Miss Seattle. I could go hang out with your folks. Could be like a kinda exchange,' and he laughed.

Hannah touched his hand. 'But you're not moving there for good, are you?'

'Only for a few months to work everything out. Managed to get some gigs set up already. Just think, I could be the new Clint Black.'

'I guess,' said Cody. 'Seeing as all your songs already sound like his.'

Fleur looked up, face flat and angry. 'That's not true. Why do you have to say things like that? Anyway, what would you know?'

Cody raised both hands. 'Hey, there's a similarity. I was just pointing it out, all right?'

'You're always so down on everyone, Cody. You could just be pleased for him instead of criticising.'

Beside her Teresa put down her glass. 'You're not being fair, Fleur.'

'Even if he thinks it, why say it?'

'Can't he say what he thinks? I mean, it's not like things have been easy in the last year.'

'No one's had it easy,' said Hannah, 'but we've all tried to help each other out.'

'Have we?' and Teresa blinked. 'I mean, what have you all done for Cody?' She looked over at Miriam. 'We helped you when you needed it, didn't we?'

Miriam put all the soup spoons in the top bowl, said, 'This isn't the time. It's Thanksgiving and I don't want a fight.'

'Come on now, Teresa,' said Jim. 'Don't be like that. If you needed money you just had to ask us. You know that.' His face was flushed from the beers he'd drunk, all the way up his scalp to where his hair had retreated.

'All we wanted was what we'd lent you paid back,' and Teresa snatched up the empty bread basket and carried it to the kitchen.

No one moved. I picked up the dirty soup bowls and followed her. She was at the sink splashing water onto her face. She must have thought I was Miriam because she turned around with her hands up to her chest as though she had to defend herself. When I slid the bowls onto the counter she sniffed and took a dish towel from a hook. 'Goddamn it,' she said. 'I don't know why we come. I try to be positive but they turn it all around.' She pressed the dish towel over her face for a moment, then leant back against the counter. 'Look at that – I'm shaking. Can you believe it?' and she held out both hands to show me.

'Do you need anything?'

'Yeah,' she said, 'to get out of this nuthouse once and for all.' She scowled at herself. 'Miriam's got them all running around doing what she wants. All except Ryan.'

'And Cody?'

'You'd better believe it. Who else would be dumb enough to lend his sister three thousand dollars without agreeing when she'd pay it back? She and Jim had just lost the house – didn't that prove enough about them? She said it was to tide them over. Who else would need that much to tide them over?' She tugged a tissue from a box and blew her nose. 'Back then we both had good jobs, but now I'm in school and Cody's sick. You wouldn't think we'd even have to ask, right?'

'Right.'

'Cody must have known what she's like. He could have told her no.'

I said, 'But maybe it was difficult – they didn't have anywhere to live.'

'There's always a way to say no – hell, Miriam manages to say it just fine,' and she went back out to the dining room.

When Miriam brought the turkey to the table she set it down telling us it was overcooked. She passed Jim the knife though from the way he lurched as he pushed back his chair it didn't look like he was going to stay standing long enough to carve it. Surprisingly he deftly cut away legs and wings, and thin slices of breast that he lifted gently onto our plates, fishing out stuffing for those who wanted it, finding dark meat to go with light. 'Where did you learn that?' I said.

'I was brought up on a turkey farm.'

'More than a farm,' said Cody. 'Turkey factory, wasn't it?'

'We didn't assemble them,' he said, 'we just fattened them up then turned them into turkey patties and turkey sausage and anything the heck else you can make with turkey.'

'Didn't you get sick of it?' I said.

'Oh no. Turkey's good meat. I got sick of steak. Dad wanted it

236

every night. Said turkey was poor folk's food.' He dropped a slice onto my plate. 'I was the one used to bring home turkey for dinner.'

Miriam passed around the vegetables. 'I can't believe he let you work in his factory like that. You could have done a lot better.'

'But I've told you – I liked it. Heck, when I was in high school that's where everyone else spent their vacation. What's the point in hanging out on your own? Besides, it was kinda fun.'

'Great fun,' muttered Ryan.

Miriam said, 'But on the factory floor? He could have given you something so much better.'

He shrugged. 'I was sixteen. I just wanted to be with my buddies.'

When Jim had finished the turkey sat between us with its cut sides pale in the light, steam still leaking from the stuffing. He laid the knife back down and said, 'Well, let's hope it's a good one,' then he topped up his beer. He ate carefully, carving pieces off his vegetables and sliding them through the cranberry sauce and the gravy.

The whole time Ryan's voice slanted out over us from the speakers. Nothing like his speaking voice at all, much richer and more soulful. Most of the numbers were straight country songs about lost love and lonely roads, but two were about Alaska. One about gold mines and *hard, cold livin'*; the other about a veteran living out in the bush with his gun and his dogs because *he cain't look anyone in the eye no more, he's killed a man he shouldn't have and now he's all froze up inside*. Old Mitchell, I thought, and all the others like him, veterans come to Alaska to get away from a world they couldn't live in any more. I wondered if that's how Fleur thought of herself – coming home to escape.

Ryan sang along to his songs between mouthfuls of food, and Hannah leaned towards Teresa to ask how her degree was going and when she expected to finish. Not for a while apparently, what with time being short, and money being short, and having other things to worry about – she glanced at Miriam and Jim, but they didn't seem to notice. Cody didn't look up while she rushed through all this, and Miriam took Lucas on her lap to feed him because he was pushing his food around rather than eating it. 'I don't like it,' Lucas said, 'why do I have to eat it?'

'Because it's good for you,' Miriam told him, and his mouth turned down as she held the fork out to him.

'Go on,' said Jim, 'it's Daddy's favourite food,' but that didn't convince him either.

Earl's fork clattered against his plate. 'Let him alone. Turkey's not to everyone's taste. What do you want to stuff him full for?'

'He's getting too fussy,' and Miriam kept the fork in front of Lucas's mouth though he had his lips tight closed. 'And I don't like food going to waste.'

'Come on,' said Ryan, 'let him enjoy his Thanksgiving. What does a bit of food going to waste matter?'

'It matters to me.'

'Well, in that case,' and Ryan grabbed the fork from her, 'I'll help you out, Lucas.' He ate the turkey on the fork, speared up the rest and ate that too while Miriam glared at him. Lucas giggled until he realised that his mum was furious.

'You have to interfere, don't you?' and she lifted Lucas down from her lap and carried his empty plate to the kitchen. The door swung closed behind her. Lucas hid under the table, then peered up over the edge with his eyes and fingers showing, watching us all to see what he should do.

'The two of us better lie low,' Ryan said, 'because your mom's mad at us.'

'I guess,' whispered Lucas. Then he slid back out of sight.

The baby started to cry not long afterwards and Jim went upstairs. The rest of us passed our dirty plates along, stacked them up and Hannah took them into the kitchen. When Jim brought the baby down she was flushed from crying. She leant her face into his shoulder and wriggled, not properly awake, and Cody tried to make her laugh by tickling her but that only made her cry more loudly. Ryan leant his chair back and sang along with Lyle Lovett. When he poked Fleur in the arm to get her to sing along too she moved her arm away.

Miriam came in from the kitchen with a pie balanced on each hand and set them on the table, then came back with ice cream. She didn't say a word as she sat down but she put one hand behind

Ryan's tilted chair and pushed it straight again. He didn't miss a word, and when he closed his eyes at the end of the chorus he looked different, as though he was singing from the heart.

In the end Cody said to him, 'So when are you leaving, Ry?'

'Next week. This could be my big chance. I have to take it.' He glanced over at Fleur.

She looked back at him, said, 'It's not going to be the same without you.'

'Yeah,' and he grinned. 'I can believe that.'

Fleur had been toying with her dessert fork. Now she raked it across the tablecloth, over and over. It grated softly and she watched it as though there was nothing in the world so fascinating. I felt sorry for her – Ryan excited about leaving for Seattle when she'd just left. Her own life going backwards not forwards.

'And when are *you* leaving?' Teresa asked me.

'I've got a job at the university now. It's not much, but I have to stay until the end of the semester. Not that that's far away.'

Miriam was slicing up the pies. 'I can't imagine why you've stayed so long. You're not doing yourself any good by hanging around here.' She looked up. 'I love Alaska, but what is there for you here? You should have left months ago.'

'She's right,' said Hannah. 'I worry about you being here, honey. Look at what happened to you, getting yourself frost-nipped like that.'

'She's a real worry,' said Fleur, and poked at her pie.

Teresa scooped some ice cream onto her slice. 'What were you doing before you came up here?'

'Moving to Arizona,' I said.

'So you ended up going in the wrong direction. Well,' and she picked up her fork, 'you've been here for months now. You must like it.'

'More like I can't afford the flight home,' I said. 'But then, you know all about that,' and I glanced over at Miriam. Fleur shifted beside me, uncomfortable I was sure. But I wasn't going to lie, not when she was sniping at me every chance she got.

Earl looked at me. 'You broke? That can't be right. Ted wouldn't let any family of his run short. He's doing well enough, ain't he? You said he was. But then maybe you didn't tell me the whole story,' and he chuckled.

'He's careful with his money.'

'Oh,' said Earl. 'So is that the word you use for it now? In my day we just straight out called it being stingy.'

Teresa passed Cody the ice cream, said to me, 'Well, you were crazy to come without enough money. Alaska's one of the most expensive states in the country.'

Miriam handed me a slice of pie. 'We're all grateful for what you've done for Fleur, but isn't it about time you stood on your own two feet?'

'There's no point me renting a cabin when we're so close to the end of the semester.'

'But you can't keep living off Fleur,' said Hannah.

Miriam sat down. 'Don't you think you should be giving her something towards rent? I mean, you've been living rent-free for some time now.'

'Yes,' said Hannah. 'It doesn't seem right.'

Ryan poured himself more beer. 'Come on, you guys – she drove Fleur all the way up here.'

'But that was months ago.' Miriam folded her arms on the table.

'Listen,' I told them, 'we have an arrangement. Besides, this is between me and Fleur.'

'Had,' said Fleur. 'We *had* an arrangement.'

I put down my fork. 'We can talk about this later.'

Fleur ignored that. 'If you want to stay, you need to pay your own way.'

'Just like you paid your own way up here?' and I glared at her. 'You've taken your time to pay me back that thousand dollars, haven't you? I haven't seen a single penny of it, and now it's nearly the end of November.'

She flushed. 'I told you, I'll pay you back.'

'And how are you going to manage that when a thousand dollars is disappearing out of your account every month? You could have paid me back months ago if you'd wanted.' I hadn't meant for it to come out, but there it was. The rest of them stared at us.

'You went through my things? What the hell kind of a friend are you?'

Miriam was scowling at me. 'You know Fleur's got other commitments, so why are you pushing her like this?'

Hannah put a hand on mine. 'Fleur's had it hard. You know that.'

Jim wiped the froth of his beer off his lips. 'A thousand a month? What are you spending money like that on, Fleur?'

'I think,' and Miriam folded her arms, 'that we should leave this for another time. It's Thanksgiving. I don't want another fight.'

It would have died right there but Ryan said through a mouthful of pie, 'Yeah, little sis, where's that money going?'

'I've had expenses.' Fleur kept her head straight, blinked fast.

Ryan leant forward on his elbows. 'Like what?'

She glanced at Miriam who stared straight back at her. Ryan frowned. Then he looked back at Miriam and grinned while she pushed the lid back on the ice cream and stood. He said, 'Wait a minute. Let me guess. You've put the diner in Fleur's name? She's paying the rent?'

'Don't be ridiculous,' said Miriam. 'It's my own business. I've worked hard for it.'

Fleur sat back. 'This house,' she said. 'It's mine. I mean, I pay the mortgage.'

As she said it Miriam spun around, snapped out, 'That's a goddamn lie.' But the way her face flushed as she stood there with the ice cream in her hands we all knew it was true.

Jim said, 'Miriam?' but she was on her way to the kitchen. 'Miriam!' he shouted. 'You just wait now.'

The baby started crying again and Jim rocked her saying, 'Come on now, Sonia, don't you start.'

From the kitchen we heard clattering, the freezer door slamming, water running, then the gurgle of coffee through the machine. Miriam the perfect hostess putting on coffee in the middle of a row. The rest of us ate our pie and ice cream, waiting as though this was an interlude. Then she was back with a jug of milk and a jar of sugar, heavy items that she weighed in her hands as though she was planning to throw them. She slid them onto the table but didn't sit down.

Jim said, 'What's going on, Miriam?'

She took the baby out of his arms. 'No one was going to give us another mortgage. Where were we supposed to bring up our children? Family's supposed to help each other out.'

Beside me Cody pushed his hand through his hair. 'You fool,' he told Fleur.

'What was I supposed to do? Leave them with nowhere to live? This is my place, I can sell it whenever I want. That's the arrangement.'

Ryan was grinning. 'And just let me guess how much rent Miriam and Jim are paying you.' He stared up at the ceiling as though he had to think about it.

Miriam stood over him, said, 'You don't understand, none of you do.'

'Oh, I understand,' he told her. 'You have to keep up with your fancy friends and their fancy houses. Thing is,' and he wagged a finger at her, 'they can afford their own places. Not like you.'

At the other end of the table Cody was looking across at Teresa. He told her, 'And they still couldn't pay us back our money? Christ.' And he threw his napkin onto his plate.

Jim had his hands in the air as though he could push all of this back into the dark where it had been hiding. 'It's OK. After all, this place is an investment. Look at it. How much do you think it's worth now? She'd make a killing if we sold it, no doubt about it,' but no one answered him.

Beside me Fleur was blinking fast, her eyes gleaming as she stared down at the remains of her pie. 'Come on,' I said softly, and put my hand on her shoulder. 'Let's go home.'

'Yeah,' she murmured and pushed back her chair.

The music had finished. Only the coffee bubbling through the machine broke the silence.

'Well, happy Thanksgiving everyone,' and Ryan lifted his glass and drank down the rest of his beer.

*

That night there was no moon. When the lights of the house fell away behind us there was nothing but the gleam of the truck's headlights on the packed snow covering the road, and the dark shapes of trees just beyond.

Fleur said, 'Shit, how do things get so messed up?'

'It was a family holiday,' I said. 'What did you expect?'

She rubbed her mitten on the inside of the windscreen, trying to clear some of the ice. 'It doesn't ever end up this bad. Usually everyone just gets mad at Ryan. Today was something else entirely.'

'More exciting than Thanksgiving in Seattle,' I said. 'Plus we didn't have to listen to Frank Sinatra all day.'

'I miss that. Those Thanksgivings were always fun.'

'Yeah. I suppose they were.'

She sped up a little as we crested the hill. 'I didn't know we were all so mad at each other. We had to be, didn't we, for things to get so bad?'

I tucked my scarf more tightly around my neck. The air in the truck was so cold I could feel every small gap where it leaked through. Already the frost-nipped skin on my face was aching. I said, 'Why didn't you tell me about Miriam and the house?'

'You wouldn't have understood.'

'No, I probably wouldn't. But then do even *you* understand?'

She kept driving, taking her foot off the accelerator for a sharp bend rather than hitting the brakes, accelerating out of it carefully. Then she glanced over, told me, 'I'm not sure I do. The whole thing made sense way back when we arranged it. Me helping them out because Miriam was pregnant and I could afford to, and because they were living in that cruddy motel. But now – ' and she swallowed. 'Now they expect me to keep helping them out like nothing's changed.'

'And you've been going along with it.'

'I thought things would be different. I thought I had it all worked out: Miriam and Jim would start paying rent on the house, I'd buy Mom and Dad's furnace for them, I'd help Cody with his medical bills. And I'd pay you back, just like I promised.'

'You were hoping for too much, believing you could do all that. You're not earning anything like what you used to.'

'You've gotta try, haven't you? No harm in that.'

'Except things didn't turn out how you wanted.'

'Miriam wouldn't pay me any rent at all. She said the diner wasn't doing well. That screwed up my plans.'

'It's doing fine. But I bet Jim's business isn't.'

'Yeah, he doesn't have any business sense at all.' She slowed at the junction, waited for a low-slung car to turn past us and up the road, then followed its tail lights into the darkness. 'That's why Miriam wanted to put the house in my name, so that he wouldn't put it up as collateral. They were supposed to live there rent-free for a year to get back on their feet, then start paying me rent to cover the mortgage. Never worked out that way, and I guess she never told him exactly how it did work out.'

The aurora was out that night. Fleur pulled over and we got out to watch though the night had a sharp coldness to it, colder than anything I'd ever felt. I pulled my scarf over my face and stamped my feet. Above us green lights wobbled across the sky in unsteady waves, curving and twisting, turning to pink and violet then back to green.

Standing there on the hard-packed snow I leant back to watch the lights. 'But why that house? It must have cost a fortune.'

'I should have said no when Miriam told me how much the mortgage would be,' she said. 'But at the time I couldn't. She said it was the only decent place they saw.'

'It's decent all right.' I tucked my hands into my pockets because even with my mittens on the cold was getting to them, making the joints ache as though they still hadn't properly thawed. 'The way she kept it quiet she must have known she was taking advantage of you.'

'More than anything she wanted to prove everyone wrong about Jim, and about how they were doing now. That's important to her, doing better than the rest of us, keeping up with the people she went to school with who're lawyers or doctors now. It's like she promised herself she was going to get somewhere, and when she married Jim everyone thought she had it made, him coming from a rich family. We didn't know they'd bought him out of the business. Maybe she didn't either.'

The aurora had curled into a half-crown overhead. 'Just look at that,' I said. 'It's magnificent.'

'I used to go skiing at night. Had to take a flashlight if the moon wasn't out, but there's no better way to see the aurora.' She kicked at the snow. 'Guess I've lost my nerve for things like that. Before it was like nothing could hurt me. Now I'm afraid everything'll turn into some kinda disaster.'

'Like today?'

'Nothing was said that hadn't been waiting to be said.' She leaned against the truck. 'I was hard on you though. Thing was, I got the feeling you were careless, not just about yourself and Bob but about me too. Telling Miriam about the accident, like that – I couldn't understand why you'd do it.'

'But I told you – I was only guessing. You hadn't told me anything about what had happened.'

'Yeah,' she said sadly. 'Anyway – Miriam said to me, "How could you try and hide something like that?" and all I could say was that I didn't want people to think any different about me. But it wasn't just that – I was ashamed, like it was all my fault.'

'He'd been drinking and pulled out in front of you.'

'I know it. But it doesn't help. It's like I brought down on myself something I can never get out from.'

'But you will, eventually.'

'No. Not the way you mean, I don't think so. It's like he's part of me now, whether I like it or not. Maybe this is what it means to be haunted.' Above us the lights bent into a wavy arc that trailed streamers of pink. 'You know, Miriam said she couldn't trust me any more. Because I hadn't told her, and because ever since I came back I've been asking her for rent. She thought I wanted it so I could pay you back – she was right about that.'

I stamped my feet. Despite my snowboots already my toes were going numb. 'No wonder she was so pissed off with me. She's been telling me you'd never pay me back and I should just earn enough for a flight and go home.'

'She probably thought that that way I wouldn't keep asking her for the money to cover the mortgage – maybe I wouldn't have. I've never stood a chance against her – she always gets what she wants because she doesn't give up.'

'So what's going to happen now?'

'I don't know,' she said. 'But things are gonna change, don't you think? After today they have to.'

245

Twenty-seven

I knew spring was on its way when I caught the smell of damp earth. The first time I'd smelled it in months. I turned off the heater and propped the door open, found a chair to take outside and whistled for Bob. At the end of the porch the sun was strong and warm, and the two of us sat there listening to water drip from the eaves while above us the ice on the roof shifted and creaked. Through the trees I saw Robin come past with her three huskies. She saw me and called over with a laugh, 'Hey, what's all this wet stuff that's dripping off the trees?'

'Could be nasty – I'm keeping an eye on it.'

She grinned. 'Don't forget to come by tonight. Seven o'clock, OK? Brandon wants to go out for Thai food.' The dogs had grouped around her, paws raised, heads high to watch me. They still weren't used to me though I'd been to Robin and Brandon's a dozen times for dinner and beers. But then they were outdoor dogs, not pets like Bob.

I shouted over, 'He wants to go to the White Lotus *again*?'

'It's his birthday so I guess we'll let him have his way. Besides, where's another good place to eat in this town?'

'Yeah, really,' and I waved as she turned into her driveway, her dogs grouped around her in a pack, the greys and whites of their fur splendid in the sun. Bob scratched at my leg. 'I know,' I told him, 'you're a magnificent dog too – in your own little way.'

I was going out more often than I had in Seattle. Birthday dinners, potluck dinners where everyone brought a dish, pretzel-making parties, anniversary parties, just-for-the-hell-of-it parties. Coats and boots and hats dumped next to the front door, everyone in their socks sipping beer and reaching for tortilla chips, dogs running around, sometimes children running around too. And at the end of the evening someone usually volunteered to take everyone's keys and get their engines running so that they wouldn't have to wait for them to warm up sitting around on cold car seats. None of it what I was used to but it was fun. In just a few months it felt as though I knew as many people here as I had in Seattle. I certainly knew a lot more dogs.

The breeze was cool but not cold, nothing like the biting cold we'd had during the winter when it had been down to forty below for days at a time. I put up my feet on an old coffee table and leant back. The first time I'd sat outside in months – many months. The air swayed the branches of a spruce, a squirrel leapt from one tree to the next with paws outstretched. Bloody things, nesting in the insulation because Ryan hadn't netted off their hole into the roof. One of the many things he hadn't done before he left. No contract yet, just gigs around Seattle. Maybe that was as well. If things had been more certain he'd have taken everything down south with him: his pots and cutlery and TV and truck. I'd have been left with an empty cabin and no way of getting around.

Sunday afternoon, and I should have been washing up while I waited for Fleur. The heat from the sun felt too good though. Besides, if I was going to take more pictures while we were out skiing that would count as work: finding shots I could use for paintings because, as Sheryl at the shop had said, I'd better have a stock in by the summer as they were going to sell like crazy. Paintings of snow and birches and moose were getting too monotonous; I was going to try something different and when I'd told Sheryl she'd raised one eyebrow, said, "Well, honey, you're the artist. Just bear in mind most tourists don't come here to buy Jackson Pollock."

Getting fired from the diner back in November had been the best thing to happen all winter. The day after Thanksgiving Miriam had phoned to say, 'I won't be needing you,' and that turned out to mean permanently. I hadn't seen her since except for running into her in the supermarket when she'd stood holding onto her trolley while Lucas rolled a tin of peaches on the floor. 'Well,' she'd said, 'I heard you were still here.'

She was wearing a business jacket and skirt, and she looked younger and less happy. I told her, 'I've got so much work it wouldn't make sense to leave.' And I had. Menus for restaurants, occasional pictures for the *Daily News-Miner*, even a couple of cover illustrations for a book publisher in town. All that on top of teaching two classes, and the artwork for the shop. I didn't ask Miriam how she was. I already knew: the house had been sold; she and Jim had moved into a much cheaper place on the condition that Fleur bought it. Not much of a deal for Fleur though at least now they were paying her rent on the new place. Getting them to do that had been a struggle back when Cody was in hospital and we all thought he wasn't going to make it.

Miriam pushed back her hair and said, 'All that talk about Arizona and here you are, still in Fairbanks.'

'It'll be summer soon and after getting through the winter I wouldn't want to miss it. I might even drive down to Denali and do some camping.' I leant onto my trolley. 'How are things with you?'

'Better than ever,' she said. 'The diner's doing just great.'

I knew that wasn't true. I'd run into Bud downtown one evening. He'd squinted at me through fast-falling snow, said, 'That place is leaking dollars like a goddamn torpedoed boat.' Nothing new about that, except this time there'd been problems with suppliers who hadn't been paid, and now more often than not the staff got their wages late. 'It ain't gonna last,' he said. 'I should quit right now. Thanks to Jim that place'll have gone under by the end of the summer and we'll all be out on our asses – and that's no time to be looking for work.' He walked off, shaking his head at himself as though he couldn't believe he hadn't left the diner already.

Lucas pulled out another couple of tins and piled them on top of each other. 'That's good, Miriam,' I said. The tins fell over with a dull clatter. We both watched Lucas stack them again. 'And how are you getting on in your new house?'

I meant it just for conversation, but she stooped to pick up the tins and pulled Lucas to his feet. For a moment she didn't seem sure what to say. Then she told me, 'You don't have a shred of sympathy in your heart, do you?' She lifted up Lucas and walked away down the aisle with her trolley squeaking. Lucas watched me over her shoulder, his hand lifted to say goodbye. I waved back.

It must have been hard for her, moving to that smaller place – but then she'd set herself up to be something she couldn't afford: businesswoman Miriam with her diner, her magnificent house, her business-dealing husband. None of it was what it seemed. And who was she pretending for? The other businesswomen in town that she had lunch with once a month? Her friends from school who'd gone to university and had careers she envied? Or was it all for herself, to prove she'd made it, as though she could fool herself?

The sun was so warm I started to doze. Through my eyelids it glowed a beautiful blood red, and I let myself drift until I realised: I had the wrong wax on my skis. I shook Bob off my lap and fetched them, spent ten minutes scraping off the –22 to 5°F wax and putting on something that would stick on snow that was starting to melt. I'd just propped them against the porch railing when Fleur pulled up. Jeans. Jacket. Checked shirt. The cute black fleece hat I'd bought her for her birthday. She'd tried it on and said, 'Next thing, you'll buy me a skirt. You'll never see me in one, you have to believe me,' and I did.

'Hey,' and she slammed her truck door, 'you ready?'

'Been waiting.'

'That'd be a first. Come on then.' She pulled off her hat and ruffled her hair. It looked better short. 'I guess today'll be our last time on the river this season. The ice can melt fast and you don't see it because most of it melts from underneath.'

'You've already told me that.'

'I know it,' and she smiled. 'Just wasn't sure if it had sunk into that hard head of yours.'

I fetched my camera, plus my hat and mittens. I called over, 'Did you drop in to see Cody today?'

'Only for a few minutes. He's not looking any better, and Teresa's talking about taking that grant-writing job down in Oregon and finishing her degree part-time. It'd be good money.'

'Think they'll really go?'

'Neither of them have ever lived anywhere but here. They should go, just to see what the Lower Forty-Eight's like.'

She didn't say he should see it while he could, but that's what I thought. His chances of making it had got smaller since his relapse. If his treatment didn't work this time there wasn't much they could do.

I carried my skis over and put them in the back of the truck, grabbed my poles and my ski boots, told her, 'Bob's coming too,' just to hear her groan. But he was good when we skied, didn't run off, didn't bark, didn't chase after moose. She was just embarrassed to be seen with such a small dog.

'I'm gonna get you a proper Alaskan pup for your birthday,' she said. 'One you don't have to carry home because it's tired.'

'Hear that, Bob? You'll have to stay home and guard the house instead.'

He didn't seem impressed. He jumped up into the truck and stood between us with his front paws on the dashboard. I started the engine and eased the truck out of the driveway. As we drove past the neighbours' cabins he craned his neck, eager to see who we passed. A couple of times he let out barks as other dogs looked our way, then he settled down onto the seat.

Fleur pushed her hat back. 'I could get you a pup from Cody and Teresa's neighbour. One of his dogs is going to have a litter soon.'

'One of those sled dogs? Whatever would I do with it when I moved down to Arizona?' and I looked at her out of the corner of my eye.

She laughed. 'You? You love it here. Look at you – skiing every weekend, talking about camping down in Denali this summer. And I haven't seen you in that miniskirt of yours in months.'

'Oh, I'm saving that for effect. It's been so long since anyone saw a miniskirt in this town I'll get mobbed by men.'

'Oh,' said Fleur, 'that reminds me – Doug's got a friend who wants to meet you.'

'Another?'

'I checked him out. He doesn't listen to country, and he knows about art and stuff.'

'Fleur, I can't spend another evening with someone who wants to tell me all about graphic user interfaces.'

'You know your problem? You're too picky. All these men in Alaska, and you find something wrong with all of them.'

'That's because half of them have got beards and missing teeth, and the other half came up here to get away from their mothers.'

'I even looked him over for you. He puts gel on his hair.'

'Really?' and I shifted into fourth. 'Well then, maybe there's a chance. Hey, you can be my bridesmaid if it all works out.'

'OK,' she said. 'But only if I can wear pants.'

We passed a few shops, took a road down to the river with the sun shining through the bare birch branches and the road slick with leaves that should have fallen in the autumn. 'Have you decided?' she asked me at last. 'Are you gonna go?'

'I'll go,' I said. 'Matt's practically family. Besides, there are things at home I need to pick up. Like my car.'

'That little Dodge Colt? You're gonna drive it all the way up here?'

'I can't keep driving Ryan's truck – last time he called he said he might fly back this summer and pick it up. Anyway, I like small things. And the trip would be an adventure.'

I caught her smiling at that but she didn't say anything, just flipped down the visor to keep the sun out of her eyes. 'Maybe it's on the rebound, Matt getting married when you only left last fall.'

'No, it's what he's wanted all along. He's bought into the practice, now he wants a wife who'll talk mortgages and buy matching tableware. I don't know why he ever thought that could be me.'

When Mum had phoned to tell me she'd left lots of pauses. I suppose she thought I was going to tell her it was ridiculous him getting married so soon, and him wanting to have the wedding over at the house. 'We do hope you'll come,' she'd said uncertainly. 'I mean, we thought you'd only be away a few weeks. Now it's been months.'

Later she'd passed me to Ted who said, 'How are things? Have you decided when you're moving?' as though I hadn't already told him that Arizona was out of the question now, that I had more work than I could handle right here in Fairbanks.

He'd tracked down some old classmate, he said, and he had contacts at some magazine in Tempe that might be useful. Still not listening until I said, 'You haven't got around to telling Mum, have you?' and knew from the way he paused that he was never going to.

The third time I'd brought it up and this time he said, 'Can't do it, not after all this time. How would she ever trust me again?' And maybe he was right. The time had passed for that kind of thing. He sighed, told me, 'She's a great girl, Matt's fiancée. We're just sorry things didn't work out with you. You know, your mom misses you, Sandy. She'd be so pleased if you came down for the wedding.'

I said, 'I don't know – it's so expensive.'

'We never did lend you that thousand dollars. Maybe we could see our way to sending it to you as a kind of not-getting-married gift.'

'Oh, a consolation prize?'

'Something like that,' and I heard his breath soft on the receiver. Then he asked me, 'How did things get so crazy back in the fall? I didn't mean for you to end up stranded in Alaska like that.'

'We disappointed you – me and Fleur. Neither of us turned out quite how you expected.'

'I guess,' he said, and he sounded sad.

*

I pulled up at the end of the car park closest to the river and we got out. In front of us gleamed the flat expanse of the river thick with snow, the gentle hills on either side with their dark spruces, the sky a baby blue overhead. I lifted my camera and focused, and though I could see nothing except snow and trees and sky the view was beautiful, not empty but full of hope. I took a couple of shots, then turned and pulled Fleur into focus: her hand up to keep out the sun, her eyes squinting against the brightness, her head tilted back as though to breathe in the spring air more deeply. She heard the shutter click and glanced over with a smile. 'Hey,' she said, 'that wasn't my best side.'

Bob lapped up snow while we hopped around changing into our ski boots, clipping them onto our skis, hooking our poles around our wrists.

252

'Ready?' called Fleur.

'Ready.'

We side-stepped down the bank and onto the river itself. Then, with Bob chasing after us, we took off across the snow.